LEISENRING №1

Jim Oglethorpe

Leisenring No. 1 is a work of fiction. Apart from the well-known actual people, events and locales that figure in the narrative, all of the names, characters, organizations, places and incidents portrayed in this novel are either products of the author's imagination or are used fictitiously. Any resemblance to current events or locales, or to living persons, is entirely coincidental.

Published by Aetna Street Publishing

A Division of Jamonya Enterprises Inc.

Fort Myers, FL

Library of Congress Control Number: 2013907064
ISBN: 0988729202
ISBN-13: 9780988729209

Dedicated to all of the miners, cokers, and their families who worked the Connellsville Seam

ACKNOWLEDGMENTS

Penn State Fayette, The Eberly Campus
Coal and Coke Heritage Center

Raymond A. Washlaski and his
Virtual Museum of Coal Mining in Western Pennsylvania

Daughters Laura Borrego and Alice Oglethorpe
for sending me to school

My wife Jean Oglethorpe for her encouragement and support

"The Connellsville Coking Coal Fields contain a seam of coal more persistent in its bed and more uniform in quality than any other at present known field in the world. Late science has brought forth a vast knowledge upon coal, and our civilization recognizes it as the material energy of our country, the universal aid, a factor in everything we do."

(Connellsville Weekly Courier, 1914)

Chapter 1

Leisenring, Pennsylvania, was a dream town, but its dreams were well hidden. They were concealed along the dirt streets and within the ragged little houses that lined them. They were mostly obscured by the smoky haze that hung in the air. They were there, but held close in the hearts of the hardworking men and women who called Leisenring home. It was the vision of a better life, but for most of them it was a dream they would never see.

Zoran Gondik was one of those dreamers. He shuffled slowly down the dusty road, past the slate dump and the Union Supply Store. It was just before 4:00 a.m. on a Saturday, August 4, 1900. Dawn was still an hour away, but it was time for his workday to begin. *It's already hot as hell*, Zoran thought.

He stopped for a minute, pulled out a dirty red handkerchief, and wiped his face. The handkerchief was stiff and foul, washed but once a week, and Saturday was washday. Stuffing it away again, he surveyed the scene across the main road.

Before him stood the Leisenring No. 1 Mine and Coke Works, stretching for more than a mile along a little stream. The mine shaft was in the middle. Two rows of coke ovens squatted in long lines away from the shaft. In front stood the tipple, a tall wooden structure where the mined coal was dumped.

The predawn sky glowed red and orange, lit by the flames that shot from the open tops of the ovens. Thick smoke hid much of the details—lorry cars shuttling back and forth from the tipple, railroad engines shuffling cars around the yard.

Zoran sighed, and slowly shuffled on. *Only one year here...*He found himself thinking of Slovakia. *Am I really better off?*

Zoran pulled coke at Number One, the toughest job in the works. He expected to work hard when he came to America, but the reality of the labor was beyond his worst imaginings. He toiled ten hours a day, six days a week, in the smoke and heat of the ovens, unloading and moving tons of coke every day. His lungs ached. His face and arms were scarred. Only twenty-eight, he looked much older.

Number One was owned by the H.C. Frick Coke Company, one of many mines it owned in the Connellsville Coal Field. Frick also owned the houses across the street and the store; it was employer, landlord, and merchant to the workers, an efficient and profitable arrangement.

Zoran reached the road, crossed the trolley tracks, and approached the ovens, feeling the heat strengthen. Walking around to the front of the ovens, he watched the other men work. Coal was being dumped into empty ovens. Some men were leveling out the loads. Masons were busy bricking up the door in front of others. And oven tenders circulated, checking the smoke to tell when the load was done.

"Hey, Gondik, get yer ass in gear. Three is ready to go." That was Zoran's boss, Moses Evans. He was a "company man," paid by the day, not by the ton like Zoran and most of the others. Arrogant and contemptuous, he drove the men hard. Zoran spit in his direction as he walked to the oven. *Some day you will pay, you piece of shit.*

What Moses meant was that the coal was done baking and it was time for Zoran to unload the oven. A water boy had already doused the load, cooling it some. Zoran used a long-handled hook to break out the bricks that sealed the front door. Then, using a long rake, he began pulling the coke from the oven.

It took Zoran almost four hours to unload an oven, first raking some coke out, then shoveling it into a high-sided wheelbarrow that he pushed over to the pier and dumped. This oven was almost empty and he was a sorry sight, drenched in sweat and grimy faced. Head down, he leaned on his rake. One more load and he could take a break.

"You wanna sleep, go home, you Hunkie bastard." Zoran jumped as Moses loomed over him. Dropping the rake, he clenched his fists.

"Get going or get out. There's plenty just off the boat looking for work."

Zoran's fists opened and his shoulders sagged. He was stuck here and they both knew it. He bent down and picked up the rake as Moses moved on.

The oven had cooled and Zoran was able to rake it clean. One last pile of coke strands fell at his feet. He picked up his fork and shoveled until only a small pile remained. As he bent to load it, something caught his eye. There, in the middle of the pile, sat a curved object. *That's not coke.* Curious, he scooped it up with the fork and dropped it at his feet. Kicking it over, he saw three holes.

He squatted for a better look and picked it up. *Smooth and hard. What the hell is it?* Finally his tired mind understood. Zoran dropped it and backed away slowly, making the sign of the cross. *God in heaven, it's a skull!*

"The coke from this region has a silvery luster, metallic ring, is cellular, tenacious, comparatively free from impurities, and is capable of bearing a heavy burden in the furnace. Its hardness, well developed cell structure, purity and uniform quality have given it a great reputation as a blast furnace coke."—*Bituminous Coal Losses and Mining Methods in Pennsylvania*, 1924

Chapter 2

Joe Zajac's sweat-stained shirt stuck to his chest. He'd been inspecting the Whitney Mine and Coke Works near Latrobe, Pennsylvania, for several hours. As security supervisor for the H.C. Frick Coke Company, these examinations were a part of his work. Frick recently purchased this mine, and several others in the area, from a smaller company. Joe had to inspect them all, and make sure they met Frick's standards.

"Hey, Zajac, over here." Across the coke yard he spotted Wesley Burdett, newly appointed mine superintendent for Whitney, standing near the coal tipple. Wesley waved him over.

Joe took a moment to untie the blue bandana he wore around his neck and wipe the sweat off his face before joining the other man. "What's up, Wes?"

"We need to get this barrel of lamp oil under lock and key. You find anything?"

Joe nodded. "Most always do. Nobody runs a mine like Frick." He pulled a small notebook from his pocket. "I found an unlocked boxcar, some leaky pipes, and a few other concerns. I'll put them all in my report."

"OK, buddy. Let's go over to the supply shed and finish up. Once we inventory that, we can call it a morning."

And a hot August morning it was. By eleven they finished counting the supplies. By eleven thirty Joe finished the report and delivered it to Wes. He left the office and walked to the streetcar stop. Taking a seat on a bench there, he stretched out his six-foot frame, hands behind his head. As he waited for the next car to Connellsville, his mind wandered.

Joe remembered little of his early life in rural Poland. *There was never enough food. The winters were hard*, Joe thought. His mother passed away when he was thirteen, sick one day and dead soon after. *Dad was never the same, and neither was I.*

In 1885, at age fifteen, Joe and his father, Karol, came to America, where there was plenty of work. Karol's brother Stanley had come over in 1880 and lived near Philadelphia. After a few weeks there, Karol found a coal mining job near Scranton.

The clanging bell of the approaching trolley snapped Joe out of his reverie. Its brakes squealed as the car came to a stop. Joe boarded and took a seat up front near the operator, watching with interest as the man released the brake and throttled up. The countryside rolled by as they cruised down the line. The scenery was a mix of rolling hills and farms tucked between the Laurel and Chestnut Ridges of the Allegheny Mountains. A smoky haze hung in the air.

It was almost one o'clock when they arrived in Connellsville. Joe jumped off the car at Brimstone Corner and walked down Main Street. His long strides moved him swiftly through the shoppers that packed the sidewalk. The street was clogged with parked delivery wagons, some nearly on top of the streetcar tracks that ran down the middle.

Joe ducked into Davidson's Grocery Store to pick up this week's edition of *The Courier,* then continued down Main. His destination was City Lunch, where he ate most every day.

I'm ready for a break from this heat, Joe thought as he pulled out his bandana and doffed his cap. Mopping the sweat from his face and neck, he entered the restaurant. Waving at Tony Molinari, the chief cook and bottle washer, he headed to his favorite spot at the far end of the lunch counter. He rarely sat anywhere else. Tony knew that and tried to always save his stool. Joe sat down sideways, with his back to the wall, and surveyed the room. As was his habit, he checked out the other customers.

Joe had a number of reasons for sitting at the end of the line. He was likely to be left alone, which suited him just fine, and as a former cop, he always felt safer with his back against the wall. His cop years also left him a habitual people watcher. He couldn't stop observing the crowd, and liked to keep an eye on the door. He could also see out the rear window, where the Main Street Bridge crossed the Youghiogheny River.

City Lunch was a decent place, nothing fancy but clean and neat. A row of smoke-stained windows let in plenty of light. Three ceiling fans turned lazily, moving the hot air around a bit. Faded red-and-white-checkered cloths covered the wooden tables. A small vase with a few snapdragons sat in the center of each one. More flowers sat in vases along the counter.

"Ah, Giuseppe, how's my favorite Polack?" Tony was a happy fellow, but why, Joe never could figure out. He was married to a gruff Italian woman and had nine kids. He worked six days a week over a hot stove, and if he wasn't in the restaurant he was tending his garden. But Tony almost always had a smile on his face and a friendly greeting for his regulars, and Joe was one of his best customers. He'd eaten here hundreds of times since moving to Connellsville.

"I'm doing better than my favorite Dago. What's the lunch special today?" Joe asked, even though he knew the answer. Every Saturday it was always the same.

"What you think? Spaghetti and meatballs! And fresh apple pie for dessert."

"Someday you're gonna surprise me and have something else on special, like maybe a nice plate of pierogies. I guess another plate of your greasy noodles won't kill me. Bring it on, and a big beer to wash it down."

Joe picked the bloom off a snapdragon and squeezed it, making the mouth open and close. "These flowers from your garden, Tony?"

"You know it, Joey. My tomatoes, peppers, and onions all come in nice, too. Everything fresh in my sauce today. I got a regular green thumb."

Joe again surveyed the room, and focused on a young couple at a table near the door. The man was frowning and talking a mile a minute. The woman looked sad and near tears. *Don't need to be Sherlock Holmes to figure that out*, Joe thought. *It's the end of the line for those lovebirds.*

Joe turned to the back window. It was miserable even for August, and the heavy haze that hung in the air was persistent. Twenty thousand coke ovens were in operation in the region, spewing tons of smoke and gas every day. There were times, if the winds were calm, you couldn't see the sun at noon. But the mines and coke works of the Connellsville region were thriving. More coal was mined here than anywhere in Pennsylvania, and no place in the world made more coke. Fortunes were being made. The foul air seemed a small price to pay.

Joe watched the West Penn Railway streetcar cross the bridge from New Haven. On Saturdays it was filled with the wives of the mine and coke workers. This was their day to come into the city from the "patch towns" built near almost every Frick mine. Everything could be bought in town at a lower price than at Frick's Union Supply Store.

Turning back to the counter, Joe picked up *The Courier* and started reading the front page.

"Here you go, Joey. Mangia!" Tony set a steaming mound of noodles and red sauce on the counter. Two giant meatballs perched on top. He returned in a minute with Joe's beer and two thick slices of crusty bread. From the smell of the place, Joe could tell it was fresh from the oven. "A big plate of pasta and gravy for a big hungry fella."

Tony knew him well. Joe had a big appetite. He carried his hundred and eighty pounds with ease, a busy life keeping him trim and fit. He took the beer and drank half. "Ah, that's good. Thanks, Tony. You got any cheese?"

Tony returned with some grated Parmesan. "So what you reading, Joey?"

"An article about coal mined in 1899. America leads the world. Pennsylvania mines produce more than the rest of America, and the Connellsville Field is tops in the state."

"That's some big news. You know, someday I'm gonna learn to read English. Maybe you can teach me?"

"If you're looking for a teacher, you better go back to school. Now leave me alone so I can eat in peace."

Tony smiled and shook his head. "Maybe I'll ask you again after you eat. I bet you missed your breakfast."

Now how'd he know that? Joe dug in and enjoyed his meal, cleaning the plate in just a few minutes. He wiped up the remaining sauce with his last bite of bread, then washed it all down with the rest of his beer. "That was pretty good for a change, Tony. I think I'll skip that apple pie, though. Don't want to get fat."

"You no got to worry about that, my friend. See you for breakfast Monday."

Joe paid the bill, picked up his paper, and left City Lunch, walking back up Main. The street was paved with red bricks. Stores lined both sides of the block from Arch to Pittsburgh Street, green-and-white-striped awnings shading the fronts. The sidewalks were crowded with shoppers, mostly women, the city ladies in long dresses and wide-brimmed hats, some carrying parasols.

He stopped outside of Featherman & Frank, one of Fayette County's largest dry goods stores. Its "August Clearance Sale" was in full swing. The miners' wives crowded around tables stacked high with fabric, clothing, and towels. They stood in contrast to the city women with their long black skirts, homemade blouses, and babushkas.

Joe had been in Connellsville for over two years. Despite the foul air, he found it a good place to live. It was a big change from Philadelphia, though, where he lived for fourteen years. The people were friendly and hardworking. The town, once a sleepy agricultural center, was undergoing a transformation driven by the coal and coke boom. Most of the downtown streets were paved. Many new buildings lined the streets, with more under construction. Just outside the city line in the South Side, ornate Victorian mansions lined Pittsburgh Street, evidence of the new money in town. All of Fayette County and Western Pennsylvania was the same. The superior coke made with coal from the Connellsville Field fueled the Pittsburgh steelworks. They in turn produced the rails and building girders that were tangible evidence of America's ongoing industrial revolution.

Joe stopped at the Royal Bakery on Main Street. Behind the counter a pretty young woman was bagging a loaf of bread for an old man. Her long brown hair was pinned in a bun on top of her head. "What's fresh from the oven?" Joe asked.

Helen Hudacek looked up, smiling. "I wondered when I'd see my man today." She finished with her customer and turned to Joe. "Are we still going out tonight?"

He'd been seeing her since they met at a Fourth of July church picnic. The last time it was dinner with her folks. *When did I become her man?* Joe mused. *She's getting serious.*

"I'm still game if you are. There's a new show opening at the Colonial Theatre. See you at seven."

She gave him a little wave as he left. "'Til then, Joe."

Heading north, Joe crossed the street and almost ran into a cop, who turned out to be his buddy, Johnny Davidson. "Joe, did you hear the news? They pulled some bones out of a coke oven out at Number One."

Chapter 3

When something went wrong at a Frick mine, it was Joe's job to investigate. He was in a hurry to get to Leisenring but wanted to stop by his apartment on Pittsburgh Street first. He washed his face and combed back his brown hair, then changed into a fresh shirt. Over it he wore a plaid vest. Stuffing a small notebook and pencil stub in the vest pocket, he grabbed his cap and hustled out the door. *The big shots at Frick will be riled up over this.* While deaths around the mines were all too common, no one had ever ended up in a coke oven. Remembering his planned date, he stopped by the bake shop to tell Helen the news.

The store was empty when he walked in. The little bell over the door jingled and Helen came through the curtains behind the counter. She smiled at Joe and joined him in front of the display cases.

"Back so soon?"

"I have some bad news, Helen. Johnny told me they found some bones in a coke oven out at Number One. I'm on my way out there now. I doubt I'll be back in time to make it to the Colonial tonight."

Helen's smile turned into a frown. "Oh, poo. And I had a new dress to wear, too. You sure?"

Joe nodded. "I'll make it up to you tomorrow. How about we spend the afternoon out at Soisson Park?"

"All right, Joe, I guess that's better than not seeing you at all this weekend." She placed her hand on his arm. "You be careful now."

Joe put his hand on top of hers. "I will, Helen. Say, how about one of those little poppy seed rolls for the ride?"

Helen's smile returned as she walked behind the counter and wrapped up a roll in brown paper. "Here you go. My treat. See you tomorrow around one."

Joe left the store and hurried to the streetcar terminal on Arch Street. *Helen is a good woman, but a bad match for a thirty-year-old dog like me*, Joe thought. Within a few minutes, he was on a West Penn streetcar bound for Leisenring.

The orange trolleys were a fixture in the Connellsville region. West Penn served the string of mines in the area that ran from Latrobe to

Uniontown. Joe loved riding on trains of all kinds, but these little streetcars were his favorites. Powered by electricity, they ran smooth and quiet.

Twenty minutes later Joe was at Number One. The trolley stopped on the main road by the tipple and Joe jumped off. He walked up the hill toward the mine superintendent's house. Located close to the company store, the house stood in stark contrast to the miners' homes. It had eight rooms, with a broad front porch, where at the moment a man sat. A freshly painted white picket fence ringed the lot. A neatly tended garden filled the side yard. Behind the house, Joe could hear children playing.

The man on the porch was Jim Thornton. Joe knew him well. He'd been with Frick most of his life, starting out as a miner. He was a true company man now, but never forgot his roots. Jim was a fair boss, respected by his workers and sympathetic to their circumstances.

Joe walked up to the foot of the porch steps. Jim was slouched in a wicker chair, shirttails out, with a white handkerchief tucked into his collar. His face was pale and sweaty.

"Afternoon, Jim. Want some company?"

"Sure, Joe, come on up."

Joe walked up the steps and lowered himself into the chair next to Jim. They sat for a minute, watching the action down at Number One. The wind had shifted, blowing the smoke away from the house. A pitcher of water stood on a small table between the chairs. Jim leaned forward, wiped his face with the handkerchief, and poured them both a glass.

"I reckon you heard about the bones," Jim said.

"I did. Came out straight away."

"This has been a bad day, started damn early, too. This doesn't figure. Nobody ever ended up in a coke oven in my thirty years working around them."

Joe picked up his glass and took a long swallow. "I'm no old-timer but it looks impossible. No man could stand the heat." He fanned his face with his cap. "The Frick big shots will shit a brick."

"Don't I know it? We need to get to the bottom of this quick."

"So where do we stand?"

"The county sheriff's already been here, name of Tom Miller. You should call on him come Monday. It looks to me like he doesn't want any part of this. He's ready to call it an accident, like maybe the fellow got drunk and fell in."

Joe took another sip of his water and nodded. "Any idea who the fellow is?"

"It's most likely George Goretsky. 'Big George'—as the men called him—was the fire boss at Number One. His wife reported him missing this morning. We found his clothes in the bathhouse."

Joe was no miner, but he did know that the fire boss was an important job at every coal mine, usually the first man in every morning. He checked for the buildup of explosive gasses, and made sure the mine was well ventilated. *If the bastard in Scranton had the sense to hire one, my father might still be alive.*

"What can you tell me about him?"

The supervisor loaded his pipe and leaned back in the chair. "Big George wasn't the most popular man in Leisenring. In fact, many a man hated his guts. He was a heavy drinker, spent a lot of time in the bars around town. The Star was his favorite joint, I hear."

Joe leaned forward and emptied his glass. He knew The Star well, probably had even seen Goretsky there. "Why was he hated?"

"George was a tough man to work with. He was a big-mouthed bully and mean as a snake. But he knew his job and came to work sober every day. He was rough on many a miner at Number One, though, and more than once it's come to blows."

"Anything happen lately?"

Jim nodded. "Last week George had a run-in with a new miner, name of Tomas Smida. Way I hear it, George called him a dumb Hunkie in front of the whole crew. Tomas came after him with his shovel and swore that he'd kill George if he didn't shut his mouth."

Joe knew recent immigrants from Eastern Europe were often called Hunkies, and it was no compliment. These Serbs, Slavs, Slovaks, Hungarians, and Poles were the underclass, valued less than the earlier English-speaking immigrants. It was an insult, fighting words.

Joe got out his pencil and started making entries in his notebook. "Does Tomas live in Leisenring? I'll need to go talk to him."

"No, he lives with his family over at Monarch. Let's stop by the store and I'll get his house number from the bookkeeper."

Monarch was the company town at Leisenring No. 3, another Frick mine a few miles down the road.

"What exactly did you find in the oven?"

"The biggest piece was a skull, but we found a few other shards, too. I'm surprised it didn't all get burnt up. It couldn't have been in there too long or nothing would be left."

Joe and Jim walked down the hill to Frick's Union Supply Store. It was a fixture in coal country, and made good money for the company. New workers had to buy their own tools, and a man needed a lunch bucket. You could get those at the store on credit. If you worked for Frick, you could also get a weekly advance on your wages in the form of scrip, good only at the store. Then, on payday, what you owed was deducted from your earnings. Your house rent was also withheld. Most weeks, little cash remained. The system left the workers at the mercy of the company, little better than indentured servants who would never pay off their debt.

The mine's offices were located in the store building. Joe soon had Tomas's house number in Monarch. He and Jim continued down the hill to the mine and coke works. Their first stop was the new bathhouse, a squat brick building with a boiler outside.

"This here's the pride of Number One, Joe, loved by the miners. It sure beats going home dirty and getting scrubbed off in a washtub by the stove."

They entered the bathhouse. One wall was lined with hooks, another with showerheads. Two rows of benches filled the middle. George's clean clothes were still there, hanging on a hook in the corner. Joe examined the contents of the pockets. There wasn't much to look at: a Frick ID card, a few coins, some pieces of wire. He took out his notebook and made another entry.

"Did the sheriff see this?"

"He did, but like I said, he's not much interested in any investigation."

"There's not much here. Was George doing anything special in the mine on Friday?"

"I don't know, but if you come back on Monday, you can ask the mine boss. He'll show you around the mine, too."

Joe felt his heart pound. He'd never been down in a mine. The thought of entering one made him sweat. He couldn't let Jim know that, though. Leisenring was a deep-shaft mine, the coal seam and working face over three hundred feet below ground.

"OK, Jim. Let's go look at where the skull was found."

Joe and Jim left the washhouse and walked over to the double bank of coke ovens. The wind had shifted and the two men were enveloped in a cloud of heavy smoke. Joe felt lightheaded. *How can a man stand this all day?* If it hadn't been for Uncle Stan, this could have been his life.

"Pity the poor buggers that work here. I tended the ovens when I started with Frick. The smoke and heat are hard to take."

Joe and Jim walked down the track used by the lorries to load the ovens. "How'd the body end up in the oven?"

"Had to be dumped through the top. The oven was charged and sealed Thursday."

Joe inspected the oven. It had a small opening on top where the coal was dumped in. "Would Big George fit through the hole?"

Jim nodded. "They called him Big George but he really wasn't. He barely topped five feet, and was skinny as a rail."

At this hour most of the men still working were the oven tenders. They'd be here all night, watching the smoke coming from each oven, occasionally adjusting the draft holes. "Would these same men have been working on Friday night?"

Jim nodded. "Let's go round and talk to them."

For the next hour Joe and Jim questioned each worker. None remembered seeing anything or anyone out of the ordinary on Friday night. And, as the sun began to set, Joe could understand why. With the heavy smoke blowing across the tracks, he could barely see ten feet in front of him. And the tenders mostly worked down in front of the ovens.

Joe was starting to feel sick. *I need to get out of the smoke.* "I've seen enough here for the day. I'll go see Tomas tomorrow. Tonight I'm going to see if I can run into any of Big George's friends down at The Star."

Joe and Jim walked up to the road, where they parted. "Thanks for coming out, Joe. See you bright and early on Monday."

Joe sat down on a bench at the trolley stop. While he waited for the streetcar, his thoughts turned to his fear of mines.

Life was hard in Scranton. His father, Karol, worked six days a week, ten hours a day. Their home was in a shantytown near the mine, a two-room shack with an outhouse in back. Water came from a pump down the dirt road. Karol came home every day black and tired, barely able to get cleaned up. Joe did the cooking, using a coal stove that also heated the shack.

They were better off than the other miners with big families to feed. There was always food in the house. Karol insisted that Joe stay in school. He learned to read, write, and speak English. After school, in the summer, he tended the garden. In the winter, he picked coal from along the tracks. Time passed and Joe grew into a tall young man, able to look out for himself. Fights in the shantytown were common. Joe was a target of the older boys because of his height.

All mines are dangerous places, some worse than others. Karol's was a small operation, run by a man with little concern for safety. Accidents were common. Men lost fingers and toes to falling rock. At times they worked in water up to their waist. The shaft was poorly ventilated, the air stale.

One day the local priest stopped by Joe's one-room schoolhouse. He interrupted the class and said a few words to the teacher, who then asked Joe to come with them.

The priest put his arm around Joe's shoulder. "I have something very bad to tell you. There's been an accident at the mine, an explosion. Three men were down there. I'm sorry to tell you that your father was one of them."

Joe stared at him for a moment with tears in his eyes, then ran to the mine. There was nothing to see but smoke.

The mine owner stopped by the house and gave Joe ten dollars. Joe wanted to shove it down the bastard's throat. He'd heard his father say many times that the mine was an accident waiting to happen. More angry than sad, Joe shoved the money in his pocket. The bodies were never even recovered. The mine flooded and was closed, a small wooden sign at the shaft the only reminder of the three men buried there.

Joe shook his head. His thoughts returned to the murder of Big George. And murder it was; George didn't fall into the oven by accident. He was dead by then.

Joe heard the streetcar bell clang. Looking up the tracks, he saw it coming around a curve. Its lone headlamp cast a dim light through the gray dusk. The car came to a screeching stop. Joe boarded, paid his fare, and sat up front close to the operator. With another clang they departed for Connellsville.

Chapter 4

Joe watched the streetcar operator get the trolley going again. He liked talking to the men who ran the trains. "How you doing, buddy?"

The operator gave Joe a quick glance. "Too damn hot."

"What's new at West Penn?"

"There's talk of building a power plant up at Ohiopyle Falls and starting a line in the mountains."

"Maybe I can catch on with them. Running one of these might suit me."

"Ain't so bad most times, 'less they run off a trestle or the brakes go. Damn sight better than working for Frick."

Joe left the man to his work, moved to the rear, and planned the next few days. Tonight he'd try to track down some of George's friends at The Star. Tomorrow he'd promised Helen a trip to Soisson Park, but in the morning he could squeeze in a trip to Monarch. Monday it was back to Leisenring to talk to the mine boss, and for Joe's unwilling descent into the mine. Maybe he'd try to see George's widow, too. After that, if he had time, he'd go up to Uniontown and see the sheriff. He supposed eventually he'd have to go to Scottdale and meet with the Frick bosses. *Hope I got something to go on by then.*

Looking out the window, Joe was surprised to see that they were already crossing the Youghiogheny. The river separated the boroughs of Connellsville on the east side from New Haven on the west. Joe enjoyed fishing the Yough upstream for trout a bit, above the Trotter Water pumping station where the water was clean.

The Monarch line ended at the terminal on Arch Street. Joe got off and walked to his apartment. It was almost 9:00 p.m. but the sidewalks remained crowded, the street still filled with horses and wagons. It was payday, and for the Connellsville working men, Saturday night was for drinking. Sunday meant church for most, and one day to rest.

Joe stopped by his apartment to clean up again. The short time spent near the coke ovens was enough to leave him grimy and reeking of smoke. He took a few minutes to read his notes and add a few thoughts. He started a page for Monday, listing "mine visit" and "Sheriff Miller." When finished, he combed back his hair, put on his favorite cap and a fresh vest, and headed out for the evening.

Joe heard the noise from The Star a block away. It was one of the most popular taverns in town. *Bars and churches*, thought Joe, *there's one or the other on every corner.*

Joe had been in The Star many times. He walked up to the end of the bar, ordered a beer, and surveyed the crowd.

It was one big smoky room, with a bar on the right and a collection of mismatched tables and chairs on the left. A brass foot rail ran the length of the bar, with matching brass spittoons placed every few feet. The high ceiling was covered with tin tiles. A tall mirror ran the length of the wall behind the bar and an assortment of whiskey bottles lined the cabinet top under it. All in all it was a friendly joint, and usually peaceful.

Joe started coming to The Star shortly after moving to town. He'd met his friend Lloyd McCormick here early on. They started as drinking buddies and over time grew into close friends, spending countless nights together, shooting the bull, and getting drunk. It was no surprise when he heard Lloyd's booming voice.

"Hey, Zajac, long time no see! Where you been hiding?"

Joe turned to his buddy and they shook hands. "Howdy, Lloyd. I was hoping to run into you. How's life treating you?"

Lloyd was about Joe's height but heavier. He had copper-colored hair, a full beard, and big ears. Tonight he wore a derby tilted at an angle, almost resting on the top of his ear.

"No complaints. You ain't been around much since you started seeing the girl from the bakery. What's it been? A week? I thought you were sick or something."

Joe nodded. "It's been about that long, maybe longer. What's new at the brickyard?" Lloyd was a boss for the Soisson Brick Company and worked at the plant in South Connellsville.

"What with all the new ovens being built, and the building boom, we can't make them fast enough. We're opening another plant at Dutch Bottom. And guess who's going to be the running the joint? Yours truly."

"That calls for a celebration, my friend." Joe slapped his palm on the bar. "Bartender, another for me and one for Big Red here. And two shots of Old Overholt." The bartender pulled the beers and poured the shots.

"Here's looking at you, Boss Man," Joe said.

They raised their glasses and drank half, then downed the shots and finished the beers.

"Damn, that's tasty. Bartender, another round."

"You know, Joe, if God made anything better than beer, he most likely kept it for himself."

"Amen, brother. You look hungry and I could sure use a bite to eat. It's been a long day." The bartender brought their drinks and they took them to an empty table in the corner.

A waitress Joe recognized approached. "How about a couple of roast beef sandwiches, Nell?" Joe said.

With a nod and a smile, Nell wrote down their order and headed to the kitchen.

Joe took a sip of his beer and shook his head. "I'm getting a funny feeling about 'that girl from the bakery,' like I'm a fish on the hook, and she's starting to reel me in."

"I figured you were only in it for the pies."

Joe laughed and raised his glass. "And the jelly rolls."

They clinked mugs and drank deep.

"I heard about them finding the bones in the oven out at Number One. What's the skinny?"

Joe took off his cap and scratched his head. "I'm not sure yet, but I don't think it was an accident. You know a fellow name of George Goretsky?"

"Big George? Yeah, I know of him. He's a real loudmouth. Been coming in here for a while. Rubbed me the wrong way the first time he opened his trap. Was it him that got it?"

"Looks like it. You know who he drank with?"

"He had a few mine buddies that could put up with him. No one I knew, though."

"Let me know if you see any of them come in. I'd like to ask a few questions."

Their sandwiches arrived, thick slices of beef, raw onions, and mustard between slices of crusty rye bread. Joe and Lloyd polished them off, and their second round of drinks.

"More beer, Joe? It's my turn to buy." Joe drained his glass and handed it to Lloyd.

"I could use another shot, too."

Lloyd walked up to the bar to get their refills. Joe leaned back in his chair and stretched out his legs. The day's events were fading fast.

Lloyd returned with round three and sat down heavily. "Here you go Joe. This should get you where you want to go."

"You're only here for a little vacation, Lloyd. Might as well try to enjoy yourself. I heard Pap say that many a time, and he was right."

"Thirst is a shameless disease, so here's to a shameful cure. That's a bit of old Irish wisdom for you." Lloyd looked toward the door and let out a low whistle. "There's a fine-looking woman for you."

Joe turned to the door. A well-dressed woman stood just inside, talking to some of the customers. A moment later, she walked over to the bar and talked to the bartender. Tall and slim with her auburn hair up in a bun, she wore a long blue dress and a matching wide-brimmed hat. Joe guessed her to be about his age. She finished her conversation with the bartender and quickly disappeared into a small office in the rear of the tavern.

"Who is she?" Joe asked.

"That's Peggy Patterson. Her father owns the joint. He fell sick and she's been helping to run the place for the last couple of weeks."

"Single?"

"Yep, and damned if I know why. Good-looking, smart, and her pappy owns a saloon. Sounds like a dream walking."

"Perfect as a woman can get."

"I gotta beat it. I'm feeling no pain, and I promised Mom I'd come over for Sunday breakfast."

Lloyd finished the last of his beer and, after making plans to get together with Joe again on Wednesday, said good-bye and left. Joe enjoyed Lloyd's straightforward ways. Good or bad, you always knew where you stood with him.

Joe sat alone at the table, gauging his condition. He'd had plenty, but always could hold his liquor. He felt damn good, enjoyed the sense of recklessness the booze created. But he'd learned that drinking could also bring out his dark side. He'd thought often about killing that bastard mine operator in Scranton. *It would be easy to do now. Enough time has passed; no one would ever make the connection.*

But tonight Joe's thoughts turned to Peggy Patterson. *I wonder if she could shed some light on who Goretsky drank with.* He finished his beer and sauntered back to her office.

Joe approached and knocked on the half-open door, cap in hand. "How do, Miss Patterson. May I have a word with you?"

She looked up and motioned him in. "One minute, please. I need to finish these entries. Have a seat." She had half glasses perched on her nose. *The picture of a bookkeeper, and a pretty one at that*, Joe thought. He looked around the office, waiting for her to finish.

The walls were covered with pictures and papers, some looking quite old and others more recent. There were several pictures of baseball teams. The Star had sponsored a club in the city merchants' league for years. The Yough Beer calendar was still on July. What looked like old bills were hanging punched on a nail. The desk, however, was neat and well organized.

Peggy finished writing, took off her glasses, and looked up, smiling. "There, now. Books all done for another day. What can I do for you, sir?"

Green eyes and red hair—my favorite color scheme. "My name is Joe Zajac, Miss Patterson. I'm employed by the Frick company, in charge of security and the like."

"Pleased to meet you, Mr. Zajac. What can I do for you?"

"We've had an unfortunate incident at Leisenring No.1 today. The remains of a body were pulled from a coke oven. From all indications, it looks to be a man named George Goretsky."

Peggy's lips tightened, her cheeks flushed. "What brings you to The Star?"

"Well, first off, I'm one of your best customers. But I also heard that George came here on occasion. I was hoping that you might be able to show me some of the fellows he drank with."

Peggy sighed, stood up, and closed the door. She leaned against the front of the desk, arms folded. "I knew George. He was a pest."

Joe smelled roses. "How long had you known him?"

"George has been coming in here off and on for a long time, as I understand it. He and some of the other mine bosses were regulars most Saturday nights. I only met him about a few weeks ago, when I started coming in to keep the books. My father owns this place. That first night George was with a fellow I knew, Charlie Kurtz. I sat down at their table for a bit and Charlie introduced us."

"You say he was a pest. How so?"

"George took a fancy to me that night, I could tell. Kept on about what a fine figure of a lady I was, couldn't keep his eyes off me. He made me feel quite uncomfortable. I didn't stay very long."

"Was that the only time you spoke?"

"No. He came back the next Saturday, and the Saturday after that. Both times were the same. He even had the nerve to invite me to a show, and him a married man! Last weekend he was here again. I happened to be sitting with a gentleman, name of Henry Brooks. He and I have been friends for some time. Henry has timberlands up in the mountains. He's big and strong as a horse. Well, George came over to our table and started up again, and Henry didn't care much for it. The two of them started arguing. George made the mistake of telling Henry where to go. So Henry picked him up and pitched him out the door, told him that if he ever came near me again, he'd fix him good."

"Have you seen Henry since then?"

"No. He mainly comes down to town on Saturday, and not every Saturday at that. He may be by later on tonight, though. He's had his share of fights, but he'd never kill a man. He's not that kind."

"I'm only trying to find out as much as I can about George and what he's been up to. If Henry comes by, mention that I'd like to see him. I have rooms at the White Front Apartments."

"I'll do so if I see him."

Joe got up and put on his hat. "Thank you for your time, Miss Patterson, and a good evening to you."

"And to you, Mr. Zajac. Good luck with your investigation."

Joe left The Star and walked up Pittsburgh Street, weaving slightly.

Chapter 5

Joe drifted awake early Sunday morning, feeling groggy and dry-mouthed. *You did it again, Zajac.* He got out of bed, stood for a moment, then sat back down on the edge of the mattress. It was just after six o'clock in the morning and already too hot to stay in bed. His head clearing, he got up and walked to the open window, white curtains hanging limply across it. Parting them, Joe surveyed the day. The sun had been up for almost an hour but it still looked like dawn. The incessant haze hung in the still air.

Last night had been a good time. Lloyd always makes him laugh. The only hitch was that they always ended up drunk. And meeting Peggy Patterson was an unexpected pleasure. Most women his age were married. The single women in town were younger, or older widows. He'd want to talk to her old boyfriend about George, but Joe doubted that Henry Brooks came out to Leisenring to stuff Goretsky in the coke oven.

Joe pulled on his pants, grabbed the water pitcher, and walked down the hall to the bathroom. He returned, poured himself a glass, and dumped the rest in the washbasin. Fifteen minutes later, Joe was clean and shaved. Dressed in his Sunday best, he headed out.

Connellsville had many Catholic churches, each serving a different group of immigrants. The Irish, Italians, and Hungarians all had their own parishes. But there was no Polish church. So when Joe went to Mass, it was usually at the Slovak parish, St. John's, in New Haven, on Seventh Street, just off of Main. If he hurried, he could make the seven o'clock Mass before going out to Monarch.

Joe believed in God, but his faith wasn't strong. And it troubled him to see the dirt-poor workers putting their money in the collection basket, money they could better use to feed their families. *Now, their faith is strong. There are better days ahead for them, if not here on earth, then in Heaven.*

Joe went to church because it reminded him of his mother. Some of his earliest memories were of going to Mass with her. They didn't go every Sunday; it was a five-mile wagon ride to the closest church. But they went on Christmas, Easter, and a few other times during the year. *Those were the good old days.*

Heading down Main Street, Joe decided to walk the eight blocks instead of waiting for the streetcar. The trip would clear his head. Only a few businesses were open at this hour. There was a little café around the corner from the church that opened early. He'd go there for breakfast afterward.

St. John's was a growing parish. Even the early service was a full house. More Slovaks arrived in Fayette County every day to work the mines and ovens, and almost all of them attended St. John's. Joe arrived at the church fifteen minutes early, and found a spot in the last pew.

The two front rows were filled with old women, all wearing long black dresses and babushkas on their heads, widows for the most part. They prayed the rosary in Slovak, heads bowed, fingers working the beads. No matter how early Joe arrived, they were always already there. The chanting was rhythmic; the women swayed as they prayed. Joe watched and listened, engrossed by the ritual.

A few minutes later, he saw Helen come in with her parents. She smiled at him and gave a nod as they made their way down the aisle. Soon after that, the servers came out and lit the candles on the altar. Mass would begin shortly. Joe sat quietly and observed the parishioners.

The church reflected the social classes of the town. Some of the families had been here for twenty years or more. The ones who spoke English well worked their way up the ladder at the mines. They were easy to spot—better dressed and well fed. Many had escaped the patch towns.

The more recent immigrants spoke mostly Slovak. Their clothes were worn and patched. Many of the men sported handlebar mustaches. The women's clothes were mostly what they had arrived in America with—peasant garb from the old country.

Then there were a few families who had worked their way out of the mines, or knew trades that gave them a leg up. That was the Hudacek family story. As bakers, they were able to open up shop and join Connellsville's growing merchant class.

The priest and servers entered the vestibule and, as the parishioners sang the opening hymn, proceeded up the aisle to the altar. The mass was in Slovak, but you didn't really need to understand the priest to follow the service. It was the same, no matter what the language. Joe knew enough Slovak to join in the responses. The service ended with a final blessing, and Joe slipped out. He was ready to get back to the job of figuring out who killed Big George. *All I have to do is find out why.*

Before leaving, Joe remembered his date with Helen and waited for her to come out, waving as she came down the steps with her mother and father. Doffing his cap, he greeted her parents, then turned to Helen. "Ready for an afternoon at Soisson Park?"

"Sure, Joe. When can I expect you?"

"I'll be by your place around one o'clock."

With the plans made, Joe walked up to the café on Main Street for his breakfast. He was back on the street twenty minutes later, waiting for the Leisenring streetcar already heading his way. The end of the line was about a mile from Monarch, where Tomas Smida lived. Joe boarded and took a seat alone in the back for a change. The car was only half full this morning, mostly with families going back home after church. Joe watched the scenery go by, and in a few minutes they were back at Leisenring. The mine and coke works were mostly deserted today. Only a few oven tenders were visible as the streetcar traveled past the long row of ovens.

The trolley stopped at Leisenring and most of the passengers got off. No one got on and soon they were back under way. In just a few minutes they arrived at the end of the line, a bit past Little Summit Road.

Joe and the rest of the passengers got off. He hung around for a minute to watch the trolley operator reverse the electrical contact arm above the car, allowing it to change directions without being turned around. The car could be operated from either end. The operator accomplished that with a long pole that was usually stowed under the car. It looked like an oversized clothesline prop. The operator flipped the arm backward, and soon he and his passengers were on their way back toward Connellsville.

Joe walked down the lane toward Monarch, the Leisenring No. 3 company town. The Leisenring No. 2 mine was further south, about two miles away. The three mines fed almost fifteen hundred coke ovens.

Joe approached town, past the mine entrance and coke works. The layout was almost identical to Number One. The smell of the ovens overpowered what had been the cleaner air Joe enjoyed as he approached from upwind. Picking up the pace, Joe hurried past the works and entered the patch.

Tomas lived in house number seventy-nine, on the far side of the village. Joe walked slowly, admiring the big gardens most of the homes had. The fences and foundations had all been recently whitewashed. The whole place had a neat and well-kept appearance, despite the modest nature of the homes and the near poverty of the workers. The people took pride in what they had.

The gardens were important to the families, providing a big part of their food supply. The women worked hard to keep them weeded and the plants healthy. Frick awarded prizes in September for the best gardens in each patch. While the prizes were modest, it was a great honor to have your garden named the best. Joe could see beans, tomatoes, peppers, and cornstalks sprouting from each plot.

Joe approached number seventy-nine. An old woman in a long dress was weeding the garden. Joe called to her from outside the fence. "Is Tomas around?" The woman eyed Joe up and down, then turned away and kept weeding. In a minute Joe heard a screen door slam. A young man approached him from the rear of the house. "I'm Tomas. Who's looking for me?"

Tomas was shorter than Joe, and very skinny. He had short black hair that looked even darker against the pale skin of his face that marked him as a miner. He wore black trousers with suspenders over a sleeveless undershirt.

"My name's Joe Zajac. I work for Frick. I'm here to ask you a few questions about George Goretsky."

Tomas opened the gate and motioned Joe in. They sat on the front porch steps. Tomas pulled out a bag of tobacco and rolled a cigarette. He lit it, took a few deep drags, and fixed Joe with a cold stare. "I heard about Big George. Someone turned him into coke, eh?"

"That's right, Tomas. Somebody roasted him good."

Tomas leaned back, resting on his elbows. "I'm gonna go light a candle for the prick. I hope they can clean the shit out of the oven." He took another drag and gazed across the yard at the old woman working in the garden. Tomas said a few words to her in Slovak. She nodded, wiped her hands on her apron, and walked to the backyard, where she sat on a swing by the grape arbor.

"She works too hard for an old lady."

"I heard that you told George you'd kill him. Now, a week later, he's dead. What do you know about it?"

"Yeah, I told him I'd kill him, and I meant it, too. But I didn't get the chance. Someone beat me to it!" Tomas started laughing, then coughing. He spit a black gob of phlegm on the wooded sidewalk. "A prick like George, he asked for it. He thinks just because he speaks good English, and got off the boat before me, he can treat me like shit, call me names. He got what was coming to him."

"Have any idea who might have done it?"

"Every man that had to work with him hated his guts. I bet his family won't even miss him. All I know is, it wasn't me." Tomas took a last drag from his smoke and flicked the butt away. He stood up and turned to Joe.

"I gotta go finish the garden work. And we got a big baseball game this afternoon. Monarch against Leisenring, the loser buys the beer."

"One more question, Tomas. Where were you Friday after your shift was over?"

"I came straight home and had dinner with my family."

Joe got up, dusting off the seat of his good pants. "Do me a favor—keep your ears open. If you hear anything, let the supervisor know. He'll get in touch with me. Prick or not, I need to find out who killed Big George."

Chapter 6

Joe retraced his route back out of Monarch and waited near the end of the line for the return car. They ran every hour on Sunday and he'd just missed the noon departure. With some time to kill, he decided to walk to Billican's Tavern a bit down the road.

Joe helped himself to some water from the pump outside, wetting his handkerchief and wiping the sweat and dust from his face. Then he drank a ladleful and entered the tavern. A few men stood at the bar, eyeing him as he entered. It was a local joint; very few strangers came out this way. Joe bought a shot of whiskey and a beer and sat at a table. He drained the shot and stared out the window, his back to the bar.

Billican's catered mostly to the mine bosses and other company men. The tonnage men and other laborers couldn't afford to drink in taverns for the most part. They usually stayed around the patch, downing whatever homemade wine was available, or maybe some corn whiskey.

Joe didn't know what to make of Tomas Smida. The man hated Big George, that was clear, but enough to murder him? Tomas had threatened to kill George, Joe couldn't ignore that. And if he did murder George, he wouldn't be confessing to it.

The men at the bar were an angry lot. Joe eavesdropped on their conversation while continuing to stare out the window.

"I tell you, Frick sold us down the river. This deal with Carnegie Brothers is a blow. Frick's not a coke man anymore. He sold us out when he let Carnegie take over his company. Who can make a living with the price of coke so low?"

Henry Clay Frick was one of the most powerful men in America, and by most accounts, also the most hated. He was a local boy made good, born and raised in Westmoreland County, not far from Connellsville. Starting with just a few mines and coke ovens, he'd built the H.C. Frick Coke Company into the largest and most profitable coke operation in Western Pennsylvania, and the world.

The man who had been talking continued. "Frick wasn't happy being the prince of Coke. He wanted to be a steel man. Now look what he's left us with. Selling to Carnegie for a dollar thirty-five a ton, with the other operators getting almost three dollars! And you and I are paying the price."

Joe knew the miners and cokers were paid on a sliding scale, based on the selling price of coke. At a dollar thirty-five, the men could barely keep food on the table. He understood some of the manipulations that created these hard times for the Frick workers, but most of it was beyond him.

The relationship between H.C. Frick and Andrew Carnegie was long and fractious. At times they were the best of friends, at other times near enemies, but their partnership helped make them both among the richest men in America. Which was the most callous could be debated, but the truth was, they made millions off the backs of the poor immigrants who labored in their mills, mines, and coke yards.

Frick was ruthless in his dealings with the workers. In 1892, while in charge of Carnegie Brothers Steel, his refusal to recognize a labor union precipitated one of the most violent strikes ever to hit the steel industry— the Battle of Homestead. The conflict killed ten workers and Pinkerton guards. The strike was broken after a failed assassination attempt against Frick turned public opinion against the union. Nonetheless, Frick was hated by most working men, especially his own.

When he thought about it, Joe had some sympathy for these workers, even though he was a Frick company man himself and made a good living. Only by the grace of God, and the help of his Uncle Stan, had he escaped the life of hard and risky labor that was the lot of so many men like Tomas Smida.

The clang of the streetcar bell ended Joe's reflections. He drank up and walked back to the end of the line, once again watching the operator use the long pole to flop the power pickup, preparing the car for the return trip. Joe settled into a seat up front and they were soon under way back to town.

"How you doing, buddy? What's new at West Penn?" Joe asked.

The operator gave Joe a quick look and a nod but had nothing to say. *I guess he's the quiet type.*

Before long, they passed the power station that supplied the electricity for the local West Penn operation. Like most everything else, here and all across America, it ran on coal. The smokestacks belched more smoke into the cloudy sky.

Joe jumped off the streetcar at Fourth and Main, and walked the two blocks to Helen's house, arriving right on time. The Hudaceks lived in a gray two-story frame house with a white picket fence around the yard. Like most every home, it had a big garden in the back. Joe waved to Helen's father, Frank, who was picking tomatoes, then came through the gate, walked up the front steps, and knocked on the front door. Helen's mother, Sophie, answered the door and led him to the parlor. "Hello again, Joseph. Helen will be right with you. Take a load off. I'm just finishing up the dishes."

Joe sat on the edge of the sofa, holding his hat. He inspected the room. Little doilies adorned the tops of the end tables. A small tea table sat in front of the sofa. It was well furnished, with gaslights. Managing the bake shop, while hard work, allowed the Hudaceks to live a decent life.

Joe was soon joined by Frank, who sat down across from Joe, wiping his head with a white handkerchief. "That's another hot one out there today, but the garden is doing great. Did you see the size of my tomatoes?"

"Sure did, Mr. Hudacek. You're as good in the garden as you are in the bake shop. What's your secret?"

"Plenty of horseshit. And after you bring my daughter back this evening, I'll have a bag of tomatoes for you sitting on the kitchen table." Frank finished wiping his face and put his handkerchief in his pocket. "So I heard about the body out at Number One. Was it an accident?"

"He was the fire boss at the mine. I don't think he ended up in the coke oven willingly. I spent yesterday with the superintendent. The man wasn't very well liked, so I already have some suspects. I have plenty to keep me busy for a while."

"Well, if you ever get tired of being a Frick cop, let me know. I could always use some help at the shop."

Joe heard footsteps on the stairs and rose as Helen entered the parlor. She looked great in a long gingham dress and big straw hat. She carried a parasol and a little bag.

"Are you ready to make up for breaking our date last night, Joseph? Let's go have some fun."

Joe and Helen walked back to Main Street, and then decided to walk over to Connellsville instead of waiting for the next streetcar. They would have to change trains for the South Connellsville line at the terminal anyway.

"I heard that the show at the Colonial was a good one, Joe. I'm sorry we missed it. Did you have to work late last night?"

"I got back in town around eight. Then I ended up stopping by The Star for a sandwich and ran into Lloyd. I was home by ten or so."

"Did you and Lloyd get drunk as usual?"

What is it with women that they always want to know how much you drink? How much he drank was his own business. "Yes, Helen, they had to roll us out of there on a wagon."

"Very funny. So tell me about your little mystery. Have it all figured out yet?"

"The man's only been dead a day. Even Sherlock Holmes needs time to sort things out. This is the roughest thing I've had to handle since I joined up with Frick. I have a busy week ahead of me."

Helen hooked her arm through Joe's, shading them both with her parasol. "Not too busy to see me, I hope."

Joe forced a smile, but was getting an uneasy feeling about him and Helen. She was a nice, smart girl, and pretty. He'd been seeing her for a month now. They got along fairly well, except for her nagging about his drinking. The problem was that at twenty-one, Helen was looking for a husband, and at thirty, Joe was on the verge of becoming a confirmed bachelor. In fairness to her, he'd have to end it soon.

"You know I couldn't go too long without something from the ovens at the Royal."

Joe and Helen crossed over the Yough, arm in arm. The new bridge was quite a change from the old suspension bridge it replaced. The streetcars couldn't use that one; it wasn't strong enough. This steel replacement, supported by two big stone piers, was built to last.

Reaching the Connellsville side of the river, they turned onto Arch Street and waited at the West Penn Terminal for the South Connellsville car. It soon arrived and they boarded along with a dozen others, all likely heading out to Soisson Park for the afternoon. Better yet, they were riding in an open summer car, enjoying a cool and breezy trip as they headed up Arch Street hill.

The South Connellsville line ran up Arch Street and through South Side, past the Colonial Theatre. Riding out Race Street, Joe eyed the many homes being built on what had been mostly open farmland until a few years ago. *If I ever settle down, I'd like to live in South Side.*

After a few more turns, the line ended up on Pittsburgh Street and entered South Connellsville. A mile later their ride—and the line—ended at Soisson Park, a sign proudly proclaiming it THE PEOPLE'S PLEASURE RETREAT.

Joseph Soisson started his brick business in 1865. Although he had several competitors, most of the bricks used to build the coke ovens, and now to pave the city streets, were made by his company. They had a manufacturing facility nearby, complete with company housing for many of the workers and bosses. The park, nestled in Longabough Hollow, had become wildly popular, the place to go on a Sunday afternoon.

"Let's go for a boat ride, Joe. The lake isn't too crowded yet."

"How about we get me a beer first? Then I'll row you around all afternoon."

Helen's smile disappeared as she shook her head. "Can't you even take Sunday off?"

Chapter 7

Joe was dreaming about his father. They were together in a coal mine, pitch-black except for a small pool of light thrown by their miner's lamps. "I told you, Joe—no matter what, don't ever go to work in the mines. It's too risky." Joe heard a rumble, felt the ground shake. "Run for it, Joe, before it's too late!" Another rumble, this one closer. Then a loud explosion.

Joe woke up, wet with sweat. He saw a flash of light. A loud bang shook the room. *Thank God it's only a thunderstorm.* He'd dreamt about his father before, but this one was the worst.

He got up, closed the window, and sat back down on the edge of the bed, head in hands. It looked like a change of weather was blowing through. *Maybe the heat will break for a bit.* At least the rain would clear the air for a few hours.

His thoughts turned to last night. *You screwed that up, Zajac.* He'd had more than one beer at the park, each chased with a frown from Helen. On the ride back, she started talking about how much she loved children, how anxious she was to start a family. Joe made no comment, she pouted, and they finished the trip in silence. On her front porch, Joe gave her the news: He wasn't ready to get married. There would be no more going out.

She burst into tears and slammed the door in his face. He could hear her mother asking what was wrong. He hadn't meant to just blurt it out like that, but now that it was over he was relieved. Almost giddy, he ran from the house. His next stop was The Star, where he sat alone for some time, drinking and thinking. His conclusion: He was a prick, but an honest one. Comfortably numb, he swayed back to his room and passed out.

Now he was awake and feeling sick. It was a combination of things: regret for the way he handled Helen, too much whiskey, the crazy dream. And today he had to go down in the mine. He needed to understand what Goretsky had been doing on Friday, and he hoped to talk to the miners. Very soon his boss would want to know what was going on, and Joe needed some answers.

Joe got up, rubbed his face, and tried to shake it all off. He wouldn't let anybody see him sweat. His reputation was at stake. And he was running late.

An hour later Joe was back at Leisenring. His first stop was Jim Thornton's office.

"Glad to see you finally made it, Joe. I just got a telegram from Cliff Sellers, wanting to know what's going on and I got nothing to tell him. He wants to see you later this week so he can give the muckety-mucks a report."

Sellers was Joe's boss, security superintendent for all the Frick properties. His office was at headquarters in Scottdale. "I've nothing to tell him. I went down to The Star Saturday night. People knew of George but I couldn't find any close friends to question. All I have is one fellow that tossed him out on his ear one night for running his mouth. I'll track him down, but I doubt he's involved in murder."

"How about Smida?"

"I talked to Tomas. He admitted he hated Goretsky but denied killing him. And he says he went straight home after his shift on Friday. Unless I find someone that saw him around here Friday night, I have nothing on him."

"Here's something for you to look into. We hired a new brattice man two weeks ago, Walter Krupp. He worked with George and didn't show up for his Saturday shift. He's not here today, either. I'd say that sounds a mite suspicious."

"What's a brattice man?"

"They work with the fire boss. You'll see for yourself today what they do."

"Where's he live? Anybody go see if he's around?"

"Walter boards with Anna Gmitter up at house forty-seven. I sent a boy up there to check. She hasn't seen him since Friday, either."

"Maybe we'll have something for Mr. Lynch after all. Say, Jim, what's this I hear about Frick screwing the workers by selling coke to Carnegie on the cheap?"

"It's the truth, and it's not just the workers getting the shaft. There's a lawsuit been filed. Some of the smaller shareholders of Frick stock are crying foul over the deal, claim they've been cheated out of their share of a million dollars. They got a good case, too. Carnegie might run Frick now, but the directors are still duty-bound to do what's best for all of the shareholders."

Joe didn't understand these business deals. He'd have to study up on the case. He did know that hard-nosed men like Carnegie and Frick looked after themselves first. Their self-interest trumped all.

"Thanks for the dope, Jim. I guess it's time I see what Number One is all about."

"You ever been in a mine before?"

Joe gave him a weak smile. "Only in my dreams."

Jim walked Joe down to the tipple, where he introduced him to Bob Finnerty, Leisenring No. 1's foreman. Bob looked to be about Joe's age, but was bald and pale. He was slim but had a big belly riding over the top of his denim pants.

"Take good care of him, Bob. This is Joe's first trip into a mine."

"Will do, Mr. Thornton. We'll try to keep the roof from falling on him."

Joe could feel his heart race.

They stood by the shaft entrance, waiting for the lift to come down from the tipple. They'd be riding down with an empty coal wagon. The lift house towered over the mine shaft, and contained a huge spool, wrapped with two thick steel cables. Each was connected to a cast iron lift cage. Powered by electricity produced at the nearby generating plant, the lift was in constant motion, lowering empty coal wagons and pulling up full ones.

A new sign had been posted above the shaft: Safety First, Quality Second, Cost Third. It was Frick's new company slogan, thought up by the president of the company himself. The signs were going up everywhere.

Bob pointed to the sign. "See Joe? H.C. Frick is making your safety its number one priority."

"Makes for a good slogan, I guess."

Bob looked at him with a frown. "I take safety seriously. You can depend on that. I'm down in that mine every day with the rest of them." He pulled out a bag of Mail Pouch chewing tobacco and stuffed a wad in his mouth. "Now, what do you know about Number One?"

"Not much. It's just another Frick mine."

"Well, here's a few facts for you. The shaft is three hundred and seventy-four feet deep. The mine property covers twenty-six hundred acres, over half of that coal bearing. We've got a thousand acres of coal to mine here, over ten million tons. The seam is eight feet high, making it easier to work than some of the other mines."

The cage rumbled to a halt next to them.

"Here's our ride. Let's go." Bob gave Joe a miner's cap with a little kerosene lamp attached to it. "Put this on."

The miners called them sunshine lamps. This was all the light they had in many parts of the mine. Joe and Bob entered the lift and descended into the mine. It was soon pitch-black except for the small circle of light cast by the lamps.

Joe fought off his fear as the hoist dropped the lift down the shaft. He needed to keep his mind off the trip.

"What can you tell me about George's last day, Bob?"

"The fire boss is the first man in the mine in the morning and often the last man out. He makes the rounds of the mine, checking mostly for proper ventilation and gas buildup. Any explosion down here would be a disaster. The mine has two main ventilation shafts where fans draw fresh air down. George had helpers that hung canvas tarps across different room openings to keep the fresh air flowing to the working face."

"Is that what Walter Krupp did?"

"Yes, Walter and another man worked with George."

"What can you tell me about Krupp?"

"Not much. He hadn't been here very long. He was older than most newcomers, didn't look like he'd spent much time in the mines. But he did understand ventilation."

The lift slowed, and stopped at the bottom of the shaft. The area closest to the shaft looked more like a big room. Bricks had been laid, covering the walls and ceiling. The air was cool and musty. Joe followed Bob off the lift and down the tracks used by the coal wagons. This part of the mine had a string of electric lights running down the tunnel.

"This here's the mine's Main Street, the first row of rooms mined. We work out from here in all directions. Right now we have over thirty working headings. We use a code to number each room. Once you figure it out, you won't get lost in here."

Joe's heart was still racing but his mind had calmed. The roof was over a foot above his head. The rooms were big and open. Still, he'd be happy to get out.

"As we work the coal vein, we leave big pillars of coal between the rooms to hold up the roof. These timber posts help, too."

At this point Joe had no idea where he was, or how to get back to the main shaft. They'd made several turns and it all looked the same. The electric lights had ended back at the last tunnel. *This is how the old man made a buck.* Up a ways Joe could see a dim light.

"We're almost to one of the working headings now," Bob said. "We just fired a cut and the loaders are shoveling up the fall."

Two men worked side by side. One was using a pick, the other a shovel. The men were black with coal dust, the floor wet. A half-filled coal car stood nearby. Joe could only imagine how many shovelfuls it took to load the car. The men glanced up at Joe and Bob briefly, then continued their work. Paid by the bushel, loaders worked nonstop to make a living. *Any man would be dead tired after ten hours of this.*

They left the men and walked deeper into the mine. Twenty minutes later they reached a dead end.

"This is the end of the line, Joe. The coal seam peters out here. We're at the far south edge of it. George was most likely here on Friday. There's a ventilation shaft close by that he watched over. He ran a regular route every day, checking for trouble, once in the morning and again at the end of the shift."

Joe looked around the room. He could see where the coal ended, mixed with clay deposits.

"Can you think of anything he said on Friday that might help us figure out why he got it?"

"I only saw him first thing. Nothing special was mentioned."

"When's a good time to talk to the crew?"

"Come by at the end of the shift. I'll hold them at the bathhouse."

"One last thing—I'd like to retrace George's regular route."

"I'll get the new fire boss to show you around."

Chapter 8

Joe finished his mine tour, and rode out with a full coal wagon. As the lift cleared the shaft entrance, the permanent darkness of the pit gave way to a hazy morning light. The tightness in his chest lessened; he had survived the trip.

Joe promised Thornton that he'd go to Uniontown to see Sheriff Miller. He still had time to visit Anna Gmitter, though. Maybe she could tell him something about Mr. Krupp. Crossing the road, he stopped for a moment to watch some dirty-faced kids playing on the slate dump. *God save the children.*

He entered the patch and found house number forty-seven down a dirt street, at the end of a row of identical "double houses." Each had two bedrooms, a kitchen, and a parlor, with a duplex outhouse/coal bin in the back. A woman he thought might be Mrs. Gmitter was hauling water from the pump shared by the houses.

All of the patch women look alike, Joe thought, as they exchanged a stare. The woman wore a long black dress and scarf tied around her head. She had on a shabby white apron cinched around a thick waist, and worn black shoes. *They all look old. She could be thirty or sixty.*

In their own way, the women worked as hard as the men. Up at five to see their old men off, they'd make a big breakfast and pack their husband's lunch bucket. If they had boarders, the women packed those men's lunches, too.

Monday was washday, and that's why Mrs. Gmitter was hauling water. After heating it on the coal stove, she'd use it to scrub the clothes on a washboard, then hang them out to dry. Joe could see some work clothes already hanging in the yard.

"Mrs. Gmitter?"

She looked Joe up and down. "Yes, that's me. Who are you?"

"My name is Joe Zajac. I work for the Frick police. I'm here about Walter Krupp."

She put down her bucket and used the apron to wipe the sweat from her face. "What about Krupp? I don't know nothing about him, just boarded him for two weeks."

"When did you see him last?"

"Friday night, late. He even missed his supper."

"You didn't see him Saturday morning?"

"No. He went back out Friday night and never came back. His blankets and such are all put up still."

"Did he leave anything behind?"

Mrs. Gmitter looked around, her eyes narrowing as she stared down the street. Joe turned to see a man standing down at the end. With a nod, she picked up her bucket and headed through the gate into the yard. "Come on."

Joe followed her around the side of the house, past another big garden and an outside brick oven. They entered through the back door into the kitchen. She poured the water into a huge pot sitting on the coal stove, then motioned for Joe to follow her.

The front room was where the boarders slept, usually on a bedroll. Mrs. Gmitter pointed to a small pile in the corner. Joe knelt down and went through it. The bedroll was on top, then a few articles of clothing and a small bag containing a razor, a tin of salve, and a few coins. On the floor were two books.

Joe picked up the first: *Elements of Coal Mining, Mathematics, Ventilation, Geology, and Prospecting.* The smaller book was a companion volume: *Tables and Formulas.* Joe mused, *What would a newly hired brattice man want with these coal mining textbooks?* He leafed through the big book. Stuck inside was a folded piece of paper. Joe pulled it out and opened it. It was a diagram of something.

Joe studied it, examining the notations and symbols. *This looks like a map of the mine. Why would he take the time to draw it?* Joe was beginning to think there was more to Walter Krupp than met the eye.

"How old do you think Walter was?"

"Older than you, I'd say, maybe forty, maybe older. I never asked no questions. He paid for a month in advance."

"Looks like he was up to something. Can you tell me anything else about him?"

Mrs. Gmitter pursed her thin lips together, frowning at Joe. "I don't want nothing to do with this business."

"It's important, Mrs. Gmitter. Maybe Krupp killed Big George, or knows who did." By now everyone in Leisenring knew about the bones in the oven.

She stood thinking for a moment, arms folded across her chest. "I tell you one more thing. He had a regular visitor, usually after dark. I only saw him good once, but I recognized his voice after that. Krupp called him Kurt."

"What did he look like?"

"A slim man but not so tall, young like you. His hair was short and blond, maybe. Like I say, I only saw him good one time. They always went out on the street to have their talks."

Joe gathered up the books and map. "I need to keep these for my investigation. Many thanks for telling me about Krupp and his friend."

Mrs. Gmitter frowned again, shaking her head. "Don't tell nobody. Now I got to get workin'."

Joe left by the front door and walked to the company store. *Jim needs to see this before I go to Uniontown.* As he walked up the steps, he saw a man leaning against the stable fence down the hill, staring at him. *That's the character was down the street. He's no miner, looks more like a farmer.* Joe stared back until the man turned and walked away. Joe shook his head and went up to Jim's office, knocking on the open door.

Jim looked up from his papers. "You survived your trip to the mine, eh, Joe?"

"I did. It wasn't as bad as I expected." He didn't tell Jim that he'd expected to die.

"Try it ten hours a day, six days a week for a few years. The men go all winter without seeing the sun." Jim looked at the books Joe was carrying. "What that you got there?"

"I called on Mrs. Gmitter. Krupp most likely hightailed it out of there late Friday night. He must have been planning on returning because he left a few possessions, these among them."

Joe placed the books on Jim's desk. Jim picked them up, read the titles, and set them back down. "These are study books for men looking to move up in the mine, usually after a few years' experience. Krupp was far from ready for that."

Joe nodded and handed Jim the paper. "What do you make of this?"

Jim unfolded the map, studied it for a moment, then set it down. "This is a rough layout of Number One. Look here—there's the main shaft, and these little squares are ventilation shafts. Why would he be drawing this layout?"

"Your guess is as good as mine, but I'm beginning to think that Krupp wasn't your common brattice man. I'd say it's no coincidence that he disappeared the same day George was done in."

"What's your next move?"

"I'm going to talk to the Connellsville police about keeping their eye out for Krupp. Then I'm going to Uniontown to tell the sheriff and the police there the same thing. Put these books and drawing in a safe place."

Joe trotted down to the streetcar stop and caught the noon car back to town. He tracked down Johnny Davidson walking his beat on Pittsburgh Street.

"Hey, Joe, what's the news from Leisenring?"

"Been a busy day for me, Johnny, with more to come. I got a favor to ask. Turns out we have a suspect, a Mr. Walter Krupp. He's about forty or so, dark hair, wears spectacles. He was working with the fellow whose bones they pulled out of the coke oven. His name was George Goretsky, a fire boss at Number One. Krupp didn't show up for work Saturday or today, and the woman where he boarded said he left Friday night and never came back."

"I knew Goretsky. He'd gotten into more than one scrape around town. What's the angle?"

"I'm still trying to figure that out, buddy. From what I know, Krupp wasn't what he was making himself out to be. Maybe he hated Goretsky like most everybody else, or there might be more to it."

"OK, Joe. I'll ask around and pass the word. Check back with me tomorrow."

"One more thing—whatever the angle, Krupp wasn't in it alone. I'm also looking for another fellow, about five eight or so, short blond hair, about my age. First name's Kurt."

"I'll put the word out on him, too."

As Johnny headed to the police station, Joe pulled out his pocket watch. Twelve thirty, just enough time for a bite to eat before the one o'clock streetcar to Uniontown. He headed for City Lunch.

Joe entered, nodded to Tony, and took his usual spot at the end of the counter. "What's for you today, Joey?"

"A beer and a bowl of minestrone, Tony. Presto."

"Right away, boss man."

Joe drank half his beer, lost in thought. *What was Walter up to? Who's this Kurt guy? Why kill George?*

"Hey, Joe, mind if I join you?"

He looked up to see Dave Norton, another local friend and a teller at the First National Bank, where Joe had a small account. "Take a load off, Norton. Buy you a beer?"

"No, thanks, but I'll have lemonade. The bank president has some old-fashioned ideas about his head teller drinking at lunch. I guess Frick doesn't mind." Norton sat down at the counter next to Joe. "Say, what's all this about one of your men getting burned up out at Number One?"

"Tony, lemonade for my friend. Bring him a bowl of the soup, too." Joe turned his stool to face Norton. "That's a fact. It was a fellow name of George Goretsky. Don't know exactly how or when he died, but he ended up baking with a load of coke. All that's left is a few bones."

"So Zajac's on the case. Made any headway?"

"I have a suspect that disappeared, and plenty of questions, but I can't get a handle on it." Joe paused for a moment. "You keep up with local business. What do you know about Frick's problems with his shareholders?"

"It's a big story hereabouts, big news all over America. Even the *New York Times* is following it. I'm surprised you haven't heard about it."

"And you'll be surprised to know that the big shots down at Frick don't take me into their confidence much. I do remember seeing something about it in the *Courier* a few months back, but wasn't much interested. Sounded like a bunch of rich men arguing about money. What's your take on it?"

"You aren't far off. I have some appreciation for men like Carnegie and Frick. They're changing this little corner of Pennsylvania and the whole of America, too, and growing wealthy in the process. But when greed becomes your god, you're playing the devil's game. There's a whole lot of bad mixed in with the good."

Tony brought the soup. Joe wolfed his down and checked his watch again. "I'm going to Uniontown to see the sheriff. Say, how about meeting me for supper tonight and telling me more about this Carnegie deal?"

"Martha's making my favorite pot roast tonight, but I can probably get out after supper. Say we meet at The Star around seven thirty?"

"See you then, buddy."

Joe finished his beer, paid his bill, and hurried to catch the one o'clock car to Uniontown.

Chapter 9

Joe barely made the one o'clock car, jumping on as it left the terminal. Uniontown was twelve miles from Connellsville, a forty-minute ride by streetcar. Joe took an open seat in the rear of the car. His favorite spot up front was already taken. The car was nearly full as they crossed the Yough.

Joe prided himself on having an organized mind. He took out his notebook and pencil, determined to sort out some of the facts. *What do I know and what's missing?* He headed up page one with "Walter Krupp." *Don't know much about him.* He'd get Krupp's work file, but doubted there'd be much to go on. Whatever was in there was most likely lies.

Page two was labeled "Frick shareholders." *There's big money involved, and the workers are agitated. People been killed for less. I've nothing to go on, just a hunch.* He'd know more about that after talking to Norton tonight. He turned back to page one and wrote, "Any connection to a shareholder?"

The streetcar picked up speed as it crested a hill and coasted into Dunbar. It stopped in the middle of town, bell clanging and breaks screeching. Dunbar was another small industrial center, growing like the rest of the towns around Connellsville. Long a center of iron manufacturing, Dunbar was now home to a glass maker, quarries, a brick works, and its own mine and string of coke ovens.

A minute later, the car was under way again. Joe turned back to his notebook. Page three was headlined "Kurt." All Joe had there was a big question mark. Kurt was surely involved; maybe Johnny Davidson would get lucky. Joe closed the notebook and put it back in his coat pocket.

The streetcar arrived in Uniontown on time. Joe hopped off and headed for the Fayette County Courthouse. He hoped to catch Sheriff Miller in his office.

Uniontown was the county seat and the biggest city in Fayette County. Joe counted seven buildings under construction as he walked down Main Street. Arriving at the Courthouse a few minutes later, he found the sheriff's office on the second floor. Sheriff Miller was sitting behind his desk, a pistol disassembled in front of him.

Joe knocked on the doorframe and went in. "Sheriff Miller?"

"That's what the sign on the door says, son. What can I do for you?"

Sheriff Tom Miller was an institution in Fayette County. He'd been sheriff for ten years and, at sixty, would probably be sheriff until he died. *He doesn't look like Dad to me,* Joe thought, but bit his tongue and doffed his cap.

"I'm Joe Zajac. I'm work security for Frick here in Fayette County. I'm here about the bones in the oven out at Leisenring."

"You're gonna have to wait until I finish cleaning my pistol. Have a seat. Make yourself at home."

Joe looked around the room. Sheriff Miller's substantial rear end occupied the only chair. Joe stood there, hat in hand, watching the older man clean the gun. "I guess you don't get many visitors, eh, Sheriff?"

Sheriff Miller looked up but offered no comment. *This is one cold fish,* Joe thought. After five minutes of rubbing and polishing, Miller reassembled the gun and slid it into the holster hanging low on his hip.

The sheriff got up, practiced a quick draw, and smiled. "You look like you could use a drink, Zajac. Let's go."

Maybe I got him figured wrong. He followed Miller down the steps, out the door, and around the corner. Halfway down the block, the sheriff turned into Greenie's Tap Room, which was almost empty this time of day. They headed to a table in the rear, the bartender already on his way with two beers.

"Thanks, Eddie. How about a plate of sausage and kraut?"

"Sure, Sheriff, right away."

Joe liked Miller a lot better already. The man had keen powers of observation, to be sure. "Here's to you, Sheriff." Joe hoisted his glass and drank the beer in one long pull.

"I knew you looked thirsty, son. To you, too." The sheriff drained his beer and slammed the empty glass on the table. "Two more, Eddie, when you get the time."

Eddie brought the beers and a big plate of sausages and sauerkraut for the sheriff, who dug in as Joe took another drink. "What's on your mind, Zajac?"

Joe watched half a sausage disappear in one bite. "What's your take on this? I know you've been out to Leisenring and talked with the superintendent."

Miller stabbed the other half of the sausage, along with a forkful of kraut. "I did, and I talked to Tomas Smida yesterday afternoon just like you did. He might've done it, might not have, either. I don't suppose we'll ever know, and I'm not inclined to spend much time looking into it. Might have been some kind of accident."

Joe shook his head. "That's not likely. Here's something for you." Joe told him about the departure of Walter Krupp and his visit with Mrs. Gmitter.

"That's all well and good, Zajac, but I'm still not all hopped up about it. Men quit the mines all the time. Maybe Krupp didn't like the work. And a few books don't make him a killer."

"You might be right, but I'm thinking he's involved somehow. I need to find out more about him. Frick doesn't like people ending up in its coke ovens. It looks bad on the safety record."

Miller cleaned his plate, drained the beer, and let out a big belch. He hooked his thumbs behind his red suspenders and leaned back in the chair. "That's their problem. I got more important things to do than try and run this down. This is an election year."

"I guess you have your priorities, Sheriff. Can you do me one favor? See if you have anything on the Krupp fellow. I'd hate to see someone get away with murder."

"I'll have my deputy check tomorrow, but then you're on your own. I'll let Thornton know if we find anything."

Joe walked back down Main Street and caught the three o'clock car back to Connellsville. He was due back at Leisenring to speak to the miners at six. That gave him time to stop by his place.

After washing up, he stopped by The Star. He got a shot and a beer from the bartender, drained the shot, and took the beer to the corner table. Taking a long swallow, he surveyed the room. The place was already mostly full and it was only four thirty. *A heavy drinker has plenty of company in this place.*

"Look who's here. Getting an early start on it today, Mr. Zajac?"

Joe looked up from his beer. Peggy Patterson was standing at his table. Joe stood up, hat in hand. "How do, Miss Patterson. Care to join me?"

Peggy pulled out a chair and they both sat down. "Just for a minute."

Joe smiled as he removed his cap. "How's business?"

"The Star does all right, but I'll never get rich running a bar. In fact, it's about the last thing I'd pick to do. But I'm stuck with it for a while."

"Why's that?"

"This is Daddy's place. He's not been well and it's up to me to take care of the business. I hope he gets better soon. I'm no saloon keeper."

"You seem to be doing a right smart job of keeping this one, ma'am."

Peggy seemed to weigh his words. Finally she cracked a bit of a smile and rose from the table. "Thank you for your expression of confidence, Mr. Zajac. Now it's time for me to get to work. If I don't check the books every day, I'll get robbed blind."

Joe rose as Peggy left. She headed back to the office and closed the door. He scratched his head and sat back down, motioning to the bartender for another beer.

Real slick, you jackass. That's the best you could figure out to say?

Joe was no longer hungry. He drank up and headed back to Leisenring. He was waiting at the bathhouse with Bob Finnerty when the miners ended their shift. The men milled around the door grumbling, ready to get cleaned up and home for supper. Bob held up his hand, quieting the crowd.

"Men, some of you may know Joe Zajac here. He's a Frick man, works security. He's trying to figure out what happened to George Goretsky and needs a few minutes of your time."

Some of the men grumbled again, tired and edgy from their ten hours of work.

Joe spoke up. "I won't hold you up long. Just know this—Big George was murdered, most likely on Friday after the shift ended. I know he wasn't the most popular man in Leisenring, but prick or not, I don't think he deserved to die."

A few of the men laughed. A voice from the rear called out, "Who says?" Joe saw Tomas Smida among them, smiling. Most just stood there, coal-blackened faces emotionless.

"All I'm asking is that if you saw anything on Friday, let me know. And if any of you know anything about Walter Krupp, I'd be much obliged if you'd share that, too. I'll be up at Jim Thornton's office for the next hour."

The crowd drifted away, most entering the bathhouse. Joe started up the hill toward the store.

"Hey, Zajac, hold up."

Joe stopped and turned. A lanky young miner approached.

"I got something for you. I seen George coming out of the mine on Friday. He was all steamed up about something, going hell bent for leather. I never seen him so mad."

"What's your name, son?"

"Billy Kapustic. I'm on the track gang."

"You know anything about Walter Krupp?"

"No, sir. I never even met him, wouldn't know him from Adam."

"Did you see anyone with George?"

"No, sir, he was alone."

"Which way was he headed?"

"Toward the bathhouse, best I could tell."

Joe pulled out his notebook and made an entry. "Thanks for the help, Billy."

Billy headed into the patch. Joe continued to the store and Jim's office. Jim was still at his desk studying some reports when Joe arrived.

"Have anything to report, Joe?"

Joe told him about his meeting with the sheriff and the news from Billy.

"It's no surprise that Miller is shying away from this. He has nothing to gain from it. Something tells me if we could find out why George was so mad, we might get on track to figuring this out."

"I told the men I'd be here for a while in case they wanted to share some information in private."

"I've had enough for today. Just lock the door when you leave."

Joe sat down at the desk and put his feet up. He closed his eyes, letting his mind wander. He was still thinking about his conversation with Peggy. *The next time I see her I'll try to relax some.*

A knock on the door ended Joe's brooding. He looked up to see a young mine worker standing stoop shouldered at the door, his hat in his hand.

"How do, Mr. Zajac. I'm Mickey Flynn."

"How do, Mickey. Come on in."

Mickey looked over his shoulder, came in, and closed the door behind him. He sat down across from Joe and fiddled with his hat, alternately looking at the floor and Joe.

"What can I do for you, Mickey?"

"Mr. Zajac, if I was to tell you something, can it stay just between you and me?"

"Call me Joe, and yes, unless you tell me that you killed George, I'll keep it to myself."

Mickey stared at Joe for a bit, set his hat on the desk, and took a deep breath. "Well, it's like this. I'm a brattice man, too, worked for George since I hired on here at Number One. I know for a fact he was one hard-assed son of a bitch."

"So I heard. So what's on your mind?"

"George and me had a talk Friday morning right after the shift started. He asked me a lot of questions about Krupp. Did he ever talk much to me, did he ask any questions, did I see him doing anything funny, like that."

"Did you?"

Mickey nodded. "Krupp was an odd duck, that's for sure. He didn't talk like no miner, didn't act much like one, neither. Funny thing is that George hit the nail on the head. Krupp did ask me plenty of questions."

"What about?"

"Mostly about how the mine was laid out. He seemed mighty curious about how George did his job, too."

"Did you tell George that?"

"I did, and I thought he'd get mad at me, but he didn't. Just nodded and got a fierce look about him. He told me to keep an eye out for Krupp and to let him know if he did anything funny."

"Anything else?"

"That's all. You think Krupp kilt Big George?"

"After what you told me and seeing as he's gone missing, I'm getting mighty suspicious. I'm much obliged for your help."

Mickey pulled out a dirty red handkerchief, mopped his face, and grabbed his hat. "Just don't let on where you heard it. Whatever's going on here, I don't want no part of it."

Joe pulled out his notebook and made a few more entries. He closed up the office and headed down to catch the next streetcar back to town and his meeting with Norton.

Chapter 10

Joe hustled down Pittsburgh Street and into The Star, a few minutes late for his meeting with Norton. The place was quiet for a change, only a few tables occupied and the bar rail half full. Norton wasn't there yet, so Joe edged up to the end of the bar closest to the door.

"Hey, Hiram, long time no see. Where you been hiding?" Joe's favorite barkeep, Hiram Kane, was working the night shift. Bald with muttonchops, he had a white apron tied around his ample belly.

"Me and the missus took a little trip to see her sister up in Cleveland, just got back this afternoon." He put a beer and a shot of Old Overholt in front of Joe.

"You're an angel of mercy for sure." Joe drained the shot and half the beer. "One more time." Hiram brought over the whiskey bottle and poured Joe a refill. "Here's to you, Hiram."

Joe felt a hand on his shoulder. "That stuff is gonna rot your guts out if you keep it up."

"Norton, how'd you manage to sneak up on me like that? How was the pot roast?"

"I'd say Martha makes the finest pot roast I've ever had. Of course, my mother wasn't a very good cook."

"How about a shot and a beer for you?"

"I'll have a beer, but you'd need to put a gun to my head to make me drink that rye whiskey you love so much."

Joe slugged down the rest of his beer. "Two more, Hiram, if you please."

"Let's grab a seat." Joe threw a quarter on the bar and grabbed the beers. They sat at Joe's favorite table in the far corner.

"What a day, buddy. I've been running around like a chicken with its head cut off."

"You making any progress?"

"I am, but not much. I've got a hunch who did it. Now all I have to do is find him. Figuring out why it happened might help me do that."

"And you think it's got something to do with Frick's shareholder problems?"

"I might be, but I don't know enough about that. I'm much obliged if you could tell me more. Who's involved?"

Norton took a sip of his beer and leaned back in his chair. "How much do you know about your employer, Joe?"

"You mean Old Man Frick himself? Not too much."

"I mean the company."

"Hardly anything, except that they pay me regular. I do know H.C. Frick started it up from scratch, and built it into the biggest coke operation in America, and maybe the world."

"True enough, but it's been some time since Frick really owned the company outright. To grow like they have, he's had to bring in investors along the way. A few of them have been with him since almost the beginning, and made a pretty penny off of their investment."

"So what's their beef, then?"

"Frick is smart and ambitious. It didn't take him long to figure out that the big money was in the steel business. He met Carnegie and they were two peas in a pod, both worshiping at the church of the almighty dollar. If anything, Frick is even a tougher son of a bitch than Carnegie. It didn't take long for Carnegie to realize this, and he put Frick in charge of the whole shooting match."

Norton took another pull on his beer, wiped the foam from his lips with the back of his hand, and continued. "But that wasn't good enough for old H. C. He wanted to own a piece of the action. So he starts selling Carnegie his shares in Frick, and uses the money to buy shares in Carnegie Steel. Before you know it, Carnegie owns a majority of the stock in Frick. That's when the trouble really began."

"How so?"

"Frick may not have owned a majority of the shares, but for a while Carnegie let him run the company as he saw fit. But they had more than one falling out, and eventually Carnegie expands the board of directors and puts his men on it, so they can take full control of the business. The first thing Carnegie gets them to do is to sign a long-term contract with Carnegie Steel to sell them coke at a dollar thirty-five a ton. It turned out to be a great deal for Carnegie, and a bad deal for Frick when coke hit three dollars a ton. Carnegie's able to keep his steel prices low and beat down his competition."

"OK, I think I got it, Norton. The smaller Frick shareholders get screwed because of all of the lost profits from coke selling elsewhere for three bucks."

"Very good. So then what do you think happens?"

"They get pissed off."

"Right again, my friend. And although at times it seems that anything goes in business, they have a legal case. Even though Carnegie owns a majority interest in Frick, the board has a clear duty to act in the best interest of all the shareholders."

"How long has this been going on?"

"The papers were filed in February. The case has been dragging on since then, with no end in sight. Carnegie has plenty of lawyers and seems willing to drag it out as long as possible. He's probably hoping that these guys kick the bucket before it gets anywhere."

Joe got his notebook out and began writing. "Who's involved?"

"Two men I know of personally, and a third I don't know much about. There's S.L. Schoonmaker and John Pontefract. They're both older men, local fellows. Word is they'd be happy to cut a deal with Carnegie and sell out."

"Either of them ever been accused of dirty dealing?"

"Just the opposite. They're both God-fearing Christians, made their money honest-like. I don't see either of them involved in anything underhanded."

"Who's the other bird?"

"That would be Wendell Sykes. He inherited his money and his Frick shares from his father. He's from over Latrobe way, but lives in Pittsburgh now. He hates both Frick and Carnegie, but again, that club has plenty of members."

Joe finished writing, put his notebook away, and drained his beer. "Ready for another, Norton?"

"No, thanks, Joe. One's my limit during the week, and I promised Martha I wouldn't stay long."

"I guess they're right when they call marriage an institution. Sounds like it got you all locked up."

Norton gave Joe a little smile and shook his head. "You should be so lucky. Still seeing the young bake shop woman?"

Joe shook his head. "Not anymore. I did her a favor and ended it. She's a mite better off finding herself a young man more settled in his ways."

"Or maybe it's time for you to settle in yours, my friend. Enjoy your evening."

With that, Norton tipped his hat to Joe and headed out the door. Joe returned to the bar and gave Hiram a wave. The crowd had thinned out. Joe stood alone, contemplating the truth in his friend's observation.

"Here you go, Joe. Want another shot with that?"

"No, thanks. I'm trying to cut back."

"That'll be the day."

"Say, Hiram, did you hear about the goings on out at Number One?"

"About Big George getting done in? Sure did. Your buddy Davidson was around earlier asking questions, too."

"What about it, then? Ever hear tell of this Walter Krupp? Or his pal, this Kurt fellow?"

"Not a thing. If they came in here, I never got their names, but there's plenty of men come through here in a week I don't know."

"OK, Hi, let me know if you hear anything."

"Will do."

"Well, look who's here, my best customer. Good evening, Mr. Zajac."

Joe turned to see Peggy Patterson standing behind him. "And a good evening to you, Miss Patterson." Joe doffed his cap and bowed toward her. "And Joe is just fine."

Peggy gave him a little smile. "It's bad policy to get too familiar with the patrons, but in your case, I guess I'll make an exception."

Joe gestured to an empty table. "Care to sit with me for a bit?"

Peggy looked to her office door, and then nodded. "Just for a minute. I still have my books to do and it's getting late."

Joe left his beer on the bar and led Peggy back to his table. They both sat down, Joe on the edge of his chair. After a moment of silence, he sat back and put his hands on the table.

"I was wondering, would you like to go see a show or maybe grab a bite with me come Saturday?"

Peggy just stared at Joe for a few moments. He could feel sweat popping out on his forehead, his face flushing.

"Like I said before, it's bad business for me to become too familiar with the patrons."

"Well, how about I stop coming in here, then?"

Peggy smiled. "You are a smart one. I could tell that the first time we met."

"Mostly, but with a mean streak of horse's rear-end."

That got a laugh out of her. "And funny, too, I can see. Are your intentions honorable?"

"My intentions are as pure as the driven snow."

Peggy nodded, then tucked a wisp of hair behind her ear. "I should have my head examined, but I accept your invitation. I'm not sure about Saturday, though. I'll let you know the next time I see you in here. Now I have to get to work."

They both stood up, Joe fiddling with his hat. "See you tomorrow, then."

"I may not be in tomorrow, but Wednesday for sure. See you then, Joe."

Joe watched her walk back to the office and shut the door. After staring at it for a moment, he got up and returned to the bar, where Hiram stood staring at him. He grabbed his beer and took a long swallow.

"What are you staring at, Hiram?"

"The slickest fellow in town, I'm thinking. Did you just get Peggy to go out with you?"

Joe smiled and leaned forward on the bar. "I did."

"You know how many men in here tried to court her since she started running the joint?"

"A substantial number, I'd say, if they have any sense."

"All the single ones, I reckon. She turned them all down."

"She's a fine figure of a woman, that's for sure. You know much about her?"

"Not much, just a few things I heard her father mention."

"She ever had a serious suitor?"

"I hear that she did, some time ago, but he died in an accident."

Joe stroked his jaw, nodding. Then he finished his beer and tipped his hat toward Hiram. "Much obliged, buddy. You have a good evening." He finished his beer and departed, whistling as he walked up Pittsburgh Street.

Chapter 11

Tuesday started all too soon for Joe. He'd left The Star early enough, intending to go straight home. But he ended up stopping at Rocky's Saloon, one of the toughest joints in town. Its usual clientele is an assortment of drunks, toughs, crooks, and other lowlifes. He'd gone there in a happy mood, and didn't even remember leaving.

He had woken in a cold sweat, and now sat on the side of the bed, trying to get his bearings. After a haphazard shave, he hauled himself out the door and headed for Tony's. It was 7:00 a.m.

"Joey, what you doing here so early? You're my first customer," a smiling Tony greeted him as he walked through the door.

Joe just looked at him, and took his usual seat at the end of the counter.

"Whatsa matter? You look like shit warmed over."

"I must have tied into a bad pickled egg down at Rocky's last night. You got any coffee back there?"

Tony's smile faded. He poured Joe a big mug of coffee and set it in front of him. "How long I know you, Joey? Maybe two years now? We friends, right?"

"Yeah, Tony, we're friends."

"So why you want to hang around that dump? You gonna get knocked in the head there some night."

"That's a good question. If I knew, I'd tell you. Now how about you make me a couple of eggs, over easy?"

Tony just shook his head. "I think you need to get your head inspected."

The bell on the door rang. Joe looked up to see Johnny Davidson walk in. He walked back and sat down next to Joe.

"You're up and at them early, Joe."

"Yeah, it's too damn hot to sleep in. Buy you a cup of coffee?"

"Tony gives me my coffee for free, but you can buy me a doughnut."

Tony brought Johnny a cup of coffee and Joe his eggs.

"Give my favorite cop a doughnut on me, Tony."

"Sure thing, boss man."

"What are you up to today?" Johnny asked.

"I need to set this murder investigation to the side—for the morning, at least—and catch up with my regular work. I'm bound for Alverton, got a meeting with my new night watchman over there. How about you, any luck tracking down Krupp or his friend Kurt?"

"I spread the word as best I could. Nobody on the force heard of them. I hit most of the bars around town, too. No luck there, either. I don't think this Krupp fellow was spending his free time in town."

"Thanks for your help anyway." Joe finished his coffee and pushed his half-eaten plate of eggs aside. "Time for me to get to work." He tossed two dimes on the counter, nodded to Tony, and left.

Joe hopped the next streetcar heading for Mt. Pleasant, located about eight miles from Connellsville in Westmoreland County. A West Penn line ran right past Alverton. Like Leisenring, Alverton consisted of three mines, with three hundred fifty coke ovens, a medium-size operation by Frick standards.

Frick acquired the mines from the McClure Coke Company in 1895. The year before had seen a vicious miners' strike in the Connellsville coal field over wages, and Alverton had seen its share of the action. A pump house had been dynamited, and a strike-breaking coker was killed by a mob of Hungarian women. The strike was broken, and the miners returned to work, but they neither forgave nor forgot the brutal treatment received from Frick, McClure, and the other mine owners.

Joe arrived at Alverton No. 1 at eight o'clock. He headed to the Union Supply Store and the office of Ed Connelly, supervisor for all three of the mines. That's where he was to meet Caleb Johnson, his new night watchman.

Joe walked upstairs and into Ed's office. Ed was at his desk, talking with a man Joe assumed to be Caleb.

"Morning, Joe," Ed boomed. "You're right on time."

Ed was a huge slab of a man, big all over. He was as tall as Joe, but with a wide body, muscular arms bulging under the tight rolled-up sleeves of his shirt. He had a thick bull neck and a big head. A red-veined nose stood out in contrast to his pale mottled face. Joe knew him to be a tough hard-drinking Irishman, and had enjoyed spending a few evenings in the local tavern with him over the years.

"Morning, Ed, good to see you fat and happy."

"Watch that fat shit, buddy, or I might have to dance a jig on your little Polish ass."

Ed got up and walked around the desk. He and Joe shook hands, smiling at each other.

"This here's Caleb Johnson, your new night watchman. Caleb, meet Joe Zajac, Frick's security man hereabouts."

Caleb got up from his chair and extended a bony hand toward Joe. "How do, Mr. Zajac. Glad to know you."

Joe eyed Caleb up and down. He looked old, very old. So old, in fact, that it was hard to guess his age. He was short and scrawny, with skin that looked like shoe leather. He wore denim work pants over bowed legs, and had a big blue handkerchief sticking out of a back pocket. Little tufts of white hair perched over big ears, but his blue eyes were clear and his voice strong.

"How do, Caleb. You ready to make the rounds?"

"Darn tootin'. The day's getting away from us."

Ed laughed and clapped Joe on the back. "I have to tell you, this man has known me most of my life. He and Pap go way back. Don't you worry about him none, either. He'll still work the pants off of men half his age."

"OK. Ready if you are, Caleb."

Joe and Caleb were soon walking the road that ran by the coke batteries, trying to stay upwind from the smoke belching out of the ovens in full blast.

"Mr. Zajac, this here job Eddie gave me ain't no charity case. I know all three of these mines like the back of my hand."

"You've been at this awhile then, eh?"

"Might could say that. I was mining coal when Henry Frick was still drinking his mother's milk. I was born in these parts, right down the road, in fact, in a little spot called Hawkeye. The Fricks lived a few miles past, down West Overton way."

"How long you been working the mines?"

"That's all I done my whole life, fifty years' worth, I reckon. Pappy worked the mines, too. That was before these boom times, though, and before big shots like Frick took over everything."

"You knew the Fricks?"

"Yep. Not Henry so much, but his momma's dad, Abe Overholt. Ever hear tell of him?"

"The whiskey maker?"

"That's him. We was chums back a ways. He's gone now, some thirty years."

"You like his whiskey?"

"I did have a strong taste for it, but gave it up some time ago. Figured I'd live longer if I did, and so far looks like I was right."

The two men walked in silence to the end of the row, then turned and started up the railroad tracks behind the ovens. Men were busy pulling coke and loading railroad cars. They were downwind of the ovens now, walking in the smoke.

"I tell you, it's some sight at night when these ovens are going full blast."

"Sounds like you were a trailblazer in this business, Caleb. I'd enjoy hearing more about the old days sometime. Maybe I could buy you breakfast some morning after you get off."

"I ain't never turned down a meal in my life. If you're buyin', I'm eatin'."

Joe smiled at the old man. "OK, let's go over what it is you need to watch at night."

"I reckon the supply yard, the stables, the tipple, and them railroad cars we just walked past, for starters."

Joe laughed out loud. "I'd say that's a good place to start. Let's go and sit down by the store. I agree—you'll not be needing much hand-holding."

"Don't suppose I will, Mr. Zajac. You strike me as a decent sort. I'm much obliged, and I'll be the best night watchman you ever had."

Joe and Caleb parted, agreeing to meet again on Thursday morning for breakfast. Joe headed upstairs to check in with Ed before leaving Alverton.

Ed was shuffling some papers when Joe got there. Joe sat down and waited for him to finish up. Ed signed his name to one sheet, set the pile aside, and turned to Joe.

"I heard about your troubles out at Leisenring. Matter of fact, all of the superintendents were advised about it this morning in our weekly telegram from headquarters. They didn't tell us much about it, though. What's going on?"

"The fire boss out there got done in, not sure where or when, but he ended up in a coke oven. All's left is a few bones."

"You know who did it?"

"I'm guessing it was one Walter Krupp. He worked with the victim and hit the road some time the evening of the murder. Haven't had any luck tracking him down so far."

"Krupp. The name doesn't ring a bell. I'll spread the word over here. Maybe we'll get lucky and turn something up. You know why he did it?"

"That's the big question, Ed. I don't know yet, but it wasn't your usual crime, I'm thinking. There's some funny business behind it and I aim to figure it out."

Ed leaned back in his chair, hands behind his head. "Better you than me, Joe. Now get the hell out of here so I can get back to my production reports. I got a deadline to meet."

"OK. I'll be back out in a few days to see how Caleb is doing. I have to admit, I like the old man already."

Joe left Ed to his work and walked back to the streetcar stop. *I have time enough to stop back by Leisenring and go over Walter's books with a fine-tooth comb.*

Chapter 12

It was noon by the time Joe made it to Leisenring. As he walked up the hill to Jim's office, Jim came out of the building and hurried Joe's way.

"I got big news for you, Joe. I just got off the telephone with Sheriff Miller. They found Walter Krupp."

Joe clapped Jim on the back, the beginning of a smile on his lips. "That's great news. Did Miller arrest him?"

"No, he's not under arrest. He's dead."

Joe stepped back, frowning. "Dead?"

"Ready for the pine overcoat. A couple of hobos found him on the railroad tracks this morning."

"How'd he die?"

"I don't know anything else about it. That's all Miller told me. He said you should get on up there if you wanted to see the body."

Joe kicked his toe into the dirt. "Son of a bitch. Now we've got us two dead Frick men."

"Go on up to Uniontown and let me know what you find out."

Joe turned, ran back down to the streetcar stop, and was soon on his way. It was just past one by the time he got to Sheriff Miller's office. The sheriff was leaning back in his chair, eyes closed. Joe tapped on the doorframe.

"Sheriff Miller. Beg pardon."

The sheriff took a moment to open his eyes. "Been expecting you, Zajac." He leaned forward, rubbing his face with both hands. "Got an early start to my day and I'm not as young as I used to be. Let's go get a drink."

They walked the block to Greenie's Tap Room in silence, and sat at a table in the rear. Eddie once again had two beers for them by the time they sat down.

"Thanks, Eddie. Have any corned beef and cabbage left?"

"Sure do, Sheriff Miller. Coming right up."

"And a plate for my buddy, too."

The sheriff lifted his glass toward Joe. "Here's looking at you."

Joe and the sheriff both took several big swallows, the beer leaving foam on their upper lips. The sheriff wiped his off with the back of his hand. Joe pulled out his handkerchief and wiped his face.

"You know, Zajac, I had no intention of getting involved in this, but it looks like my hand's been forced."

Joe leaned forward, holding his beer with both hands. "I wanted to find Krupp, but was kind of hoping he'd still be breathing when I did."

"Breathing comes hard to a man that's had his head caved in."

"Jim said he was found on railroad tracks. Was he run over by a train?"

"No, but he sure would have been if them hobos hadn't come upon him. They were walking the B&O line up near Hogsett, found him lying right in the middle of the tracks."

Joe got out his notebook. "What time was that, Sheriff?"

"You might as well just call me Tom. Looks like we're gonna be working together for a spell. They found him around six. Hobos are early risers, generally speaking. These boys and a few others have a camp close by there. They pulled him off the tracks and one went for help. But there weren't no helping Mr. Krupp. He'd been long gone by then."

"You go out there?"

"Got there about seven thirty."

Eddie showed up with their lunch and two more beers. The sheriff and Joe drained their first ones and Eddie took the empties.

"I love Eddie's cooking, puts Mrs. Miller's to shame, not that I'd ever tell her. Let's get it while it's hot."

The two of them dug in, eating in silence until their plates were clean. Eddie cleared the table, and the sheriff pulled a pipe out of his jacket pocket. He struck a match and got it going, taking a long draw and blowing the smoke over Joe's head.

"I'm no early bird, but my deputy knew I'd asked about this Krupp fellow. They found a Frick ID card in his pants pocket. Once my boys realized who it was, they came and got me right away."

"You got a good look at the body?"

"Unfortunately, yes. Whoever worked him over did a good job of it. I'd say he'd been clubbed with a baseball bat or something similar. And from the looks of it, he wasn't killed there. I'd say he was dead for some time already."

"Can I see the body?"

"Be my guest. He's over at the coroner's funeral home. He might give you a better idea of when Krupp was killed."

"I'd like to go see where the body was found. You got someone can take me over there?"

Sheriff Miller nodded. "Figured you would. I'll take you myself." He drained his beer and stood up. "Ready when you are. And it's your turn to buy."

Joe finished his beer, paid the bill, and followed the sheriff out the door.

"I got us a wagon around back."

They rode out in silence. It was almost three by the time they arrived at the scene. The spot was a short walk down the tracks from the road where they left the wagon.

"That's the spot." Sheriff Miller pointed to a section of tracks about ten yards beyond where the roadbed curved around an outcropping of rock. "There's a regular supply train comes by here every Tuesday morning about six thirty, headed up to the Revere mines."

Joe surveyed the spot, stroking his chin. "So Krupp's body would most likely have been chewed up pretty good by the time the engineer got the train stopped."

"Enough so as no one would be questioning how he comes to have his head caved in. Here's something else for you. He smelled like he took a bath in cheap whiskey."

Joe took out his notebook and wrote a bit. "OK, Sheriff, I think I got the picture. We got lucky. Remind me to buy those hobos a good meal. Whoever killed Krupp had a good setup here. He gets run over by the train, obviously drunk, case closed. You'd figure he killed Goretsky in a moment of anger, then went on a bender and had the bad luck to pass out on the railroad tracks."

"You're most likely right, Zajac. I never did like opening up a can of worms. But this here's a different game now. Two murders in Fayette County in three days add up to a crime spree. I got a young buck challenging me in the primary election. If I don't do something now, he'll be saying I'm too old to do my job. Can't be letting that happen."

Joe smiled and put his arm around the sheriff's shoulder. "I'm glad to hear that. What do you aim to do next?"

"Watch you figure this here mess out, mostly. You got a good head on your shoulders, I'm thinking. Get us a last name on this Kurt fellow who was Krupp's friend. I'll get every lawman in Fayette County looking for him."

"Only one problem with that, Sheriff. Say we do track down Kurt. What then? Unless we find a bloody club or some witness saw him do it, we've nothing on him. What say we go back up the road and knock on a few doors, see if anyone saw somebody in a wagon stopped by the tracks last night?"

Sheriff Miller shook his head, removed his Stetson ranger hat, and smoothed back his damp hair. "I'm not much for more legwork. In fact, I'm close to worn out. And if you still want to take a look at the body, we better get on back to town. How about I send a deputy back out here with you tomorrow morning?"

Observing the sheriff made Joe mindful of his own fatigue. "I guess that will be soon enough. Let's go get a look at the stiff."

The two men walked back to the wagon and returned to Uniontown. Joe counted a dozen houses close to the tracks. Maybe he and the deputy would get lucky and find someone who saw something.

By four thirty they were at the coroner's office, next to his funeral home. A sign out front read JACOB FOSTER, UNDERTAKER. They knocked on the door and a man in a black suit answered.

"Afternoon, Jacob. Sorry we're late."

"I was about to embalm the victim, Tom. Who's your friend?"

"This here's Joe Zajac, a Frick man. He's helping the sheriff's office out on this one. Joe, meet Jacob Foster, the county coroner and best undertaker in town."

Jacob was about Joe's height, but older and skinny as a rail, his suit hanging slack. His coal-black hair was well oiled and parted in the middle. Wire-rimmed spectacles perched on a thin pointy nose.

"How do, Mr. Foster. We won't be delaying your work long."

"How do. Let's go, then. Momma hates when I'm late for dinner."

They followed Jacob down a hall and through a door at the end, into his workroom. A table stood in the center of the room. The naked form of Walter Krupp lay there, one arm at his side, the other hanging down toward a wash bucket. The room smelled of chemicals.

Joe stepped forward and examined the body. Krupp was most likely close to forty, and a bit thick. His body had a soft look about it, with no signs that he'd lived a life of hard labor. His hair was light brown and very short.

"How long you figure he's been dead, Mr. Foster?"

"Based on the skin color when I first examined him, I suspect he'd been dead less than twenty-four hours, maybe as few as twelve. I'd say he was killed no later than eight last night. Sometime yesterday, at any rate."

Joe walked around the body, stopping to look at the side of his head. The left half of his skull was caved in from front to back. It looked like his left arm was broken, too. Joe noticed that the tip of his little finger was missing. There were signs of bruising on his rib cage. "I'd say whoever did this was not very happy with Mr. Krupp."

The undertaker gave him a thin smile. "He was struck in the head at least three times. Any one of the blows could have killed him. Then he was beat about the torso, struck eight or ten times more. The only body I've seen looked like this was a farmer got tangled up with a big bull."

Sheriff Miller joined Joe next to Krupp. "I see the mark of a man full of rage here. Whoever did this was near crazy, and like you say, not very pleased with the victim."

The smell of the room, and of the body, was starting to get to Joe. "That's about all I can handle, Tom. Let's let Mr. Foster finish his business. Don't want to make him late for dinner."

Joe and the sheriff left the workroom and Jacob to his work. Once outside, Joe took a deep breath, and let it out with a sigh. "I'd say Mr. Krupp got his due in full measure. And you're right on the mark. The killer is a man capable of extreme violence. Krupp must have pissed him off pretty good."

Sheriff Miller nodded and yawned. "I'm done in. Let's call it a day. Come on back tomorrow by nine. I'll have a deputy waiting for you."

"OK. See you then."

Joe trudged back to the streetcar stop and was soon on his way back to Connellsville. He sat in the rear, closed his eyes, and let the motion of the car lull him into a catnap.

Chapter 13

"West Penn Terminal, end of the line."

Joe opened his eyes for the first time since leaving Uniontown. The streetcar had arrived at Connellsville. The terminal clock showed just past six. Standing up, he stretched and exited the car.

Still groggy, Joe stretched again before heading uptown. Halfway up Main Street, he saw Johnny Davidson across the way, off duty and out of uniform. Joe waved and caught his eye, then hustled over to join him.

"Almost didn't recognize you, Johnny. Got a minute?"

"Sure, Joe. I was just heading over to the new arcade. They put in a new shooting gallery I've been looking to take a crack at. What's up?"

"How about I join you? Loser buys dinner?"

"You're on."

They headed up Main, stopping to let a streetcar pass before crossing at Brimstone Corner. "I got some news for you. You can call off the search for Walter Krupp. He's been located."

"You found him already?"

"Not me. A couple of hobos found his body this morning up Uniontown way."

"His body? He's dead, too?"

"Met his maker sometime yesterday, and came to a brutal end."

"Some kind of accident?"

"Clubbed a dozen times from the look of it, and left on the B&O tracks."

Johnny stroked his chin, his head tilted to one side. "What say we hold the shooting match for another day? Let's go get some grub, and you fill me in."

"What strikes your fancy?"

"How about we head down to the Water Street Hotel dining room? The Tuesday dinner special is pot roast."

"I could use a good meal. Let's go."

The two headed back down Main Street and descended the steps from the bridge to Water Street, which ran next to the railroad tracks and along the river. The hotel was two blocks down, across from the B&O Station. They entered the dining room from a side door and sat at a corner table where they were met by a waitress. She was an older woman, short and heavy with her grey hair in a bun, wearing a long grey dress with a lacy white apron. Smiling at Johnny, she slid two menus on the table.

"Well, looky who it is. My favorite nephew."

"Hello, Aunt Mary. How's life treating you?"

"Other than my feet killing me, tolerable well, honey. Who's your friend?"

"This is Joe Zajac, a buddy of mine. He works for Frick. I brought him down to sample some of your home cooking. How's the pot roast today?"

She turned to Joe. "Hello, Joe, and welcome to The Dinner Bell. The pot roast is mighty good tonight. We just butchered the cow yesterday."

Before Joe could reply, Johnny spoke up. "Two specials, Aunt Mary, and two beers, if you please."

She picked the menus back up and tucked them under her arm. "Coming right up, boys."

"Mary is Dad's sister. She and Uncle Mahlon bought this place two years ago, right after B&O built the new station. They've earned a reputation for good food and clean rooms."

Joe looked around the dining room. The tables and chairs all matched. The tables were covered in clean white linen. The wood floor was polished and spotless. Electric lights glowed from fixtures that lined the wall.

"You Davidsons got a lot of irons in the fire. Your uncle Frank runs the grocery on Main, right?"

"Yes, sir. And Pappy just started putting up houses on the South Side. Turned half his little farm into three blocks of building lots."

Mary returned with their beers and a plate of rolls. "Made these myself fresh today." She set everything down and headed back toward the kitchen.

"Here's to home cooking, Johnny."

They raised their glasses and drank deep. Mary returned again and set two plates in front of them.

"Eat hearty, boys. We got blackberry pie for dessert if you can fit it in." She turned and disappeared into the kitchen.

Joe looked down at the mound of food on his plate. Alongside the beef were potatoes, carrots, and onions, all covered with thick brown gravy. He tucked a napkin into his shirt collar and dug in. "Don't tell Tony, but I think City Lunch just got some competition."

The dining room wasn't very busy. Joe and Johnny sat alone in the corner, eating in silence until their plates were both clean.

"Great chow, Johnny. Aunt Mary knows how to run a restaurant."

"No argument there. Now how about filling me in on your investigation?"

Joe took another swallow from his beer and pushed his chair back. "In a nutshell, I'd say that this Krupp fellow must have killed Big George, but for reasons still unknown. I already suspected that Krupp was involved in something shady out at Number One. He'd been asking a lot of questions and had a map of the mine drawn up that I found where he'd been boarding."

"Where does this Kurt fellow fit in?"

"I figure he killed Krupp, or had someone do it for him."

"Why kill him? He'd already made his getaway from Leisenring."

"The plan was for Krupp's body to get run over by the train. He'd been soaked in whiskey so as to make it look like an accident. Then the Big George case is closed. Murderer meets justice riding a cowcatcher. The whys get buried along with him."

Johnny stroked his chin and sat forward, elbows on the table and hands folded. "I think I get the picture. But what in tarnation is really going on? Two people don't get murdered over small potatoes."

"You're right. It's a big deal, whatever it is."

"What's your next move?"

"I'll try to run down this Kurt fellow. He's my only lead. And here's another thought for you. Once he knows his plan came a cropper, and I suspect he already does, he's going to be feeling pressed."

Johnny nodded, and finished his beer. "He's likely to show his hand eventually, unless he decides to call off the plan, whatever it might be."

"I doubt he'll do that. He wouldn't have done in Krupp unless he was all in."

Mary appeared at their table once again. "You boys want another beer, or a slice of that pie?"

"No more for me. Joe?"

"I'm about to explode myself, ma'am. How much do we owe you?"

"Seeing as how this is your first visit, and you're a friend of the family, it's on the house. But come back and see me sometime, and bring a friend."

Joe tipped his cap at Mary. "Much obliged. I surely will."

Johnny and Joe got up and left the dining room. Outside, twilight was falling. Gas streetlamps were being lit along the way.

"I might have room for one more drink," Joe said. "Care to join me?"

"No thanks. I promised Pappy I'd stop by tonight. And I'm on the early shift again tomorrow."

The men shook hands and parted company, Johnny heading back up Water Street. Joe headed up Peach Street, a route that would take him past The Star. On the way he passed Rocky's Saloon. He stopped at its side door for a moment, and then decided to skip The Star for the evening. He entered the saloon and staked out a spot at the end of the bar. The joint was quiet tonight, the bar only half full. The bartender was standing at the far end, talking to a patron. Hearing the door close, they stopped talking and looked his way.

The bartender approached Joe. He was big and ugly, with a scar on one cheek and a crooked nose. He eyed Joe up and down, unsmiling.

"What'll it be?"

"Shot and a beer chaser. Old Overholt if you got it."

The bartender turned, drew a small beer, and slammed it on the bar in front of Joe, slopping some on the counter. He banged a shot glass down, grabbed a bottle from beneath the bar, and filled it. Joe tossed a dime on the bar and stared at the bartender, who glared back at him for a moment then turned and walked to the other end.

His face is ugly enough to peel paint, Joe thought. He drank half the shot and half the beer and surveyed the room. Turning slightly, he saw a table of four men sitting in the corner. All of them were staring at him, grim-looking and silent. *Must be the welcoming committee.*

Joe turned back to the bar, leaned forward, and contemplated the half-full shot glass. He could hear the men at the table talking now, low and terse. Last night had been his first visit to Rocky's and he'd already had a few. He'd not really appreciated what a dive it was, worse than some of the dumps he'd frequented on the Philadelphia waterfront. Tonight he felt distinctly unwelcome. *I'll be damned if I'll let these jokers give me the creeps.* He finished the shot and beer. "Bartender, another round."

Big and Ugly repeated his earlier routine, slamming and slapping another round down in front of Joe. Meanwhile, one of the men from the table approached the bar, standing a few feet from Joe.

"Philo, another round for me and the boys."

"OK, Jake."

The man called Jake turned to Joe. "Don't mind Philo. He doesn't like most people until he gets to know them. You new in town?"

Joe eyed Jake up and down. They were about the same size but Jake was younger, and built like a farm boy. He had a thick neck, big forearms, and broad shoulders. He wore a working man's clothes, but Joe noticed that his hands were clean. Joe turned to face him.

"Nope." He turned back to his drink.

"Well, you enjoy your evening, my friend."

Jake collected his drinks and returned to the table. The low talking resumed. A minute later one of the men got up and left through the side door, brushing against Joe as he did. Turning toward the table again, Joe saw the three men staring at him. Jake smiled at him before turning to his mates, and they continued their conversation.

I think I've had enough of this place, Joe thought. He finished his drinks, tossed another dime on the bar, and left through the side door. Hands in his pants pockets, he walked toward Pittsburgh Street at the end of the block. He looked up and saw the man who had left the bar heading his way. Joe's hand curved around the sap in his pocket as the distance between them closed. The man stopped a few feet from Joe, blocking the sidewalk. Joe pulled his hands out of his pockets and showed the man his sap.

"Say, buddy, you got a match?"

Joe eyed the man for an instant, trying to gauge his intent. In that moment the man made his move, catching Joe on the side of the head with a solid blow. He followed up with one to Joe's stomach, knocking the wind out of him. Joe doubled over, and the man caught him with an uppercut to the jaw, sending him to his knees. He saw the glint of a knife in the man's hand. Joe's attacker looked down at him and drew back his arm. "As you sow, so shall you reap."

Joe rolled to his left, ending up in the gutter. The knife slashed by his arm, missing him by inches. Joe swung his sap and caught his assailant on the wrist. The man dropped the knife and stepped back, holding his arm.

"You Frick bastards belong in hell, and I'm gonna send you there."

Joe scrambled back away, able to get his legs under him as the man recovered his knife. Joe swayed from the effort, seeing stars. The man crouched low and moved forward.

"Time to face the music."

Joe kept backing away from him, trying to clear his head. He heard the clip-clop of hooves striking brick, and from the corner of his eye saw a wagon turning down the street.

His attacker turned toward the sound. Joe stepped forward and swung the sap with all of his remaining strength, striking the man a glancing blow in the ribs. Joe saw him wince in pain.

The man in the wagon was now close enough to see what was going on. "Thunderation, what's this here all about? You boys break it up." He pulled his whip from under the wagon seat.

Joe's attacker backed off, pocketing his blade. "See you again, you son of a bitch." He turned and trotted off, heading up the alley behind Rocky's.

Joe collapsed to his knees, spent and hurting. The wagon driver hopped down and approached him.

"You all right, young feller? Seems like you two had quite a tussle going there."

Joe caught his breath and stood up. He gazed at his rescuer, an old fellow with a full white beard. "I am, thanks to you. I'm much obliged."

The old man chuckled. "If'n it were a fair fight, I might've let it go, but seeing he had a knife pulled on you, I couldn't let it pass. You need some help?"

"I could use a ride home, just up by Brimstone Corner."

"Sure 'nuff, sonny. Hop on up and let's go."

Joe winced as he climbed up on the wagon. "What's your name, my friend?"

"Elijah Jones."

"Elijah, I'm Joe Zajac. You most likely saved my life tonight. I'm in your debt."

Elijah turned the wagon and headed back up Pittsburgh Street. "It weren't nothing, son."

Chapter 14

Joe drifted awake Wednesday morning, groaning. He lay in bed for a while, assessing the damage. His head throbbed, and his stomach ached. Even his teeth hurt. Swinging his legs over the side, he sat up. His head swam for a moment before clearing. He staggered just a bit when he walked over to the dresser and picked up the hand mirror.

It looks even worse than it feels, he thought, as his hands gently traced the lump near his eye, a yellow bruise showing around the edge of it. A smaller lump on his jawline had a cut in the center. He opened his mouth and grabbed a few of his teeth. They all seemed intact. He pulled up his shirt and examined his gut. It ached but there was no swelling or bruising evident.

I've been beat worse than this. I'll survive. But he knew he'd been lucky. The stakes were raised. *And I let myself get caught by surprise.*

He grabbed the pitcher and headed for the hall bathroom for water. He washed up, shaved with care, and got dressed. It was just past seven by the time he headed out the door for City Lunch.

Tony's smile turned into a frown as Joe walked in and took his usual stool. Tony poured a cup of coffee and set it down in front of Joe, shaking his head.

"So what the hell happened to you, Joey? You look like you fell off a streetcar or something."

"I got into a little scuffle down on Peach Street last night."

"Peach Street? You mean down by Rocky's?"

Joe picked up the coffee and took a gulp, then nodded to Tony.

"What I'm gonna do with you? You no listen to what I say yesterday."

Joe shrugged. "You were right. I'm too stupid to listen to good advice."

"We got plenty of toughs here, maybe even tougher than in your Philadelphia."

Joe took another gulp of coffee, looking at Tony over the cup. "I learned that lesson the hard way, my friend. Now how about you make me some pancakes?"

Tony shook his head and disappeared into the kitchen. Joe turned his gaze out the back window, trying to make some sense of yesterday's events.

Whatever was going on at Number One had taken an ominous turn, and if he wasn't more careful, he'd end up joining Krupp. *Those fellas knew who I was. I'm being watched.*

The tinkle of the doorbell broke his train of thought. Like clockwork, Johnny Davidson was here for his morning coffee. Joe turned back to the counter as the cop sat down next to him.

"Damn, Joe, what the hell happened to you?"

"Misjudged my enemies, and pret' near got stabbed for it." He recounted the events of Tuesday evening after they had parted.

"Looks like you almost bit off more than you could chew. You're lucky old Elijah showed up. You want me to go after this Jake fellow?"

"Don't waste your time. I doubt it would do much good. The part I can't figure is that 'sow and reap' crack."

"That's from the Good Book. 'Whatsoever a man soweth, that shall he also reap.'"

"I know it's from the Bible, but what did he mean by it?"

"You should get by now that H.C. Frick is despised, and in the eyes of the working men, you're one with him. His Coal & Coke Police are hated around these parts. I've seen them throw striking miners out of their houses in the middle of the winter. You weren't with them in ninety-five, the last time we had big labor trouble in the coal fields. I saw how it was."

"I started with Frick just after, and I've been in charge of protecting property for the most part, not treating workers poorly."

"I know that, and you're a good man, but that doesn't matter to the working folks. A Frick cop is the enemy."

Tony showed up with Joe's pancakes and a cup of coffee for Johnny, shaking his head as he put down the plates. "What you think of our boy here, Johnny? I seen better looking heads on a cabbage."

Joe ate a few bites of his pancakes, put his fork down, and turned to Johnny. "So I'm to blame for the misery these people suffer at the hands of Frick?"

Johnny nodded. "You're as guilty as H.C. Frick himself, and there are plenty of men itching for some payback."

Joe ate a few more bites and paused again. "I know a miner's life is rough. Hell, the old man and I lived it. I'd hoped that maybe times had changed some for the better. I guess it hasn't but I can't change that."

Johnny finished his coffee and got up to leave. "Most likely not, Joe, but that doesn't matter. Looks to me like things are heating up in the coal fields again, and there's not much middle ground. I'd be watching my back if I was you."

Joe sat thinking about what Johnny had said. His words rang true, Joe had to admit.

Tony appeared with the coffee pot and topped off Joe's cup. "I been listening, Joey. I hope you were, too. Johnny knows what he's talking about."

"I know, Tony, but I'm stuck. Two men are dead and it's my job to figure it out. As long as I take my pay from Frick, I'm bound to do my best for him. If I can't stomach that, I need to move on."

Joe finished his pancakes and coffee and settled up with Tony. "I have my own stake in this now. My friend from last night will be looking to take another crack at me."

Joe hustled over to West Penn Terminal and was soon on his way to Uniontown. He arrived at Sheriff Miller's office a bit before nine, and found him behind his desk, studying some papers.

"Morning, Tom. How goes it?"

Sheriff Miller looked up, frowning as he examined Joe's face. "What happened to you? You get kicked by one of them mules?"

"I took a good beating last night. It could have been worse."

"Barroom fight?"

"No, but it started in one. The man jumped me on the street. I believe it was because of this case we're working on. The fella knew I worked for Frick and I never saw him before."

Joe told the sheriff all about Tuesday evening's events. "I know one thing—I've not taken this seriously enough. I may not know what's going on, but with people getting killed and attacked, it has to be something big. My ass is on the line and the only way for me to stay healthy is to figure it out."

Sheriff Miller sat stroking his chin, then stood up. "That makes sense to me. The way I figure it is, this Kurt fella's been keeping an eye on you for some time, maybe even was watching Mrs. Gmitter's place. He's got some friends, too, sounds like. You carry a gun?"

The fellow standing at the end of the street and by the stable. "Didn't think I needed one to this point."

"I'd arm myself if I was you."

Joe nodded. "I need to keep on digging. Your deputy ready to go back out to Hogsett?"

"He should be downstairs."

Joe and Sheriff Miller left the office and went out the back door of the building. A fair-skinned young man was sitting on the steps, two horses tied to the rail.

"Joe, meet Horace Etling. He's my best deputy, and also my son-in-law, so try not to get him hurt if you please."

Horace stood up and offered Joe his hand. "How do, Joe. You ready to ride?"

Joe looked at the horses, then back at Sheriff Miller. "No wagon today?"

"You men need to move fast. You ever been on a horse?"

"I have, but I'd be lying if I claimed much experience. Mostly I get around on West Penn, or a buggy."

"You'll be fine, then. Old Sarge is as agreeable a piece of horse flesh as you're apt to run into. Try and get back by noon. I'll be back in my office by then. I need to be kept up to date."

Sheriff Miller reentered the building. Horace untied the horses and handed Joe the reins to Sarge, a big black stallion. Horace swung up into the saddle of the other horse, a chestnut-brown mare. "Ready when you are."

Joe climbed atop Sarge, who was snorting and sidestepping away from the rail.

"You just follow me and Daisy here. Giddy up."

Horace and Daisy trotted off at a brisk pace and Sarge fell in behind. It took them twenty minutes to get out to Hogsett. They dismounted near the tracks and tied the horses to a tree.

Joe pulled out his handkerchief, wiped his face, then turned to Horace. "How much do you know about what we got going on?"

"Sheriff Miller explained most of it, and I was the one came out here yesterday morning."

Joe looked up and down the road that crossed the tracks. "Let's see if anyone remembers seeing anything Monday night or yesterday morning. Let's start with the houses that are within sight of the tracks. You head north and I'll go south."

"OK, Joe. Meet you back here."

Joe headed down the road. The first house was more like a shack, one room covered in tarpaper with a tin roof. He stopped at the pump by the road, took a drink, then approached the front door and knocked.

"Anybody home?" He waited a few minutes before walking around back, where he found an old woman hoeing a row of lettuce.

"Hello, ma'am. Sorry to interrupt your work."

The woman straightened up and leaned on her rake, wiping the sweat from her forehead with the back of her hand. "And who might you be?"

"Name's Joe, ma'am. I'm working with Sheriff Miller. You know that they found a body up the tracks yesterday?"

"'Course I do. Don't bad news always travel fast? What do you want from me?"

"Whoever dropped the body most likely brought it out by wagon. I'm wondering if you saw anything Monday late or early Tuesday."

"No, sir, I didn't. Now if that's all you want, my garden needs tending."

"Maybe your husband might have seen something?"

"Ain't no husband here no more. He got himself killed up at Revere."

The Revere mine, up the road a bit, was owned by Frick's competitor, W.J. Rainey.

"Sorry to hear that, ma'am."

"Left me alone and so broke I don't have a pot to piss in." The woman turned her back to Joe and resumed hoeing.

Joe walked back to the road and headed to the next house. The residents hadn't seen anything. The next four houses were the same story. He approached the final house within sight of the railroad crossing, a little bungalow set back from the road. A white picket fence surrounded the front yard. A wooden walk ran from the gate to the front of the house, under a grape arbor. Joe opened the gate and trudged up the walk. The shade was a welcome relief from the hot August sun.

An old man was sitting on the front porch in a rocking chair. He looked to be sleeping. Joe cleared his throat and the man opened his eyes. He had long white hair and was wearing bib overalls. He looked Joe over, then reached for his pipe sitting on a table next to him.

"Whatcha selling, sonny?"

Joe smiled as he watched the old man load his pipe. "I'm not a peddler. My name's Joe."

"I'm Luther Stackhouse. This here's my daughter's place. What's on your mind?"

"You heard about the body found down the tracks?"

"Sure enough. Saw the sheriff come by here yesterday, and if I ain't mistaken, you were riding on the wagon with him. You a deputy or something? I don't see no badge."

"I'm not a deputy but I am helping out Sheriff Miller. Did you happen to see anything down by the tracks Monday night or Tuesday morning?"

Luther dug a match out of his pocket and soon had the corncob in full blast. He leaned back, started rocking, smiled at Joe, and nodded.

"I was wondering if you folks would be by checking. You know, I'm in the habit of rising early, even though I ain't working anymore. Old habits are hard to break."

Joe took off his cap and sat on the step. *No sense trying to hurry him.* "I'm an early bird myself. Like to get up and get going."

"Mostly I wake up hungry, that's what gets me up and at 'em." The old man puffed away, blowing smoke rings in Joe's direction.

"So you got up early yesterday?"

"Sure 'nuff, 'round five or so. And since the grapes are coming in, I headed out to get me some ripe ones for my breakfast. The sun was just coming up."

"And you saw something?"

Luther nodded. "I was all the way down by the road. I noticed the gate was open and went to close it. We got an old dog here that likes to wander off. I checked the road for him. That's when I noticed it."

Luther paused again, smiling at Joe and puffing away.

"What did you see?"

"I seen a wagon down by the crossing, and a man getting in it. Then he turned up the road and came a blasting past here, hell bent for election."

"Did you get a look at him?"

"Just a peep as he went by, but not so's I could describe him."

"How about the wagon?"

"That, I can tell you some about. It was a delivery wagon with high sides. It had words painted on it."

"Did you make them out?"

"All I could get was 'Mining Supplies.' He was going too fast for me to make out the name."

Joe stood up and put on his cap. "I'm much obliged for the information, Luther." He pulled two bits out of his pocket and set it on the table. "You think of anything else, get word to Sheriff Miller."

Luther eyed the coin, then picked it up and put it in his overalls pocket. "I'll do that, son."

Chapter 15

Joe hurried down the walk and returned to the horses. Horace was already there.

"Did you find anything out, Horace?"

"No, sir. How about you?"

"We got lucky, I'd say. A man up the hill saw something yesterday morning." Joe related Luther's story to Horace as they untied their horses and mounted up.

"Let's ride. We got us an angle to work."

The two men took off for Uniontown, running their horses at a gallop. They arrived at the courthouse in a cloud of dust, both horses lathered up. Horace grabbed Joe's reins as he dismounted. "You go on up and tell Sheriff Miller the news. I'll walk the horses a bit."

Joe ran up the stairs and found the sheriff on the telephone. He waved Joe in and continued talking.

"Yes, Jim, they just made it back. I'll give him the news." He hung up and looked up at Joe, frowning. "That was your man out at Leisenring looking for you. I got a message."

"And I got news for you, Sheriff. We found us a witness that saw a mine supply company wagon out by the tracks yesterday morning, leaving the scene in a big hurry. He didn't get a good look at the driver, though." Joe told Sheriff Miller about his conversation with Luther.

Sheriff Miller got up and rubbed his hands together. "We got us a little something to go on. Let's check out every mine supply operation in Fayette County, and see if they got anyone name of Kurt working for them."

"Makes sense to me. Can you get Horace to start on the ones up this way? I'll go round to the ones near Connellsville."

"We'll get started on it tomorrow. Now I got something to tell you."

"What did Jim want?"

"He got news from over at Standard. Seems they had a boxcar broke into last night."

"What did they get?"

"A considerable amount of dynamite."

Joe's jaw dropped. "What the hell is going on around here?"

Sheriff Miller sat back down and laced his hands across his belly. "It's kind of suspicious, all this happening together, that's for sure. You're on your own with this one, seeing as Standard's over in Westmoreland County."

Standard was Frick's biggest mine and coke works in the Connellsville Coal Field, with more than six hundred ovens in operation. It was near Mount Pleasant. Joe stopped by there at least every other week.

"I have a good night watchman over there. I better get moving. No time for lunch today."

Joe walked slowly to the streetcar line, lost in thought. This was bad news, for Frick and him. *There's only one thing makes sense. Someone intends to do Frick harm.*

The streetcar arrived and the ride to Connellsville was uneventful. He changed cars at the terminal and arrived at Standard around two. He hurried to the company store and the superintendent's office.

Caspar Brown was sitting behind his desk talking to Isaac Gilmer, the night watchman. Caspar was near sixty, mostly bald with a full white beard. He stopped talking to Isaac as Joe entered his office.

"We got us one big mess here, Zajac, and the shit is hitting the fan."

"How much dynamite is missing?"

"Twenty cases. The order was for us, Alverton, and some other mines over this way."

"Twenty cases at a hundred sticks a case, if I'm not mistaken."

"Right. That's a thousand pounds of explosives, and they got the caps, too."

Isaac stood up and turned to Joe. He was a big man, about Joe's age and missing his left arm from an accident in the mine. "I don't know how or when they got it, Joe. I made my rounds like always. The boxcar was dropped off late yesterday. I checked it soon as I got here. It was locked up tight and parked down past the end of the ovens, close to the road."

"Let's go take a look. You coming, Caspar?"

"I saw enough of it already and have to send a report to Scottdale." He directed a scowl their way. "This makes us all look damn bad."

Joe and Isaac left Caspar to his work and headed down to the railroad siding, both knowing the superintendent was right. They were soon standing next to the boxcar, its door open.

"We're liable to be looking for work if we don't figure this out, Isaac." Joe got out his notebook and pencil stub. "Let's go over this from the start."

"I'm fit to be tied. I can't lose this job. Ain't many people willing to hire a cripple."

"There's nothing to be done except try to catch up with whoever pulled this off. What time did the boxcar arrive?"

"B&O dropped it around five yesterday evening. I started at six and checked it out first thing. I knew what was in it, wanted to make sure the wind wouldn't be blowing toward it."

"When did you make your next inspection?"

"That would have been around midnight. Everything was still secure."

Joe made a few notes in his book, then stuck the pencil behind his ear. "What time did you discover the theft?"

"I came back around just before my shift ended, a bit before six. I noticed the lock was off, and the door was slid back a bit. So I opened it all the way and saw that a big part of the load was missing."

Joe walked around the boxcar, examining the stone rail bed. He walked the short distance to the road and returned.

"I'm thinking this was a quick and organized job, no fly-by-night crooks. I'd say two wagons were involved and likely a dozen men. Look here."

Joe pointed to ruts next to the track, some on both sides.

"These tracks go right up to the road. I figure that the thieves were able to unload the crates in short order, working from both sides. Maybe took them ten minutes or so from start to finish."

"Around four in the morning, it's pretty quiet around here. Still dark, morning crew not due for an hour, ovens checked. I was having my coffee up at the supply shed."

"I've seen enough. Let's go up and talk to Caspar."

They returned to the superintendent's office and found it vacant. "You might as well go home and get some sleep, Isaac. It's been a long day for you. I'll wait for the boss."

"Much obliged. I got to be back here before you know it, and I ain't slept a minute all day."

Isaac lumbered out the door, head down and shoulders stooped. Joe sat down and leaned back, closing his eyes for a moment.

"Wake up, Zajac. We don't need any more sleeping on the job."

Joe opened his eyes as Caspar entered his office and sat down at the desk. "It's been a long day."

Caspar looked at Joe's face, spotting his lumps and bruises for the first time. "Looks like it was a rough one, too. I thought you were a tough guy."

"I might have to go back to being a cop. It's a mite safer than what's been going on around here."

Caspar leaned back and stroked his beard. "What the hell is going on? We all heard about what happened out at Leisenring, and Jim told me about that body up at Uniontown. That's two dead Frick men in four days. Now we get relieved of a thousand pounds of dynamite."

Joe explained to Caspar what his inspection of the boxcar led him to believe. "Whoever did this most likely had inside information. First off, they needed to know that you were getting that shipment in. Second, they were familiar with the layout here, and how the graveyard shift operated. Who else beside you and Isaac knew about it?"

"The bill of lading showed up around four. The bookkeeper knew. But the car had a Danger sign on it so anyone keeping his eyes open could have figured it out. And it doesn't take a genius to know when the quiet time is around a coke yard at night."

"You got that bill handy? I want to know how to identify these crates if I need to."

Caspar shuffled some papers around, found what he was looking for, and handed it to Joe. "Here you go. The dynamite was manufactured by the Vulcan Powder Company. The crates are marked and numbered. The bill lists them all."

Joe took a few more notes and handed the bill back to Caspar. "I'm going to stop down by the houses closest to the road, see if anyone spotted anything. It's a long shot but I've no other ideas at the present."

Joe left and headed back down the road. For the next hour, he visited every home within sight of the siding. No one saw anything that morning. *Can't get lucky twice in one day*, Joe thought. Tired, and his face hurting again, he trudged down to the streetcar track and waited for the Connellsville car.

The familiar gong sound announced its arrival. Joe boarded and sat in the rear. *I need to go over this with a fine-tooth comb.* He pulled out his notebook and started at page one.

Joe's ride back to Connellsville passed quickly as he studied his notes. By the time the car made town, he'd drawn up a short list of items to follow up on. He jumped off at Brimstone Corner and, after a quick stop at his place, headed to The Star.

It was after six when he got there and took his usual spot at the end of the bar. Hiram saw him coming and had a shot and a beer waiting.

"Here you go, Joe. Looks like you could use a drink."

"Evening, Hiram. You got that right."

Joe knocked back the shot and half the beer, took a deep breath, and slowly exhaled. Then he finished the beer and threw a quarter on the bar. "One more time, if you please."

Hiram brought Joe another shot and a beer, which he took to a table in the rear corner. He sat down, leaned back in the chair, and closed his eyes, hands folded in his lap.

"Wake up, Zajac. This is a barroom, not a bedroom."

Joe opened his eyes to see his friend Lloyd pulling out a chair and sitting down. He sat up and rubbed his face. "It's been a long day, Red, and last night was nothing to brag about, either."

"Did your girlfriend do that to you?"

"No. Mrs. Weimer up at the corner store caught me stealing penny candy and beat me with her cane."

Nell the waitress approached the table. "You boys need anything?"

"Bring my buddy a shot and a beer, Nell," Joe said. "No food for me at the moment. I'm planning on drinking my dinner."

"And I already had my dinner. Just the drinks will be fine."

After Nell left, Lloyd said, "That's a real pretty shade of blue you got developing there. You gonna tell me about it or make me guess?"

Nell returned with Lloyd's drinks. Joe picked up his shot glass and raised it to Lloyd. "Here's to you, and to Lady Luck."

Lloyd raised his shot and tapped Joe's. "May misfortune follow you the rest of your life, and never catch up."

The two tossed back the shots and chased them with the beers.

"I'm feeling better already, Lloyd. Just what the doctor ordered." Joe motioned to Nell for another round and leaned forward, elbows on the table. "I came close to getting myself sliced open last night, down on Peach Street."

It took Joe several minutes to bring Lloyd up to date on the events that had unfolded since Saturday. Lloyd let him speak without interruption, stroking his beard as the story unfolded.

"Great balls of fire. And here I thought you had it easy."

"Compared to being a cop, this job has been easy. But all of a sudden I'm a marked man, and I never saw it coming."

"You know that your man Frick ain't exactly loved around these parts. What's your next move?"

"I have to track down Walter's friend Kurt. I'm going to call on every mine supply house around here and see if he turns up."

"I know one thing. A thousand pounds of dynamite is enough to blow a hell of a hole in something. I'm mighty suspicious about that. You got a gun?"

"You're the second man asked me that today. I don't because I haven't needed one."

"Do yourself a favor and get one. I'd recommend a Colt .45. Momma always said that trouble comes in threes. And if you want to go to Rocky's again, let me know so I can watch your back."

Joe leaned forward. "You're right, Red. I'll get myself armed tomorrow." He stroked his jaw and yawned. "All of a sudden I'm plum tuckered out. Let's drink up and call it a night."

Chapter 16

Joe was up at dawn on Thursday. He'd fallen asleep early Wednesday night, slept soundly, and woke up well rested. He picked up his notebook and started a list of all he needed to accomplish that day. He'd promised Caleb that they would meet for breakfast, and he wanted to stop by Number One. Somewhere along the way, he was going to buy a gun and a holster. Then he would start calling on mine supply businesses.

The first streetcar to Mount Pleasant left town at six and Joe was on it. He arrived at Alverton around six thirty, and saw Caleb sitting on the steps of the company store.

"I was wondering if you forgot about buying me breakfast. I'd about gave up on you and was fixin' to head on home."

"Got here as soon as I could, Caleb. Thanks for waiting. Let's go get us some grub."

"There's a little place down the road makes a good breakfast and it opens early."

Caleb jumped up and they headed down the street to the main road. After a half-mile walk, they came upon an old log cabin with a sign out front that said EATS.

"This is Ethel's place. She's been here for years, catering mostly to the Alverton trade. Everything's farm fresh and she bakes her own bread."

Joe and Caleb entered the cabin, where they were greeted immediately by a short and slim woman with her white hair in a bun. "Hello, Caleb. How's my favorite cousin doing?"

"Just got off work up the road, Ethel. I caught on as the new night watchman. This here's my boss, Joe Zajac."

Ethel held her hand out to Joe. "Pleased to meet you, Joe. Sit yourself down and let me get you both a cup of coffee."

Joe and Caleb took a table in the far corner, and soon had steaming mugs of black coffee in front of them. "How about I get you boys our cabin special? I guarantee you won't be leaving hungry."

"Fine by me. You game, Mr. Zajac?"

"I'm game. Eggs over easy, if you please."

"Coming right up. Shout if you need more coffee." She hollered as she left, "Two specials, Albert. Easy and scrambled."

Caleb eyed Joe as they sipped their coffee. "I ain't seen a bruise like that for a while. You youngsters sure know how to have fun."

Joe gently touched the side of his face. That morning, he'd seen in the mirror that while the swelling had gone down, the bruise was growing, a faint yellow appearing around the edges.

"It's an exciting life I'm leading. How about you? Anything going on out here?"

"Well, we ain't lost any dynamite on my watch, which I understand seems to be a problem hereabout."

Joe smiled and pushed his chair back a bit from the table. He leaned forward, arms braced on his thighs.

"How much do you know about what's been going on lately?"

"Let's see—two dead men and half a ton of missing dynamite. And you got your ass whipped, I guess, too."

"That's the simple facts, but I'm still trying to figure out why and what's next."

Joe took the next few minutes to tell the story in more detail. Caleb listened as he drank his coffee.

"So the theft of the dynamite tells me that the worst is yet to come, Caleb."

Ethel arrived with their breakfast, huge platters stacked high with pancakes, eggs, potatoes, sausage, and bacon. She set them down, left, and returned with a plate of biscuits and a full pot of coffee.

"Enjoy your chow, boys. I made some donuts if you got any room left after."

Joe pulled up to the table and they both dug in, eating without talking. Before long their platters were clean.

"I love a big breakfast best of all," Caleb said. "How about you? Eat your fill?"

"And then some. Ethel's a great cook."

"She does the baking and runs the joint, but her boy Albert does the cooking. His pancakes are the best I've ever ate, and I've had my share."

Caleb took a corncob pipe and a pouch of tobacco out of his overalls, loaded it up, and was soon puffing away. He laced his hands across his stomach and stared at the cloud of smoke drifting toward the ceiling.

"You sure got a case of something here, and I'm thinking we haven't seen the last of that dynamite, either."

"Walter Krupp was in the middle of it, whatever it is. That's why he ended up dead."

Caleb stroked his chin as he continued puffing. "Krupp. That name rings a bell. There used to be a family of Krupps hereabout, had a small farm down the road. They had a daughter about my age I was kind of sweet on for a while, name of Hilda."

"It doesn't seem to be that common a name around here. We got plenty of Poles, Serbs, Slovaks, and Hungarians, but not many Germans."

"Maybe that's the case now but it wasn't always so. In fact, it was Germans from over Philadelphia way that first settled and started farming Westmoreland County, the Overholts among them."

Joe took the last biscuit from the basket, pulled it apart, and spread it with strawberry jam. "You know your local history better than me. What else do you remember about the Krupps?"

"Hilda married a man from over Greensburg way, another German farmer name of Otto Schmidt. And if I ain't mistaken, they had a boy named Walter."

Joe got goose bumps. "Ever meet him?"

"Can't recall as I did, but I think the Schmidts still run that farm. You think he's mixed up in this?"

"I wasn't able to turn up anything about Walter Krupp. Maybe I'll have better luck with Walter Schmidt."

Joe pulled his pocket watch out and checked the time. It was already past seven thirty—time to get moving. He took a half dollar out of his pocket and gave it to Caleb. "Here, buy yourself some good tobacco. That stuff you're smoking smells worse than a coke oven."

Caleb pocketed the coin, flashing a toothless smile. "Sure enough will, boss. I think there's still a few relations of the Krupps around. I'll see if I can find anything out about the Schmidts."

"Much obliged for that. Now I have to get over to Leisenring and you're due some rest. Keep a close eye out until we get this all figured out."

Joe dropped a quarter on the table and left Caleb there to finish his pipe. He caught the next streetcar back to town, changed cars at the Connellsville terminal, and within the hour was back at Leisenring. He walked up the road to the Union Supply Store and the Frick offices.

Joe bounded up the stairs and found Jim Thornton sitting behind his desk, a stack of papers in front of him. Jim looked up at Joe, shook his head, and pointed to a chair.

"Be with you in a minute, Joe. Let me finish with these."

Joe removed his cap, sat back, and tried to relax. He looked around the office, noticing for the first time an old picture of John Leisenring, the original owner of the three mines that bore his name. Although the family ran the mines for ten years, they'd never made much money off of them, and sold them to Frick at what it had cost to develop the properties. It was just one of many smart moves Frick had made as he patiently acquired coal properties during slow times, until he became far and away the dominant coke producer in the area.

Jim finished his reading, stacked the papers, and, except for one, set them aside. "Care to guess what this is?"

Joe could see that it was a telegram, but just shook his head.

"It's a telegram from Frick's president, Tom Lynch. I've been the superintendent here for five years and never had the pleasure of hearing from him direct. He wants to see you at headquarters tomorrow to meet with him and Cliff. He's expecting you there by ten."

"I'll be there."

"Ever meet the man?"

"Never have. How about you?"

"Only once at a big meeting down at headquarters, right after he took over as president. He's not as wild as H.C., but a piece of work in his own right. He's come up through the ranks and runs a tight ship. He mentioned the missing dynamite."

"Whoever did that job was well organized and knew what they were doing. They were familiar with Standard's layout, and most likely had someone inside to tip them off about the shipment. Other than that, I don't have much to tell him."

"Be prepared to get an ass chewing. You're on the spot for this, like it or not."

"I'll wear my old pants, then. Thanks for the kind words."

Jim smiled and leaned back in his chair. "You're a real wise guy." He stared at Joe's face for a bit. "Now what's happened to you? Get falling-down drunk?"

"Got bit by a snake, more like it." Joe gave Jim a rundown of the events of the last two days.

"You must have a horseshoe up your ass. You're lucky the old man came by."

Joe stroked his chin and nodded. "The part that doesn't make much sense to me is the 'reap what you sow' remark. Let me ask you something, Jim. You've been the superintendent here for a long time, worked for Frick even longer, a company man to the quick. Do the men hate your guts?"

Jim leaned back and locked his hands behind his head. "I'd have to answer yes and no. We've a hundred fifty men working here. Some know me well, some not at all. The ones that know me, I don't think they hate me. I'm a fair man to work for, and I worked in the mines, but fair or not, I got to drive them hard. I do understand this—anyone that's worked here for a while ends up with bad feelings about the company, and no wonder. They treat the mules better than the men."

"What about me?"

"You, they don't know at all. You got an easy job in their eyes, make easy money. And as far as they're concerned, you're just another Frick cop, and the Frick police are the most despised men in the company, mostly because they end up doing the dirty work. So yes, Joe, I'd say that the men most likely got no use for you."

Joe pondered Jim's words for a minute, frowning. "Thanks for the straight talk. I guess I've been walking around with blinders on. Not much I can do about it now, though. I've decided to arm myself until this all gets resolved."

Jim got up and unlocked a storage cabinet in the corner of his office. He pulled out a revolver and a holster. "Here you go, then, if that's what you decided, and I can't say as I blame you. This here's an old Colt .45 I picked up in ninety-four, the last time we had real labor trouble in these parts. You're welcome to use it until you find something better."

Joe took the revolver, opened the cylinder, and gave it a spin. There were five rounds loaded and one open chamber. Joe put the empty under the hammer and holstered the gun. "Much obliged, Jim. I hope it stays in the holster."

"I'd give it a good cleaning and pick up a box of fresh cartridges. And go shoot a few rounds before you need to use it."

Joe laid the gun on the desk and pulled out his notebook. "I intend to visit every mine supply company in these parts, see if I can get lucky and find this Kurt fellow. You must have a list of them somewhere, right?"

"Sure do. We'll stop down and see the bookkeeper. He keeps a record of our suppliers."

Joe paged through his notes. "I'm double-checking everything that's happened so far, see if I missed anything. What happened to the stuff that was in George's pockets?"

Jim pulled open a drawer and took out a cigar box. He opened it and dumped the contents on his desk. "That's one Frick ID card and some wire."

Joe checked his notes. "Weren't there a few coins, too?"

"I gave those to the missus when she picked up his belongings."

"Think we missed anything?"

"No, I double-checked the trousers before I gave them to her."

Joe picked up the wire—two short pieces of copper. "What does the fire boss use this wire for?"

"He don't. That wire's used by the blasters to rig their charge."

"So why's George carrying these around? And in his good pants, too?"

Jim scratched his head. "You know, that's a good question. There's no good reason comes to mind."

Joe took the wire and pocketed it. "But maybe a bad reason does. I'm figuring this ties into Goretsky's murder. Where's those books and the map I found of Walter's?"

Jim retrieved the books from his cabinet and spread the map out on his desk, where they both examined it.

"We know that Krupp was up to something and most likely George got wind of it. Krupp seemed to be interested in these ventilation shafts. You know where they come out?"

Jim nodded. "Let's get us a couple of horses and head on out there."

Chapter 17

Joe and Jim hurried down to the stable and had the stable boy saddle up two horses. They mounted up and trotted down the main road, past the end of the coke ovens, where they turned off and followed a narrow lane away from Leisenring. They traveled about a mile before Jim pulled up and pointed to some high ground.

"We need to follow this trail up to that hill. It's tight going so let me lead the way."

Joe nodded and followed Jim through a grove of maples that opened up into a field of corn. They skirted the rows until they arrived at a hedgerow, and then followed that to the foot of the steep hill.

"Let's just tie the horses here and walk up," Jim said.

They climbed down, tethered the horses to a crabapple tree, and hiked through tall weeds to the top of the hill. Just over the rise, Joe spotted the conical metal roof that covered the ventilation shaft. As they approached, he could hear the fan pushing the fresh air down to the mine three hundred feet below.

"Everything look right to you, Jim?"

"Sounds like it's running fine. Let's take a look around."

They split up and walked around the shaft in opposite directions in ever widening circles. About a hundred feet from the shaft, Joe came upon what looked like an old road.

"Hey, Jim, over here."

Jim came over and they both started walking down the road.

"Where does this come out?"

"This is an old construction track that starts on the back road to Monarch. It's rarely used anymore, to my knowledge."

"Looks to me like it's had some traffic of late." Joe knelt down and examined the crushed grass in the road. "These ruts look fresh."

Jim nodded. "And look here. These broken branches didn't happen long ago, either."

Joe knelt down to examine the cracked brambly branches that had grown out from the sides of the road. The breaks were still light and looked new, the leaves on the ends of the branches still alive.

"Someone's been up here in a wagon, from the looks of it. You sure it wasn't one of the crew?" Joe asked.

"We send a man up here once a month to oil and inspect the fan. He comes up on horseback, just like we did. It's a hell of a lot quicker to get here that way."

"So what do you make of it?"

"Mines can't operate without proper ventilation. Damage this shaft and we're shut down."

Joe nodded, stood up, and brushed the dirt from his trousers. "We need to keep an eye on this and all of the other ventilation shafts until we put a stop to it. I'll let Scottdale know what we've found, and get one of the Frick police shifted here full-time." He took out his notebook and made an entry. "Let's go get that list of mine supply outfits."

Joe and Jim returned to their mounts and galloped back to the Leisenring stable. They tied the panting horses to the fence rail and returned to the Union Supply Store. Joe followed Jim into a small office, where a young man stood at a desk, making entries in a ledger.

"Joe, meet Frank McCoy, our bookkeeper."

Frank put down his quill pen, pulled out a handkerchief, wiped his right hand, and extended it to Joe. "How do, Joe."

"Joe needs to call on the local mine supply companies, Frank. Make him up a list of the ones we do business with, names and addresses."

"Will do, Mr. Thornton, right away. Come back in fifteen minutes, Joe, and I'll have it ready for you."

They left Frank to his task and walked through the store. It was almost noon. The place was crowded with miners' wives. There were thirty Union Supply Stores in Fayette and Westmoreland County. They sold everything from food to furniture to carriages for babies and adults. Joe noticed Anna Gmitter standing at the butcher counter. Their eyes met for a moment before she turned away.

"Come on up and get your gun, Joe. I need to get back to work."

Joe followed Jim to his office and retrieved the revolver and holster. He returned to the store and bought a box of bullets, then went back to Frank's office and picked up the list, which he folded and slipped into his vest pocket. By twelve thirty he was on his way back to town, seated in the rear of the streetcar. He pulled out the list and read it over.

There were ten companies, seven near Connellsville, two in the Dawson area, and one in Dunbar. He'd start with the ones in town this afternoon. The rest he'd visit tomorrow after he got back from Scottdale.

Joe soon arrived at the Connellsville terminal. He headed up Main Street, crossing the street mid-block to avoid the Royal Bake Shop. Distracted, he nearly got run over by a delivery wagon, the driver cursing as he reined in the two-horse team. Joe turned down Pittsburgh Street, stopped by his room to drop off the gun, then headed back out to start his visits to the supply companies.

His route took him past City Lunch. Realizing he hadn't eaten, he decided to stop in. The lunch rush had ended. Tony was sitting at the counter eating a bowl of soup. Joe sat down beside him.

"Joey, I wonder where you been. You stop eating?"

"No, Tony. I had an early meeting over at Alverton, had breakfast over there."

Tony looked Joe over. "How's the face?"

Joe rubbed his hand along his jaw. "Not too bad, healing up fast. Mind getting me a bowl of that soup?"

Tony got off the stool and disappeared through the door behind the counter. A minute later he returned with a bowl of chicken soup and a plate of bread. "You want a beer?"

"How about just a water today?"

Tony's eyes widened. He put the soup and bread in front of Joe, poured a glass of water from a pitcher behind the counter, and returned to his stool. Joe dipped a piece of bread in the soup and took a bite.

"You find out who beat you up?"

Joe shook his head and ate his soup. He finished up quickly, wiped his lips, and turned on his stool.

"Tony, how long have you been in America?"

"I come over on the boat in ninety-two, me and my brother."

"You glad you came?"

Tony turned toward Joe, legs apart and hands on his knees. "When we first come over, we were in New York City. It was rough for us. We lived in one room with two cousins. It was OK in our neighborhood, but you had to be careful around the town. People hate us, call us greasy wops."

"How about here in Connellsville?"

"It's better, but us *italianos* still on the bottom, the last ones off the boat. Only the black man lower."

Joe nodded. "It's a funny world. Half of the people in Fayette County came over on the boat, including me."

"But you a lucky guy, Joey. You got a good job, work with your brains instead of your back."

"I know it. Lucky I got to go to high school."

Joe thought back to the time following the death of his father. Joe had used some of the money from the mine owner to send his uncle Stanley a telegram. A day later he got a reply, and the next day his uncle showed up at the shack.

"Look at you, Joseph. In one year you've grown into a man." Uncle Stanley sat down at the little table, his head in his hands. "I can't believe that Karol is gone. I'm so sorry."

Joe joined him at the table. "The mine owner came by, gave me ten bucks. That's all a dead Polish miner is worth, I guess. The greedy son of a bitch killed Dad just like if he shot him with a gun. He should be dead, too."

Uncle Stanley shook his head. "You'd just end up in jail. Let God take care of the vengeance. Pray that your father's soul rests in peace." Uncle Stanley made the sign of the cross. "What are you going to do with yourself?"

"Get out of this stinking shack. Quit school and get a job doing something. I know one thing: I'll never mine coal."

"I got a better idea for you to think about. Come back to Philadelphia with me. Take some time to think things through. You can help me in my shop."

Joe understood the offer was a good one. They left for Philadelphia that day. Uncle Stanley owned a meat shop in Conshohocken, a small town just outside Philadelphia, and lived in an apartment above it. He had never married, and treated Joe like a son. Uncle Stanley insisted that Joe stay in school, but Joe helped in his uncle's shop whenever he could. Before he knew it, graduation day arrived in June of 1888.

For the next year, Joe worked full-time for his uncle, trying to pay him back for what he'd done. Then one day in June of 1889, Uncle Stanley and Joe had a talk at the dinner table.

"Joe, you've worked hard for me for three years. You've been like a son and I love you. But it's time for you to move on."

"I'm happy to stay with you."

Uncle Stanley smiled. "You owe me nothing, and you don't want to stay with me forever. Go out and make your own life."

Tony got up, cleared their empty bowls, and brought Joe's thoughts back to the present. "You right about that. One reason I work so hard is I want my kids to stay in school."

Joe stood up and put his arm around Tony's shoulder. "You're a good poppa, and a good friend. Now I have to get busy. See you tomorrow."

Joe put a dime on the counter, straightened his cap, and headed out the door. He stopped on the sidewalk and pulled the list of mine supply stores out of his pocket. Two were located across the river in New Haven.

He started across the Main Street Bridge then paused above the B&O Railroad tracks. Smiling and waving at the engineer, he watched as a yard engine passed under, thick smoke pouring from its stack. Then he hurried on before the soot from the smoke rained down.

His first stop was Connellsville Mining and Supply, located at the end of South Third Street. It was a big operation, consisting of a warehouse, storage yard, and stable, all behind a tall board fence. They sold everything from track spikes to miner's lamp oil.

Joe walked through the gate and looked around the yard. Two men were unloading wooden posts from a big wagon pulled by four horses. Several smaller delivery wagons were parked near the fence. He continued on and entered a warehouse filled with rows of mining supplies. A soot-stained skylight provided the only illumination. A counter ran the length of the rear wall. An old man sat on a stool behind it, shuffling through a stack of papers. As Joe approached, the man looked up over the rims of his half glasses.

"Can I help you, young man?"

Joe pushed his cap back on his head and leaned on the counter. "I surely hope so. My name is Joe Zajac. I work for Frick."

The man looked back down at his papers. "We don't do much business with the Frick mines. What can I do for you?"

"I'm not here for supplies. You heard about the trouble out at Leisenring, I reckon."

The old man set the papers on the counter and took off his glasses. "'Course I did. Ain't every day someone gets burnt up in a coke oven. Get to the point, son. I got things to do."

Joe smiled at the old man. "Yes, sir. The fellow in the oven was murdered, and the man that most likely did it ended up dead to boot. They found his body up on the B&O tracks to Revere."

The old man drummed his fingers on the countertop, took a deep breath, and exhaled slowly. "I'm thinking you must have a question bottled up inside you somewhere. How's about you see if you can't just spit it out?"

Joe took a deep breath himself. The man obviously wasn't in the mood to shoot the breeze. "I'm looking for a man named Kurt, don't know his last name. He's about my height, maybe a bit older, with light brown or blond hair. He was driving a mine supply delivery wagon up near where the body was found."

Now it was the old man's turn to smile. "I'm right proud of you, son. I knew you could do it."

Joe laughed, took off his cap, pulled his handkerchief from his back pocket, and mopped his brow. "You that rough on everyone comes in here?"

"I just got a low tolerance for BS. What'd you say your name was?"

"Zajac. Joe Zajac."

"OK, Joe, here you go. No one named Kurt works here. No one looks like the man you described works here. All of my wagons get locked up in the yard at night and I don't trade up at Revere. Now, it ain't that I'm generally inhospitable, but I'm 'bout busy as a one-armed paperhanger today. That do it for you?"

"Yes, sir, it does. I'm much obliged."

The man was already back to shuffling through his papers as Joe left the warehouse.

Chapter 18

Joe visited three more supply companies that afternoon. Nobody named Kurt or anyone matching his description worked at them. By five o'clock he decided to call it a day and go to The Star for a bite and a beer. On the way, he ran into Johnny Davidson walking his beat on Main Street.

"Your face is healing up nice, buddy. You shouldn't end up any uglier than you started out."

"Thanks, Johnny. What's new with you?"

"Been quiet around town for the most part. I heard about the dynamite heist out at Standard. Somebody surely has it in for Frick."

"That's the key to all of this. I'm going over to Scottdale tomorrow for a meeting with my boss, and most likely Mr. Lynch, too."

"Your ass on the line?"

"Who knows? I'm just going to play it by ear. I'm not making any progress. I wanted to become a detective, but I'm no Sherlock Holmes."

"Good luck. You going to be down at The Star tomorrow night?"

"Most likely. You off tomorrow night?"

"Off all day. I'll see you there."

Joe and Johnny shook hands and went their separate ways. Passing by a butcher shop, Joe's thoughts again returned to his years in Philadelphia. The day after Joe and Uncle Stanley had their talk, Joe started looking for work, in the want ads of the latest edition of the *Philadelphia Bulletin*. One caught his eye. The police department was hiring twenty-five new officers. Joe had never thought of becoming a policeman, but the starting pay was good. He took the train downtown to City Hall.

There were over a hundred applicants and they all had to take a written test. Thanks to his schooling Joe had the highest score. He aced the interviews that followed. In July he was offered a job. After thirty days of training, he started walking a beat.

Joe moved out of Uncle Stanley's place, taking a room in a downtown Philadelphia boarding house. On his own, he did as he pleased. He developed a taste for liquor and nightlife; he became a man in all ways.

Joe was a good cop but had a quick temper, especially when he was drinking. His beat included one of the roughest parts of town, down by the Delaware River docks. The residents included bunco artists, pickpockets, prostitutes, thugs, and thieves. He carried a Smith & Wesson .38, which he rarely had to use, and a billy club he used frequently. His favorite weapon was a small sap that, when properly applied, would render the biggest man unconscious.

One night in early 1894 proved fateful. He was off duty and drinking in a bar near police central that was popular with the force. He was drunk and got into it with an older—and also drunk—cop. The argument turned into a fistfight, which Joe was winning until the man pulled out his nightstick. Joe pulled out his sap and cracked the older cop on the head. The man fell against the brass foot rail and died on the spot.

Life on the force was rough after that. It was self-defense, but the other cops never forgave him. He read about the coal boom going on in Western Pennsylvania, and in May of 1894 saw an ad in the paper. Frick was looking for security people. Joe sent a letter of application that day.

A week later, he heard back, and was invited to Scottdale for an interview. As a veteran policeman, he was well qualified for the work and received a job offer on the spot. He became a "plainclothes" member of the H.C. Frick coke police. He moved west in June 1894. Four years later he was the supervisor of security for all the Frick mines in the Connellsville Seam, and moved to Connellsville in 1898. Joe was happy to leave Philadelphia. The small-town life was a welcome change.

Joe's thoughts returned to the present. He was almost to The Star and could tell from the noise that the joint was already jumping. He went in and found a spot at the far end of the bar. Hiram saw him come through the door and had a beer waiting.

"Much obliged, Hiram. Might as well pour me a shot, too."

Hiram returned with a shot of Old Overholt, which Joe downed in one gulp, chasing it with half of the beer. He wiped his mouth with the back of his hand, picked up his beer, and took a seat at his table in the corner. He took out his notebook and pencil stub and turned to a fresh page, which he headed up with "Scottdale meeting."

Item number one was Wendell Sykes. Joe intended to ask about the problems with the minority shareholders that he learned about from Dave Norton. He still believed that the events of the past week could be connected to that. After his name, he wrote "address" and "visit."

Before he could write item number two, he became aware of someone standing at his table. He looked up to see a big fellow staring down at him.

"Your name Zajac?"

Joe put his notebook and pencil back in his vest packet, and stood up. The man was a head taller than Joe and half -again as wide. "I'm Joe Zajac."

"Name's Henry Brooks. Peggy told me you wanted to talk to me."

Joe looked over Henry's shoulder and saw Peggy standing in the door of her office, arms folded and smiling. Joe smiled back at her and then turned to Henry, his hand outstretched.

"How do, Henry. Join me for a beer?"

Henry shook Joe's hand and they both sat down. Joe waved the waitress over. "Evening, Nell. How about a couple of beers for me and Henry?"

Nell went to collect the beers. Joe turned to Henry, who sat unsmiling, his big arms crossed over his chest. Joe leaned forward, arms on the table.

"Truth told, Henry, I forgot all about that. I did want to ask you about George Goretsky."

"Ask away, then. I heard about the little shit ending up in the coke oven."

"He did, and my first inclination was that someone from town might have had something to do with it. But at this point, I doubt that's the case."

"I don't know anything about him anyway, except that he's got bad manners when it comes to ladies. With three sisters, I can't abide that."

Nell dropped off their beers. Joe raised his toward Henry. "To your health."

Henry raised his glass and they took long draws. Henry put his glass down and leaned back in his chair, long legs stretched out under the table.

"Peggy says you work for Frick. You one of his coppers?"

Joe nodded. "Peggy says you live up in the mountains. What brings you to town on a Thursday night?"

"I ended up bringing down a load of timber. One of my regular drivers got hurt in the sawmill."

"You run a sawmill?"

"Brooks Lumber is one of the biggest outfits hereabout. Pappy owns a couple thousand acres of good timberland up Ohiopyle way."

"You sell to the mines?"

Henry nodded. "They use all I can deliver. Frick's a big customer, but I sell to them all."

"How's business?"

"Won't be long until I run out of trees to cut down. I reckon I got enough to last a couple more years. By then I should be well set, maybe move on down to town and start me some other kind of business."

Joe nodded. They sat in silence for a few minutes, finishing their beers. Henry sat up in his chair and pushed away from the table.

"I don't envy you your job, Zajac. From what I hear, there's trouble brewing with the miners."

"Who says?"

"My uncle Buck is in the coal business. He told me that there's some new crew trying to organize the miners, or leastwise stir things up."

"Where are your uncle's mines?"

"Down Dawson way. They're just little mines, don't even have names."

Henry stood up. "Thanks for the beer. Time for me to head up the pike."

Henry turned and hurried out the door. Joe drained his beer and waved Nell over.

"What's your pleasure?" she asked.

"How about a roast beef sandwich and another beer?"

"One beer, Hiram," Nell called as she headed to the kitchen. She returned in a minute with Joe's sandwich, retrieved his beer from the bar, and set both down on the table.

Joe ate his sandwich slowly, the crusty bread the perfect complement to the tender beef. He finished, pushed his plate away, and sat holding his beer between both hands.

He seems like a no-bullshit fellow. Joe believed what Henry had said about his uncle's mines. Pulling out his notebook, he added "labor problems" to his Scottdale list. He rose, headed to the rear of The Star, and knocked on the closed office door.

"Come in."

Joe opened the door to find Peggy hard at work on her books, head down and pen moving across a ledger. He took a seat and waited for her to finish the entry. In a minute she looked up, smiling. Her smile disappeared as she looked Joe over.

"What happened to you?"

"Got beat up Tuesday night."

"I wondered why I didn't see you last night."

"I was by, but decided to turn in early."

"This beating—does it have anything to do with your troubles out at Leisenring?"

"I suspect so. Plenty has happened since Monday and none of it good. Are we still going out Saturday?"

"Yes, we're still going out. What are your plans?"

"How about we visit The Dinner Bell first, and then go to the Colonial for the show?"

"Sounds good. What time do you want me to be ready?"

"Say around six? Where do you live?"

"I'm just across the street from the Colonial, on the corner of Pittsburgh and Green. I have an apartment above the apothecary on the second floor. Number four."

Joe took out his notebook, wrote down her address, and got up from his chair. "I'll let you get back to your books. I'm off to Scottdale tomorrow for a meeting at Frick headquarters." Joe yawned and stretched his arms above his head. "I'm bushed. Think I'll call it a night."

"All right, Joe." Peggy stood up and walked around the desk, standing next to him. "Please be careful."

Joe could smell roses again. "I won't be taken by surprise a second time. Until Saturday, then." Joe tipped his hat and walked out the office door. He left The Star, whistling.

Chapter 19

Joe got up at six on Friday morning, and after washing up, spent time shining his shoes and shaking the wrinkles out of his Sunday suit. Before getting dressed, he sat down with his little notebook, and, using it as a guide, wrote a summary of the events and his activities since last Saturday. It was after seven by the time he finished. He pulled a small black leather briefcase from under the bed and loaded it with his papers. Then he finished getting dressed, slicked back his hair, and headed downtown.

A few of the stores were open on Main Street. Joe stopped at Davidson's, where he bought an apple and this week's edition of *The Courier*, putting them both in his briefcase. He continued down Main and entered City Lunch at seven thirty. As usual, Tony was behind the counter. The place was already busy, the counter half full and several tables occupied.

Tony looked Joe up and down and whistled. "What you up to, Joey? You gonna try and borrow some money or something?"

"Yeah, then I'm going to open a restaurant across the street so I can get a decent meal once in a while." Joe walked to his stool at the end of the counter and pulled out *The Courier*. The front page headline caught his eye: "Bad Week for Frick." It detailed the events since Saturday, including the two deaths and the stolen dynamite. The writer had interviewed Sheriff Miller and speculated that the three events were somehow connected. Joe was now sure of it. He was also sure that the story was on the front page of the other local weeklies, and probably made the Pittsburgh papers, too. His case had become a big story.

Tony brought him a coffee and a donut. "You a funny man. You win a free donut today. What you want for breakfast?"

"I'm not very hungry today, how about a short stack?"

"You got it, boss man. Coming right up."

Joe put cream and sugar in his coffee, took a sip, and read on. Two Slavs were killed in an explosion down at Star Junction. Seemed one of them was smoking while they were transferring dynamite from a keg to a smaller container, and hot ash fell in the cask. *I always figured smoking was bad for your health.*

Tony returned with Joe's pancakes and slid the plate in front of him. "You no gonna tell me why you all dressed up?"

Joe poured some maple syrup on his pancakes and sliced them up. He took a bite while Tony stood watching.

"I have to go to Scottdale and talk to my boss about the dead men and the dynamite and I don't have much to tell him. I figured I might as well get dressed up for the dressing down."

"You gonna figure it out, I bet."

"I'm not so sure, Tony. I was a beat cop, not a detective. I figure I'll just keep poking around until someone tries to beat me up again."

Tony shook his head and walked away. Joe ate his pancakes and kept reading the paper. Coke production was down for the week, with some operators letting their ovens go cold. Frick was still busy, though, with Carnegie Steel buying almost all they could produce.

Joe polished off his pancakes, ate the donut for dessert, and finished his coffee. Packing up his paper, he put fifteen cents on the counter and headed for the door, giving Tony a wave as he left. The Scottdale streetcar was heading out of town. Joe jumped on as it made the turn from Arch onto Main. He paid his fare and moved to the rear, where he read over his notes and questions.

Scottdale was about seven miles from Connellsville, just across the Westmoreland County line. Joe stuffed his papers away and looked out the window as the trolley left town. The still air was smoky, the day already hot.

Scottdale was a slightly smaller version of Connellsville. Frick had had its offices here since the beginning, occupying an inconspicuous two-story frame building across from the Pennsylvania Railroad station in the middle of town. The ordinary look of the structure belied the great enterprise managed from there.

When the trolley stopped, Joe jumped off, took a moment to wipe his brow, and crossed the street. Several fancy carriages were parked in front, their drivers standing in a bunch, smoking. Joe entered the building and approached the receptionist, a slim, red-haired young woman sitting behind an opening in the wall.

"Hello, Polly. What's going on today? That's some mighty fancy coaches parked out front."

Polly looked up from her work and smiled. "Good morning, Joe. Mr. Sellers told me to send you right up." She lowered her voice and looked back down at her work. "Mr. Frick is here, along with the whole board of directors and other men. Something important is going on but I don't know exactly what."

Joe whistled. "Glad I decided to wear my Sunday best, then." He removed his cap, stuffed it in his briefcase, and entered the offices proper. The inside of the building matched the outside, an unassuming collection of mismatched desks and file drawers. Cliff's office was located on the second floor at the top of the stairs. Joe climbed the steps and found him sitting behind a big oak desk reading *The Courier*.

"Morning, Cliff." Joe entered the office and sat down across from him.

Cliff Sellers was a big man. Joe guessed he was somewhere in his forties but looked older. Cliff's oil-slicked hair was grey and parted in the middle. His fat round face was pockmarked and covered with red splotches. The skin on his neck was rubbery and loose, falling over a too-tight collar. His suit looked new but fit him poorly. He looked uncomfortable and probably was. Like Joe, Cliff was a former cop, a lieutenant with the Pittsburgh force until hired by Frick five years earlier.

Cliff looked over the top of the newspaper and frowned. "Look who the hell it is—the pride of the H.C. Frick police. I was just reading about us in the paper."

Joe's face flushed. He got along well enough with Cliff, but didn't care much for the man's heavy-handed ways and mockery. Joe was determined not to rise to the bait, though. Leaning forward in the chair, he pulled his report from the briefcase.

"It's been a busy week, and I figured you'd all be pissed off over here by now. I guess I should have come by sooner, but here I am."

Cliff glanced down at the papers Joe was holding. "Let's hear what you got, Zajac."

Joe took a deep breath and set the papers down. Leaning back, he laced his hands behind his head. "You already know what happened. The question is why, and what's going to happen next."

Cliff glanced down at *The Courier* again, then folded it and tossed it in the wastebasket. He laced his fingers on the desk, and fixed a cold stare on Joe. "Two stiffs and a half ton of missing dynamite is cause for some concern, wouldn't you say, Joe? Tell me, then—why did the fire boss end up in the coke oven?"

"I'm not one hundred percent sure, but here's what I got. The first victim, George Goretsky, was Walter Krupp's boss at Number One. Walter's the second victim. He was up to something and George got wind of it. I think Walter was planning on blowing up the mine. We found some dynamite wire in George's pants pocket, and some evidence of goings-on around one of the ventilation shafts. I found a rough map of the mine among Walter's papers, which he left where he was boarding before he went missing Friday night. George most likely got stuffed in the oven early Saturday morning, or there wouldn't have even been any bones left."

Cliff stroked his chin and reclined in his chair, placing his hands across his stomach. "Now why in God's name would this fellow want to blow up the mine? You found anything out about him yet?"

"I don't know anything about Krupp, except that he wasn't working alone. And Krupp probably isn't even his real name. According to the woman he boarded with, he had a regular visitor, some man name of Kurt. I figure Kurt killed Walter because he botched the job and got caught. Whoever killed Krupp has a bad temper. Damn near beat his head off."

"You saw the body?"

Joe nodded. "Sheriff Miller has let me get involved in his investigation. We have a witness that saw a man racing away from where the body was found, most likely in a mine supply delivery wagon."

"So track down this Kurt fella, then."

"I'm trying to do just that. I've been to quite a few of the supply companies. Miller's been checking on the ones up Uniontown way, too. I'll be visiting more tomorrow. So far no Kurt has turned up."

Joe picked up his report and shuffled through it. Before he could begin again, loud voices could be heard from down the hall. The sounds of an argument continued for some time before subsiding. Joe looked across the desk at Cliff, who just shrugged.

"What's all the hubbub about? Polly says you got Old Man Frick himself here today."

"There's a board of directors meeting going on, some big changes in the works, I'd say. But I wouldn't be worrying about it too much if I was you."

Joe reached into his briefcase and pulled out his little notebook and pencil. "This got anything to do with the pissed-off minority shareholders?"

Cliff's jaw dropped. "Where'd a dumb Polack like you learn about that?"

Joe's face flushed. He leaped to his feet and leaned over the desk until his face was close to Cliff's. "How'd you like this dumb Polack to stick his foot up your ass sideways?"

Cliff jumped up, his face even redder. He clenched his fists and pushed his chair back until it crashed into the wall. "Take it easy, Zajac. Don't let your mouth get you in trouble."

"Pappy didn't raise me to be taking a bunch of bullshit. You best remember that. I'm not one of Frick's Hunkie miners."

Joe stepped away from the desk and sat back down. Cliff retrieved his chair and did the same. The two men stared coldly at each other until Cliff finally blinked and sighed. "OK." He pulled a handkerchief from his pocket and mopped his brow. "And you're right. That's what's going on here today."

Joe consulted his book. "Would Mr. Wendell Sykes be involved in the meeting?"

Cliff nodded. "He is. What do you know about him?"

"Only that he's a rich man's son and hates Frick, but I know he got a lot of company in that. Maybe he's pissed off enough to want to do the company harm?"

The loud voices could be heard again. This time they heard a door slam, and heavy steps in the hall. They both looked out the door in time to see H.C. Frick himself charge past, hat in hand.

Joe turned back to Cliff. "That's one unhappy man, best I can tell. What's really going on here?"

Cliff spoke in a lowered voice. "H.C. has lost control of the company. Carnegie took over the board of directors and his men run things now. They're trying to work out a deal to buy out Frick and the other shareholders and put an end to the legal troubles."

Joe heard more footsteps in the hall and saw Cliff look over his shoulder. Joe turned as an older woman entered the office.

"Mr. Lynch would like to see you two in his office right away."

"We'll be right there, Hope."

Cliff stood up, slicked back his hair, and hitched his pants up over his belly. "You're coming, too, Zajac. Mr. Lynch wants this shit straightened out. You better convince him you're the one that can do it."

Chapter 20

Joe and Cliff walked down the hall to the end, where the Frick officials had their offices. Thomas Lynch, the president, occupied the one at the very end. He started out as a clerk at the Broad Ford company store in 1875 when he was twenty-one years old. His standing and position grew with the company until he became the number two man in 1882. He ran the company while H.C. built it into the dominant force in the industry that it was today. Frick stepped down as president in 1896 when he became president of Carnegie Steel. Lynch had been running the company ever since.

As they approached the office, Cliff grabbed Joe's arm and pulled him to a stop. "Play dumb about that shareholder shit, and don't bring up Sykes."

Joe nodded, and they continued to the open office door. Cliff rapped on the frame and entered, with Joe right behind. Lynch's secretary occupied a small desk to the right of the door. Lynch sat at a large mahogany table, his head down as he examined plans of some sort. Two straight-backed wooden chairs sat in front of the table. A large roll-top desk sat behind Lynch, overflowing with papers.

The secretary looked up as they entered. "Mr. Lynch will be right with you. Please have a seat." She gestured to the chairs at the table.

Joe and Cliff sat down and waited for Lynch to finish. *He looks more like a schoolteacher than a captain of industry*, thought Joe. Lynch was of medium build, with white hair parted on the side and a closely trimmed white mustache. He wore frameless eyeglasses, had a thin pointy nose, and thin lips. Even in the August heat, he wore a high collar and necktie.

Joe and Cliff sat quietly for a few minutes until Lynch finally rolled up the plans and placed them on the desk behind him. He turned back to the men, pulled a white handkerchief from his coat pocket, and carefully cleaned his spectacles. When they were spotless, he put them back on and looked at Cliff.

"Good morning, Mr. Sellers. Is this our investigator?"

Cliff was already sweating and his collar looked even tighter, his face red as a fire wagon. "Yes, sir, Mr. Lynch. This here's Joe Zajac. We were just going over what he's found out."

Lynch turned his eyes to Joe. "Mr. Zajac, the events of the last week are of concern to me. Our workers murdered, our property stolen—all this casts the firm in a very poor light."

Joe nodded. He could feel the sweat popping out on his forehead. "Well, Mr. Lynch, sir, I'm working at getting to the bottom of it, made some progress, too. I have some suspicions but nothing firm yet."

"Are these events somehow connected?"

Joe's mouth was dry, his tongue thick. *In for a dime, in for a dollar.*

"I'm sure of it. Someone has it in their mind to cause harm to the company. I think our first victim got wind of it, and that's what got him killed. The second fellow that got it was most likely the murderer. Now I'm chasing down a confederate that I suspect is guilty for the second murder."

"When you say 'harm to the company,' what exactly do you mean?"

"I think they planned to blow up Leisenring No. 1."

Lynch leaned back in his chair, his hands folded in his lap. His eyes never left Joe's.

"With the dynamite stolen from Standard?"

"No, sir. I think they already had the dynamite they needed for Number One."

"You think other Frick properties are in jeopardy?"

"I do, but which ones and why, I don't know."

Lynch brought his hands to his lips, index fingers straight up, and sat staring into space. After a moment he turned to Joe again.

"Mr. Zajac, this is a significant moment for the Frick company. Events like these might have a very injurious effect on certain negotiations currently under way. It is imperative that we stop whatever plans might be in the works."

"Mr. Lynch, do you think that someone involved in these negotiations might have reason to disrupt them?"

"Most likely not. Some of the men involved have little love for our founder, but it would not be in their interests to derail the current efforts."

Joe sat silently for a few moments, then blurted out, "Would Wendell Sykes be one of those fellows that doesn't care much for Mr. Frick?"

From the corner of his eye, Joe could see Cliff almost rise off his chair, his face scarlet.

"What's Mr. Sykes got to do with this?"

"I heard he's one of your minority shareholders that's hauled you into court. Does he hate Frick?"

Lynch turned to Cliff. "Have you told Mr. Zajac about this, Mr. Sellers?"

"No, sir, Mr. Lynch. I got no idea where he comes up with his wild ideas."

Lynch looked over to his secretary. He made a motion and she got up and left the room, closing the door behind her.

"Well, Mr. Zajac, you are a better investigator than Mr. Sellers gives you credit for. In fairness to you, and with the hope that any information I can give you will assist in your getting to the bottom of this, I will candidly answer you. Please keep the information to yourself."

Joe nodded. "Yes, sir."

"Wendell Sykes does indeed harbor hatred for our founder." Lynch paused for a moment, turning in his chair to stare out the window. He started speaking again without turning back. "He claims that his dead father, Bartholomew, was responsible for most of our success. Wendell believes that Mr. Frick cheated his father out of his fair share of the company, leaving him with a small fraction of what he thinks was his due."

"Is Wendell crazy enough to start blowing mines up?"

Lynch paused again before replying. He turned back to the men and fixed Joe with a firm stare. "At one point I would have said yes. But recent events would make any such action extremely harmful to him. If the current negotiations are successfully concluded, even Mr. Sykes's small share of the company will provide him with the means to live a very comfortable life for many years to come."

"I'd like to ask him a few questions, see if I can put him on the spot."

"What kind of questions?"

"I'd like to see if he knows a fellow name of Kurt."

"Kurt who?"

"I don't know his last name yet, but he's the one I think carried out the second murder."

Lynch sat with his eyes still locked onto Joe. Finally he nodded. "While I have my doubts about your deductions, I won't ignore them. And it just so happens that Mr. Sykes and the other minority shareholders are still here, having their lunch in the boardroom and most likely discussing an offer they just received."

"Can we get Sykes alone?"

"No, Mr. Zajac, but I have a better idea. The troubles of the past week came up during our meeting and those men are as concerned as I am. How about if I go down there and offer them a private update from the lead investigator? Give them a brief report, like you just gave me, and then drop this Kurt fellow's name. I'll be watching Sykes."

Joe pulled a handkerchief out of his pocket and mopped his brow. *You'd think he'd have a fan in here.* "That's a smart plan, Mr. Lynch."

Lynch got up and left the room. As soon as he cleared the door, Cliff jumped up. "Zajac, I swear to Christ that you are the biggest asshole in Western Pennsylvania. I told you to keep your goddamn mouth shut about Sykes."

Joe stood and faced Cliff, a smile on his face. "And you are about the dumbest piece of shit I ever had to work for. I told you once to watch your mouth. I won't tell you again. You want a whipping, keep it up."

Cliff clenched his fists and stepped forward. "If you weren't in the middle of this, I'd kick your ass out the door right now. As soon as this is over, I'm going to enjoy getting rid of you. And I'll wipe that shit-eating grin off your face, too."

At that moment they heard Mr. Lynch in the hall, and both stepped back and sat down. Lynch and his secretary walked through the door.

"Mr. Zajac, our minority shareholders would appreciate a report. Please come with me."

Joe and Cliff headed out the door behind Lynch, who turned to them. "Mr. Sellers, your attendance won't be required. Thank you for your assistance."

Cliff fixed Joe with a cold stare, his lips pressed tightly together. Without a word, he turned and walked away.

Joe followed Lynch down the hall and around a corner. At the end of another short hall, double doors stood open. Through them Joe could see five men seated at an ornately carved mahogany table. Lynch stopped and turned to Joe. "Keep it brief and get to the point. I'll be watching Mr. Sykes to see how he responds."

The two men entered the room. A huge portrait of H. C. Frick hung in the middle of the wall on the left. A painting called *Clay Works*, depicting one of Frick's first properties, hung on the right. The room was austere, with a bare wood floor and no drapes on the window.

Lynch walked to the head of the table and sat down. He motioned for Joe to take the open seat to his left. Joe felt the stares of the men on him, and he returned each in turn as his eyes swept the table.

Lynch introduced the men to Joe. Sykes sat across from him; the other names Joe immediately forgot. Sykes was of medium height and build, with a soft and pampered look. He was somewhat fancily dressed, his shirt ruffled. After the introductions, Lynch turned to Joe. "If you will, Mr. Zajac, please summarize the events of the last week for our shareholders."

Joe rose to his feet without thinking and stood behind his chair. "You men all read the newspapers. Two Frick men dead and a half ton of dynamite missing, but there's more to it than that. From what I can tell, we got us a man with a plan to do the company harm."

Joe briefed them, tying the first murder to the second, outlining the evidence of a threat to Leisenring, and laying it all at the feet of his mystery man. He paused briefly, and then continued. "The good news is that I'm on the trail of our foe. His name is Kurt and he's working at some local mine supply operation. I'll have him found by tomorrow this time."

Joe watched Sykes as he spoke Kurt's name. Sykes coughed and his face flushed a bit. Joe could see sweat beading on the man's forehead. His eyes found Joe's for a moment and then he quickly looked away.

Lynch stood up and turned to Joe. "Thank you for your report." To the others at the table, he said, "You men know as much as I do at this point. Rest assured, though, that I have full confidence in Mr. Zajac, and expect that by this time next week, these events will be brought to a satisfactory and safe conclusion."

Without further comment, Lynch turned and left the room, with Joe falling in behind. They returned to Lynch's office and closed the door. Lynch sat behind his desk, motioned to a chair, and Joe flopped into it.

"What was your impression, Mr. Zajac?"

"Sykes looked a mite nervous to me. I though he was going to swallow his tongue when I mentioned Kurt."

Lynch nodded. "I'm a fair judge of men and I'd say he knows something about this. Good work in there. You trusted your judgment and it proved sound. I'd like you to keep me informed directly from now on about this. It is imperative that you find this Kurt fellow with all due haste."

With that, Lynch turned to his desk and once again unrolled the plans he'd been examining. Joe got up and left, breathing a sigh of relief as he cleared the door.

Chapter 21

Joe hustled down the hall. He passed Cliff's office without stopping and clomped down the stairs. Polly was staring at him wide-eyed as he entered the office. He gave her a smile while he pulled his hat on. "Some exciting day, eh, Polly?"

She gave him a shy smile. "Surely it is, Joe. Almost too rousing, if you ask me."

He leaned over her desk and spoke low, "You don't by any chance know where Wendell Sykes calls home in Pittsburgh?"

She nodded, and, after looking around the office, turned a piece of paper around so Joe could see it. The names and addresses of the Frick shareholders were listed there. Joe got out his notebook and jotted down Wendell's address in Allegheny City. He smiled, winked at Polly, and hurried out the door.

Once outside, he relaxed from the case of nerves he'd had while with Lynch. He'd done all right, he reckoned, no matter what Cliff might think.

As usual, the noon sun was barely visible through the haze in the air. He took a deep breath and felt a burning in his throat. He crossed the street and waited for the next streetcar to Connellsville, which was in sight a few blocks away. When it arrived with a clang and a screech, Joe boarded, paid his fare, and found an empty seat up front. The operator gave him the once over, eased the throttle open, and the little trolley departed Scottdale.

Joe knew he was on the right track. He took his pad and pencil out and jotted down a few more notes. Returning the pad to his case, he pulled out the apple, eating it as he reviewed his list of mine supply houses.

Joe finished the apple and tossed the core out the window. They were almost back to Connellsville, rolling down Main Street hill. He jumped off at Brimstone Corner, and walked down Pittsburgh Street to his rooms. He dropped off the briefcase, changed out of his suit, and washed up. Feeling refreshed, he was ready to carry on the search for the mysterious Kurt.

Joe stuffed the list of supply outfits in his vest, left his place, and walked down Main. The street was already congested with delivery wagons and men on horseback, the sidewalks and stores filled with women in long dresses and bonnets. Joe passed quickly through them, motivated anew by the day's developments. *I'm about to crack it open.* Suddenly hungry, he decided to stop by City Lunch.

The counter was packed; even Joe's usual stool in the rear was occupied. Looking over the room, he saw Dave Norton sitting at a table by himself. Joe walked back to join him.

"Mind a little company, buddy?"

Norton was eating a bowl of soup and reading *The Courier.* He looked up and smiled. "Always room for you, Joe. Take a load off."

Joe sat down across from Norton, took his hat off, and put it on an empty chair. He looked for Tony, who was busy clearing some dishes from the counter. After catching the Italian's eye, Joe pointed to Norton's soup bowl and then to his stomach. Tony smiled and nodded.

"So what's new at the bank, Norton?"

"Never been busier. I opened a dozen new accounts this morning. Deposits are up, and we're thinking about opening another bank in Dunbar."

"A smart man like you, I bet you'll be running the place someday."

"I enjoy the banking business and work darn hard at it. As we grow, I do hope to move up the ladder."

Tony brought Joe's soup to the table, along with a glass of water and a plate of bread. "You look like yourself now, Joey. How'd your meeting go?"

"I survived, Tony. I even got to meet the head man himself over at Frick."

"Pretty soon you be a big shot, too."

"Yeah, then I'll buy me one of those big houses on the South Side and hire you on as my private chef."

"You the funniest guy in town, Joey. Enjoy."

Tony hustled back to the kitchen and Joe dug into his soup.

"So what's this about you meeting Frick?"

"Not Frick, although he was in a meeting there. I met with Lynch. I had to go over to the Scottdale office to talk to my boss, and we ended up getting called in to see Lynch."

"I read about your case in *The Courier.* How are you making out?"

"Well, I got my ass kicked on Tuesday, and if I don't figure this out, I'll more than likely get fired, but otherwise I'm a happy fellow. I'm taking Peggy Patterson to the Colonial tomorrow."

"Good luck with her. She's a fine, smart woman from what I can tell, and very independent-minded. I hear her father isn't doing too well. They're trying to sell The Star."

Joe finished his soup, wiping the bowl clean with a piece of bread. "Does the old man have money?"

"He owns the building there, and a few acres on the South Side that he's started to build some houses on."

"Peggy isn't too keen on running that place anyway. She'd be happy to sell, I'm thinking. I'm much obliged for you explaining all of those Frick shareholder problems. I'm sure there's a tie-in. It came up in my conversation with Lynch, and I even met Mr. Wendell Sykes today. All of the shareholders, Frick included, were having a big powwow."

"From what I hear, Carnegie is trying to settle things between him and Frick and the rest of the shareholders."

"You got good ears, buddy."

Joe dug a dime out of his pocket and dropped it on the table. "I've more detective work to do and best get at it. I'm going out to Dunbar to see if I can track down the fellow most likely behind all this. Know anything about Keystone Mine Supply?"

"Just know of them. The owner, Paul Byers, is one of the men that wants to invest in the new Dunbar bank. His business is doing well, and sells all over the county."

Joe pushed his chair back and stood up, offering his hand to Dave. "Thanks for sharing your table and your knowledge, my friend. I'll be seeing you."

Joe waved to Tony as he left and headed to West Penn Terminal, where a streetcar to Dunbar and points south was waiting. He boarded and the car soon departed, heading across the bridge and out of town. After twenty minutes, Joe stepped off at the Hardy Hill stop. Keystone Supply was just up the road.

Ten minutes later he was standing at the gate to the supply yard. As he started to enter, a fancy closed carriage came charging out of the yard, stirring up a cloud of dust and almost running him down. Joe jumped out of the way as the carriage hurtled down the road.

No-good bastard, Joe thought as he brushed the dust from his trousers. He stood staring at the rear of the coach as it disappeared around a corner. He removed his cap and scratched his head. *I saw that rig before, this morning over at Frick. I remember the fancy lanterns.*

Joe put his cap back on and headed toward the main building, a big barn. He entered and saw a man with a clipboard standing near a barrel of spikes. He was short and slender, with long black hair parted in the middle. Walking to him, Joe prepared his little speech in his mind.

"Afternoon. You run this operation?"

The man looked up from his clipboard. "I do. What's your interest?"

The barn was hot and dusty. Joe pulled out his handkerchief and wiped his face. "Name's Zajac. I work for Frick and I'm looking into the goings-on of the last week, the murders and the like."

"Frick's a good customer of mine. What's on your mind?"

"You got a fellow works here name of Kurt? I don't know his last name. He's shorter than me, older, with blond hair."

The man put down his clipboard and shook his head. "I don't anymore but I did. And you're the second fellow in ten minutes been looking for him."

Joe could barely contain his excitement. "Was it that fellow in the fancy coach that almost ran me down?"

The man nodded. "Indeed it was. I'll tell you like I told him. I fired Kurt Straub day before yesterday."

Kurt Straub. Now I have something to go on.

Joe got out his little notebook and pencil stub. "What did you say your name was?"

"Didn't say, but I'm Paul Byers."

"Why'd you let him go, Mr. Byers?"

"Don't have any use for liars or thieves."

"What sort of lies?"

"I know he took one of my wagons out after hours a few times. One of my men saw it on the road. I asked him about it and he denied it."

"And the stealing?"

"Missing dynamite. I keep close tabs on that, and ten sticks turned up short the last count I took. All the other men here have been working for me for years without incident. It had to be him."

"How long was Straub with you?"

"I hired him on just after the Fourth of July."

"Know where he was staying?"

"No, but it must have been somewhere around here. He walked to work, best I could tell."

"Know where he came from?"

"No. He just showed up here looking for work. My business has been growing and I needed someone to make delivery runs. I don't think he was from around here, though. He got lost a few times early on."

Joe finished his note-taking and stuck his pad and pencil in his vest pocket. "Mr. Byers, I'm much obliged for the information. One more question for you and I'm on my way. The fellow in the fancy coach—he mention his name?"

"No, he did not."

"Did he happen to be wearing a fancy shirt with ruffles?"

Byers thought for a moment, then nodded. "He did indeed. He was a bit of a dandy."

Joe smiled and held out his hand. "Best of luck. I'll let Jim Thornton over at Leisenring know what a big help you've been to the Frick company."

The men shook hands and Joe left Paul Byers to his work. As he headed to the gate, a delivery wagon was pulling in. Joe waved to the driver, who reined in his horses and stopped beside Joe.

The driver was an older fellow sporting a full and unkempt grey beard. His pants were patched and dirty. His left cheek was bulged out and tobacco stains dotted his shirt. When he looked down at Joe, a few crooked yellow teeth jutted from his sunken mouth. He fixed Joe with a cold stare.

"How do, buddy. Kind of hot today."

The man held his stare for a moment, and then replied, "Got no time to shoot the breeze. Speak your piece."

"I'm looking to track down Kurt Straub. You got any idea where he was living?"

"Straub's a no-good lying thief, and I knowed it from the first."

"You're a good judge of men, then. He's also most likely a cold-blooded killer."

The man's eyes widened. "Wouldn't surprise me none. He talked crazy sometime."

"About what?"

"The evils of the rich man and such. I didn't pay him no mind until he started talking bad about Mr. Byers, then I had to shut him up. Mr. Byers puts food on my table and treated me fair for many a year."

Joe nodded. "Any idea about where he was staying?"

"He was making camp someplace, maybe with them hobos that live up the streetcar line. They's camped out about a mile south, just past the first trestle."

Before Joe could reply, the man made a clicking sound and the horses took off toward the stable. Joe took out his notebook and made a few more entries, then walked back down the road toward the streetcar line. When he reached the tracks, he turned south and walked along them. Twenty minutes later he was crossing the trestle the old man had mentioned. Looking up the ravine to the west, he spotted a man near the bank of the small creek. When Joe reached the other side, he entered the woods and worked his way down the hill toward the creek.

After slipping and sliding the last ten yards, Joe finally stood on the creek bank, looking up and down the ravine for the fellow he'd noticed. Not seeing him, Joe sat on a rock and took off his shoe to empty some pebbles. As he was putting the shoe back on, he heard a twig snap behind him. Before he could turn to look, a gruff voice said, "Take it nice and easy, Buck. Put them hands up where I can see 'em."

Chapter 22

Joe felt cold metal pressed behind his ear. He dropped his shoe in the creek and raised his hands above his head.

"There you go. Now how's about you take that other shoe off."

Joe started to reach down, and then felt the metal press harder.

"I didn't say nuthin' about you putting them hands down, now did I?"

Joe raised his hands again, and using his stockinged foot, pushed the other shoe off.

"I'm going to step back now, but don't get to feelin' froggy, Buck."

Joe breathed a sigh of relief as the metal left his flesh. Feeling more dumb than scared, he sat rock still, staring across the creek.

"Stand up and turn around."

Joe did as he was told. Ten feet away stood a short man with a small pistol. He wore a sleeveless undershirt and black trousers, with suspenders hanging down. His face was brown and weathered-looking, his hair long and hanging wetly over his ears.

"Don't you West Penn bulls got nothing better to do than rousting out men ain't doin' no one no harm?"

Joe smiled and relaxed a bit. He had been expecting to meet Kurt Straub. "I'm no West Penn bull."

"You kinda smell like the law to me."

"You're right, buddy. I used to be a cop."

"I knowed it. Old Rabbit can smell the law a mile away."

"But I've no interest in rousting out you or anyone else."

"State your business, then, and we can both be movin' on."

"Mind if I put my arms down, Rabbit?"

"Go ahead and put 'em down, but put them hands in your pockets."

Rabbit stuck his gun in the waistband of his pants and hitched up his suspenders. "Throw me them shoes."

"I'll have to take my hands out of my pocket to do that."

Rabbit smiled and nodded. Joe fished the one shoe out of the creek and tossed them toward Rabbit, who set them down next to a fallen tree. "I'll be back."

Joe watched him walk up the creek around a bend. In a few minutes he returned, hair combed and wearing an old striped shirt. He had a brown canvas bag slung over his shoulder.

Rabbit sat on the fallen tree trunk and removed his shoes. Joe could see holes in the soles. He pulled on Joe's shoes, laced them tight, and stood up.

"They's a mite big for me, but a damn sight better than what I been wearing. Now where was we?"

"I'm looking for a man name of Kurt. I heard he was making camp up this way. I saw you from the trestle and came down to ask if you'd heard tell of him."

"What's this Kurt look like?"

"Shorter than me, about my age with blond hair."

"He a hobo?"

"No, he was working up at Keystone Supply."

"I know of him. He was camped out here but no more. Haven't seen him since day before yesterday. He lit out for points unknown."

Rabbit threw his old shoes toward Joe and hitched up his pants. "Your man Kurt is an odd duck, always reading books and nary a drop of whiskey passed his lips. We all gave him a wide berth." Pulling a cap from his bag, he smiled for the first time. "Now old Rabbit's gonna jump on out of here. Nice to make your acquaintance, and thank ye kindly for the shoes."

Rabbit turned and climbed the hillside, leaving Joe smiling and looking at the old shoes.

***

An hour later, Joe stepped down from the streetcar at the Connellsville terminal. He limped up Arch Street, his bare feet black and sore. He'd tried to wear Rabbit's shoes but they were too small. The climb out of the ravine and walk down the tracks had been slow and painful. It hadn't taken long for his socks to wear out, too. Barefoot, he'd attracted quite a few stares and smiles from the other riders and didn't blame them. *I'm a sorry sight.*

Joe continued up Main with a wobbling stride and finally made it to his rooms. He collapsed on his bed for a few minutes before filling up his washbasin and soaking his feet. He cleaned himself up, changed clothes, put on his good shoes, and headed back out.

His first stop was the Johnston & Norris shoe store, where he replaced his everyday shoes with a new pair of low boots. Next he went to Newcomer's Hardware. It was nearly empty and he found the owner, Clarence Newcomer, stocking shelves.

"Can I help you?"

"I'm looking for a revolver, something small but reliable."

"Our firearms are in the rear."

Joe followed Clarence to the back of the store, where a small glass case was filled with pistols of various sizes. Rifles hung on a rack on the wall. Clarence went behind the case and pulled out a medium-sized, nickel-plated revolver.

"This here's an Otis Smith model 1249, manufactured by the US Arms Company. Holds five .32 rounds, not much bigger than some derringers but accurate at close range. What use do you intend for your weapon?"

Joe picked up the gun. The .45 that Thornton gave him was too big and had to be carried in the holster. This little number was engraved, with pearled grips. Joe liked the way it fit his hand. "We got us a rat problem at work I need to attend to." He slid it into his pants pocket, where it fit comfortably. "I'll take it, and a box of cartridges."

Joe paid for his purchases, stuffed the box of bullets in his other pocket, and headed back to his rooms. He'd gotten lucky with Rabbit but needed to be better equipped for catching up with Kurt. By the time he finished getting cleaned up, it was after five. He was ready to head down to The Star to blow off some steam. He loaded four cartridges into the revolver, leaving an empty chamber under the hammer, and slipped the gun in his right pants pocket.

Friday was in full swing on Pittsburgh Street. There were six bars in a two-block stretch. Women and children avoided this part of town, especially on Friday and Saturday nights. Two drunks argued loudly in front of The Arlington, pushing each other back and forth while a small crowd watched and egged them on. Joe stepped around them and entered The Star.

The bar was crowded and noisy, the way Joe liked it. He squeezed in at the end, his back to the wall. Hiram was hustling tonight. He eyed Joe and nodded. A minute later he put a mug of beer and a shot of Old Overholt on the bar.

"Much obliged, Hiram. Looks like you got a full house tonight."

"Full and rowdy, Joe. Watch your wallet."

Joe nodded, and picked up the shot glass. He remembered the first time he'd drunk whiskey. It had burned all the way down to his stomach, and then all the way back up. He swore he'd never touch it again, but eventually acquired a taste for it, drinking with his cop buddies in Philadelphia. He examined the brown liquid and then threw it back, washing it down with half the mug of beer.

The whiskey hit his empty stomach and he gave a shiver. "Ahh, just what the doctor ordered," Joe said to no one in particular. Hiram came by with the bottle and refilled the shot glass.

Joe felt a heavy hand on his shoulder. "You sure you can handle the hard stuff, son?"

"Drank you under the table on more than one occasion, Lloyd." Joe turned and looked up at his big friend. "First round's on me." Joe finished his beer and waved Hiram over. "Two beers and a shot for Lloyd."

Hiram brought their drinks, and Joe and Lloyd headed to an empty table. They sat down and raised their glasses, as Lloyd solemnly intoned, "My friends are the best friends—loyal, willing, and able. Now let's get to drinking. All glasses off the table!"

They clinked their shot glasses and threw the whiskey back, chasing it with big chugs of beer. Joe laughed as he slammed his mug on the table. "Where do you get those old sayings from?"

"Grand Pappy Joe had a hundred of them or more. I forgot most of them."

"Hello, boys. Looks like I got some catchin' up to do."

Joe and Lloyd looked up to see Johnny Davidson standing at the table, a drink in each hand. Lloyd kicked a chair back from the table so Johnny could sit down.

"Greetings. Here's to you." Johnny drained his shot and slapped the empty glass on the table.

Joe clapped Johnny on the shoulder. "Good to see you, buddy. It's been too long since the three of us tore up the town."

"The chief had me on the night shift every Friday for the last month. Been putting a crimp in my social life. How'd your meeting go?"

"Started out rough but ended up with a bang." Joe told his friends about his day, finishing up with his limping back to town barefoot.

Lloyd shook his head, laughing. "You sure you used to be a cop? You're lucky old Rabbit didn't need a new pair of pants."

"I sure been wandering around fat and dumb, but I'm gaining some ground on it, and taking no chances from now on. I bought a little .32 revolver that's gonna stay in my pocket until Mr. Straub is out of business."

Johnny finished his beer and leaned forward, elbows on the table. "My cousin works at *The Courier*. He told me the publisher got a letter from someone calls himself 'The Reaper,' demanding better pay for the miners and cokers, and threatening violence if the men aren't allowed to organize."

Joe took out his notebook. "You know the publisher?"

"Pap's been friends with Henry Snyder for years. I peddled his papers when *The Courier* was just getting started."

"Can you get me a meeting with him? I'd like to see the letter."

"I'll talk to him tomorrow."

Joe leaned back in his chair, surveying the room. The Friday crowd was a mix of regulars and strangers, and most were well on their way to getting drunk. He was about to order another round when he noticed three men sitting at a table in the front corner. The one sitting with his back to Joe looked familiar.

"Gents, this is my lucky day. If I'm not mistaken, those three characters at the table in the corner were in Rocky's the night I got waylaid. The fellow that done it was sitting with them before he left."

Lloyd stood up and took off his derby. "How's about we go have a little discussion with them?"

The man at the table stood up and walked to the bar. "That's him, all right," Joe said. "He tried to strike up a conversation. The bartender called him Jake. How's about you fellas just keep an eye on his mates while I have a word with him."

Joe walked over to the bar, stood behind Jake, and tapped him on the shoulder. Jake turned around, smiling as he recognized Joe.

"No Rocky's for you tonight, pal?"

"The crowd struck me as being a bit unfriendly. Where's your other associate, the fellow with the blade? I was hoping to catch up with him again."

"Don't know who you're talking about, chum."

Joe moved a bit closer to Jake and spoke in a near whisper. "Didn't expect you would, but that's not why I come over. I got a message for your pal Kurt Straub."

Jake's smile faded as Joe grinned at him. "I was out at Keystone today. Tell him I know about him and Wendell, and it won't be long until I track him down. He's not going to get away with murder."

Jake looked over at his mates and nodded. They got up from their table and approached the bar. Jake's smile returned as he stepped closer to Joe. "You'll have a chance to tell him yourself, I suspect, just before he slits your rotten throat. The time for you to reap your just rewards for the misery you help sow is coming fast."

In the mirror behind the bar, Joe could see Jake's men move in behind him, fists clenched, with Lloyd and Johnny moving in behind them. "I didn't think you'd be doing the paybacks. You're the kind of man that gets others to do his dirty work." Joe turned around and faced Jake's boys.

"Look here, Johnny. We got us three tough guys visiting tonight."

"I see that, Joe. What say we all step outside and see how tough these boys really are?"

Jake's men turned, looking at Johnny and a scowling Lloyd. Their fists unclenched and they stepped aside.

Joe gestured toward Jake, still talking to Johnny. "This here fella's the chief." He turned to Jake. "What say you? Willing to try a fair fight?"

Jake backed off, hands up and palms out. "We just stopped in for a drink, not trouble. I can see this joint ain't as friendly as I heard, so we'll just be moving on. Let's go, boys."

Jake stepped around Joe and headed for the door, his two mates right behind. As he left, he turned his head to Joe and tipped his hat, then turned down Pittsburgh Street.

Chapter 23

J oe woke on Saturday with a headache. After running off Jake and his pals, he and the boys had a few more drinks. Joe told them about Jake's threats, which hadn't bothered him much. In fact, he was pleased, since it meant he was making progress, and he was sure Jake would pass on his message.

Joe got up, performed his morning ritual, and dressed for work. After jamming his cap on his head, he slipped the pistol into his pants pocket, his notebook and pencil in his vest, and left the apartment. Even at this early hour, the sun was scarcely visible. Joe's eyes watered and, as he crossed Main Street at Brimstone Corner, he nearly stepped in a pile of fresh horse manure. The stink filled his nose as he walked down Main. It was 7:00 a.m. when he walked in the door at City Lunch. The place had just opened and, as was usually the case on Saturdays, he was the first customer.

Tony was putting fresh flowers in the vases. The little bell on the door announced Joe's arrival and Tony looked up with a smile. Joe headed down to the end of the counter and took his favorite spot.

"Hey, Joey, you right on time." Tony poured him a cup of coffee and put it on the counter in front of him. "You hungry, I bet."

Joe put sugar and cream in his coffee, blew on it a bit, then took a sip. "Ah, that's good. Just what the doctor ordered. I have to hustle out to Alverton. How about an egg sandwich, and wrap it up."

Tony disappeared into the kitchen and Joe finished his coffee, staring out the window at the river. He wanted to make sure he caught up with Caleb this morning, see if the name Kurt Straub meant anything to him. His afternoon was free, and he wanted to get a haircut before his night out with Peggy.

Tony returned with a sandwich covered in white paper. "One egg sandwich wrapped for the ride."

Joe pulled a dime out of his pocket and left it on the counter. "Thanks, Tony. Enjoy."

The Scottdale streetcar was waiting at the terminal. Joe boarded the almost empty trolley and sat up front. The operator exited the terminal building and climbed aboard, touching the brim of his hat as he eyed Joe.

"What's new at West Penn, buddy?" Joe asked.

The operator settled into his seat, released the brake, and eased open the throttle. The car accelerated smoothly out of the terminal, up Arch Street and then right on Main. "They're fixing to run a new line from Greensburg to McKeesport. If they do, I'm putting in for a transfer, get out of this smoke before I ruin my lungs." The operator pulled out a handkerchief and wiped his face as the car climbed up Main Street hill.

"Pity the cokers. Have to work in it all day, six days a week."

"I do pity the poor bastards, killing themselves for a dollar a day, and making Frick and the rest millionaires ten times over."

Joe nodded, then opened his egg sandwich and ate it as the trolley sped through the rolling hills. They arrived at Alverton just before eight. Joe jumped down from the car and headed up the road toward the supply shed. As he rounded the corner of the building, he saw Caleb locking the shed door.

"Morning, Caleb."

Caleb turned toward Joe, his pants riding low on bony hips. He was wearing a railroader's hat and had a red handkerchief tied around his neck. "Morning to you, too, Mr. Zajac. You here to check up on me?"

"Just making my rounds. You had any excitement out here?"

Caleb shook his head. "It's been quiet for the most part, boss. I been keepin' an eagle eye on the works, 'specially the explosives, mixing up my rounds, doin' a few extra, and hanging around longer, too. I'm plum tuckered out today, I got to admit. I'm ready to hit the sack and for a day of rest."

"Had any luck tracking down the Krupps?"

Caleb struck his forehead with the heel of his hand. "I pret' near forgot. 'Course I did. Let's go take a load off."

Joe followed Caleb as he limped over to a bench by the baseball field. They sat down, and Joe watched as Caleb loaded his pipe and fired it up until it was puffing like a steam engine. A sweet smell wafted down Joe's way.

"I did like you said and picked up a bag of the best 'baccy they stock downtown. I'm spoiled for the rough junk now."

"You help me figure out this mess and I'll keep you in the good stuff. What's the news?"

Caleb puffed contentedly for a bit, then put his pipe on the bench. "I was right—there are a few Krupps left hereabouts. I tracked down a cousin of Hilda's. She says the Schmidt boys still run the family farm over

Youngwood way. I'm pretty sure I know 'bout where it is. Ed's got a map in his office. Let's go take a look."

Caleb rose stiffly and headed up the hill to the Union Supply Store, with Joe right behind. Ed Connelly was opening up his office as they arrived. He nodded, unsmiling, to them both as he entered and sat down at the desk. After pulling some papers out of an old black briefcase, he looked up.

"To what do I owe the pleasure of this early morning visit?"

"Ain't nothing going on much, Ed. The works been nice and quiet all night. Me and Mr. Zajac just stopped to take a gander at your map if it wouldn't be no bother."

Ed looked toward the map of Western Pennsylvania stuck on the wall. "Have at it."

He's cranky this morning, Joe thought, as he and Caleb walked over to the map.

"The Schmidt farm is up past Youngwood, on White Hill, 'bout here." Caleb pointed to a spot on the map as Joe got out his notebook. "It's a straight shot up the Greensburg line. Just get off at Youngwood and head out Depot Street. I'm thinking 'bout two miles to White Hill Road. Their spread is on the right just up a piece, a big dairy operation. Just look for two white silos and a big red barn with two farmhouses."

Caleb stretched and yawned. "That's it for me. Good luck to you, Mr. Zajac."

Joe pulled two bits out of his pocket and handed it to Caleb. "Much obliged."

Caleb winked at Joe, tipped his hat to Ed, and left the office. Joe was about to do the same when Ed spoke up. "Hold up, Joe. I got some news for you."

Joe turned, took off his cap, and sat down across from Ed. "What's eating at you?"

"Cliff Sellers was by here yesterday afternoon. He's looking to get rid of you, wanted to know about any problems we had that might could be your doing."

Joe took a deep breath and exhaled slowly. "That rat bastard can kiss my Polish ass. He's pissed off because he thinks I made him look bad in front of Mr. Lynch yesterday, and maybe I did, but he had it coming. I about had enough of his big mouth. Tell him anything you want to, I don't give a shit."

Joe rose to leave, but Ed stood up and came around the desk. "Now hold on there, Joe, I'm on your side. Sellers is no friend of mine, and you are. But I'll not be looking to get in the middle of your troubles with him. You're a good worker for Frick and I told him as much." Ed smiled and put his hand on Joe's shoulder. "That wasn't what he wanted to hear. He up and left in a hurry."

Joe sighed and shrugged. "I'm starting to think me and the Frick company ain't long for each other, but I intend to get to the bottom of these murders and such before I make my move. Thanks for the news, buddy. I owe you a beer."

Joe headed out the door and stomped down the hill to the streetcar stop. The Greensburg car soon arrived, and in twenty minutes he was in Youngwood. This part of Westmoreland County was just northwest of the main coal field and still primarily farmland. Joe hopped off the trolley, found Depot Street, and headed out of town.

The walk was pleasant, the air here clean and sweet smelling compared to Connellsville. The road was rutted from wagon traffic. Joe enjoyed the hike, but by the time he got to White Hill Road, his feet hurt from the new shoes. He could see the two silos just up ahead.

It took him ten minutes more to walk down the farm road. At the end, two white houses flanked the barn. Joe walked up the steps to the house on the right and knocked on the door. "Anybody home?"

He could hear footsteps approaching and was soon facing a big woman in a long dress, with an apron and hands white with flour. She looked Joe over, shaking her head. "We got no use for peddlers here, mister. If we can't make it ourselves, we do without."

"I'm no peddler. Is this the Schmidt brothers' farm?"

"Who'd be asking?"

"Name's Joe Zajac, and I'm looking for information about Walter Schmidt."

The woman frowned, wiping her forehead with the back of her hand and leaving a trail of flour. She came out on the porch and turned to the barn, hollering. "Karl, Hans, kommen sie hier."

Two men came out of the barn, both big and blond, in bib overalls and straw hats. They looked like brothers and kept their eyes on Joe as they approached the house.

"Ja, Momma, what do you want?"

"This man is asking questions about Walter." With that, she returned to the house, leaving Joe with the brothers.

"What's this about Walter? We haven't seen or heard from him for over a year. Is he in trouble?"

Joe walked down the steps and stood in front of the two men. "Name's Joe Zajac. I work for the Frick company and am looking into some problems we've had over the last week. I'm not sure if Walter is involved or not. Mind if I ask you a few questions?"

The men looked at each other before one of them said, "I'm Karl and this is Hans. We got cows needing us so make it quick."

"Much obliged, Karl. Does Walter look like you fellas?"

Hans smiled and spoke up. "Our older brother took after Mother's side of the family. Walter is much shorter and thick, with brown hair instead of blond."

"What's Walter been doing of late? He a farmer, too?"

Now it was Karl's turn to smile. "There's no farmer blood in him. He left home at sixteen just to get away from it. So get to the point, man. What about Walter?"

"A man named Walter Krupp was employed by Frick at a mine near Connellsville. There was trouble at the mine—a murder, most likely—and Krupp disappeared. His body was found up near Uniontown on Tuesday."

"What did this Krupp look like?"

Joe pulled out his notebook and leafed through the front pages, finding what he was looking for. "I'd say he was about forty years old. A bit shorter than me, a bit of a belly, brown hair." He paused as the men's shoulders sagged. "And he was missing the tip of the little finger on his left hand."

The brothers walked over to the porch and sat down, each pulling out a big red handkerchief and blowing his nose. Hans spoke first. "He lost that finger when he was a boy, got it caught in a silo door."

Karl nodded. "That's why he hated the farm life. Well, it's a damn sight better than the life he made for himself. The last time we were together, I figured he was into something no good."

Chapter 24

Karl got up from the porch steps and went inside the house, returning with a jug and a tin cup. He filled it, drank it, filled it again, and passed it to Hans, who drank it with a shudder. Karl took the cup, refilled it, and handed it to Joe.

"That there's the smoothest corn whiskey this side of Dunbar. Help yourself if you're so inclined."

Joe had only tasted corn whiskey once before and hadn't thought much of it. He lifted the cup toward the brothers. "To Walter Schmidt, may he rest in peace."

He drained the cup, the whiskey burning as he swallowed. He shivered and passed the cup back to Karl.

"I'm sorry to bring you the bad news. I think he was involved in the death of the man at Number One and it cost him his life. I'm on the trail of the man I think killed your brother. Anything you can tell me about Walter might help me catch up with his murderer."

Karl put the jug and the cup down and wiped his eyes again. "I'll tell you all I know, but Walter's been a stranger to his family for many a year. Come, the cows need tending."

Joe followed Karl and Hans to the barn. Joe sat on a bale of hay and watched as they worked with their stock. After a while, Karl started talking.

"Brother Walter was always different. He was first born, six years older than us. He was a mite sickly, too, never cut out for farm life." Hans led one cow outside as Karl led another out of a stall.

"For one thing, he was afraid of the animals, and they didn't seem to care much for him, either." Karl washed off a sore on the cow's front leg, scratching the animal's ears and talking softly to her. "There now, Dolly. That feels better, don't it?" He put the rag down and turned back to Joe.

"Then he lost that finger at eleven years. After that he was done doing chores and Momma protected him. By then me and Hans were already helping Poppa. We both took to it natural." Hans came back in and Karl gave him a tired smile. "Farming is either in your blood or not."

Joe rose and approached the cow. She turned her head and looked him over with big brown eyes. "My father had animals in the old country," Joe said. "A few chickens, some pigs, but we weren't famers. We raised them to eat."

Hans came over and stroked the cow's nose. "Farming has been good to us, and it's a damn better life than working the mines and mills."

Karl finished with the cow and Hans led him out. "We were never close to Walter growing up, and at sixteen he left home. Momma cried but Poppa was glad to see him go, one less mouth to feed. We didn't see or hear from him for two years."

Joe got out his little book and started making some notes. "When was Walter born?"

"November 11, 1859. He showed up again around Christmas of seventy-seven. We were still young but I can remember like it was yesterday. Momma cried again, but this time tears of joy."

Karl sat down on a bale of hay and took off his straw hat. "Even Poppa was glad to see him. And Walter had stories to tell. He'd been working on the railroad, caught on with the B&O."

"I was a young boy in Poland then. Don't know much about America in those days," Joe said.

Hans spoke up. "Them was tough years here. Ever hear of the Panic of Seventy-Three?"

"Can't say as I have."

"We were just kids, but I can still remember Poppa talking about it. Some big shot New York banker went bust, and like to take the country down with him."

Karl took over. "Businesses going broke, no work. Wages cut back. We were lucky to be farmers. At least we had food. The summer of seventy-seven saw the Great Railroad Strike. Brother Walter was in the middle of it. He was living in Cumberland, Maryland, but the strike got going over in Martinsburg, and he was there. The B&O cut wages again and the men shut down everything, wouldn't let trains out of the yard."

Hans picked up the story. "The strike spread all over—Pittsburgh, Philadelphia, even to Chicago and St. Louis. President Hayes had to call out the army. Plenty of poor working men lost their lives, including one of Walter's best friends."

Karl continued, "The railroaders were starving, too. They finally gave in but they never forgot. Brother Walter had a deep hatred of the big companies and the men that owned them. Robber barons, he called them. And he had plenty of company."

Hans again. "He'd fallen in with a band of Germans. They called themselves anarchists. I remember him saying he'd do anything he could to bring down the big companies."

Joe had stopped taking notes and put his book away. "How long did Walter stay?"

Karl stood up and put his hat back on. "Left after New Year's and was gone for another year. Got so we'd see him once a year, and he was a firm believer in the union cause. He was part of most every strike in Pennsylvania, and there were many of them in the eighties. He hated them robber barons with a vengeance, Frick and Carnegie among 'em."

"What was he up to the last time you saw him?"

"Walter had become a sad and bitter man. He'd lost some of the fire in his belly but still believed in the cause. He'd come to the conclusion that men like Frick, Carnegie, Rockefeller, and the rest didn't deserve to live, seeing how they worked their labor into early graves."

"Any idea where he was living?"

"He was living a hobo life. Worked when he needed to and traveled all over."

"Ever hear him mention a man name of Kurt Straub?"

"No, never did." Karl turned to the stall, two cows left in it. "Now if you'd be excusing us, we got work to finish."

Joe nodded, and left the Schmidt brothers to their chores.

Ten minutes later he was heading down Depot Street hill, back toward Youngwood. He'd learned quite a bit about Walter, but nothing that would help him find Straub. The Schmidt brothers seemed like decent hardworking men.

Pulling out his pocket watch, Joe noted it was near 11:00 a.m. He wasn't due at Peggy's until six. He thought for a moment about the best way to proceed. *Sykes was looking for Straub yesterday and I got no time to beat around the bush. It's time the two of us had a talk.*

So Joe hustled back to Youngwood, caught the trolley to Greensburg, and was soon on a Pennsylvania Railroad train heading to Smoke City. As they approached Pittsburgh, Joe eyed the giant iron and steel mills that gave the town its nickname and used all of the Connellsville coke.

It was just after noon when the train rolled to a stop at Union Station on Grant Street. Joe jumped off and found a row of carriages waiting at the curb. With no time to waste, he hired one to take him across town.

"Allegheny City, Eighteen Sherman Street."

"Name's Earl. Fare's two bits, paid in advance." Joe paid the man and climbed into the open carriage.

The driver gave the reins a shake and they were under way. Allegheny City was located across the Allegheny River north of Pittsburgh. They sped through town and crossed the Sixth Street Bridge. On the other side, they turned down Ridge Avenue, known locally as Millionaire's Row. Andrew Carnegie and H.J. Heinz, along with most of the old "Iron Barons," had homes there.

Joe gawked at the mansions, impressive monuments to the fortunes being made in Western Pennsylvania. "Fantastic wealth lives here, eh, Earl?"

"Not so far-fetched when you work men to death and pay them a pittance."

Joe nodded, thinking about the little homes in Leisenring and the other coal patch towns and hard labor the workers endured. *Don't seem right somehow.*

As they traveled down the avenue, the homes became smaller. By the time they turned onto Sherman, the houses weren't much bigger than the new homes being built along Pittsburgh Street. The driver pulled to the curb. "Number eighteen, Sherman."

Joe fished another quarter from his pocket and handed it to Earl. "I won't be long. Can you wait and take me back to the station?"

Earl examined the coin, pocketed it, and nodded. Joe hopped down from the carriage and climbed the steps to the front porch of number eighteen. He turned the brass lever in the middle of the door and heard the bell ring inside. In a moment the door opened, Wendell Sykes himself standing in the entrance.

"A big shot like you answering your own door, Wendell? Must be the butler's day off."

"What are you doing here, Mr. Zajac?"

"I was just in the neighborhood and thought I'd stop by. Mind if I come in?"

"I do mind. My wife and I are expecting company." Wendell started to close the door, but Joe put his shoulder to it and pushed his way into the entrance hall.

Joe looked at Wendell, who was fancily dressed. *Expecting company, no doubt.* "This won't take long. All I'm looking for is some information about your friend Kurt."

Wendell backed away from the door. Joe saw a woman appear at the top of the stairs. "Who is it, Wen? Mother and Father will be here any minute."

"Just a man from Frick, Rose. We won't be long." He turned to Joe. "I don't know what you're talking about."

Joe moved closer and spoke in a low voice. "Stop the bullshit, Wendell. You almost ran me down outside of Keystone, in a big hurry to warn him that I was on his trail. The owner remembered your fancy shirt and I recognized the carriage. I don't exactly know what you're up to, but I know enough to cause trouble."

Wendell pulled out a handkerchief and wiped his lips. "Let's go into the library."

Joe followed him into the room, and watched as Wendell pulled the doors shut. The library, while small, was lined with elaborately carved mahogany cases, all filled with leather-bound books. They stood just inside the door.

"What do you want to know, Zajac?"

"Where is Kurt Straub?"

Wendell let out a high-pitched laugh. "I have no idea, and hope to never see him again."

"Why did you want to blow up Leisenring No. 1?"

Wendell started pacing the floor, hands behind his back. Joe let him walk for a minute, then said, "Stop the marching around and tell me the story. Either that or I go see Mr. Lynch and tell him you're in cahoots with Straub."

A look of panic crossed Wendell's face. "Please don't do that. It would queer the deal and cost me a fortune. I have money. How much to keep you from talking?"

Joe laughed and moved closer to Wendell, grabbing his fancy shirt by the ruffles. "I don't want your dirty money, and I don't give a shit about your Frick deal. You're involved of your own accord, and I promise you this—if anyone else gets hurt, their blood will be on your hands, and I'll be the one to mete out the justice." Joe released him and pushed him away.

Wendell paled, and sat down in a chair. Joe sat next to him. "I got a man waiting and places to go. Spill the beans."

Wendell wiped his brow, took a deep breath, and started talking slowly. "I hate H.C. Frick. He's a cold and arrogant bastard and he cheated my father. That I hate him is no secret. Father built the company and ended up with scraps from Frick's table."

"Where did you meet Straub?"

"He approached me right before Independence Day. I was at my family home in Latrobe, preparing it for sale. He just showed up at my door. He knew all about what was going on between Frick and Carnegie. It wasn't enough that Frick cheated me once, now Carnegie was cheating the company out of its rightful profits."

"And he had a plan?"

"He did. Straub hates Frick more than I do, although I'm not sure exactly why. He spoke of being involved with the unions, spoke of how he despised the robber barons, as he called them, but it seemed very personal, too. We sat and talked, drank whiskey."

"So it was his idea to blow up Number One?"

"He didn't exactly say what he intended to do, only that he would make Frick pay for his crimes, as he called them, and hurt the bastard in the pocketbook, too. All Straub needed from me was some financial assistance, which I provided."

"Did you meet again after that?"

"Yes. He'd show up unexpectedly from time to time. I'd see him in Scottdale—he even showed up here once—usually looking for more money."

"When did you last see him?"

"Two weeks ago. He said the plan was coming together. Today was to be the big day, and I tried to call the whole thing off. Carnegie had just made us an offer to settle the lawsuit and it was a very good one. But Straub wouldn't hear of it, said it was too late. He mentioned his job at Keystone, that's why I went out there yesterday—to try again to stop him. But as you know, he's gone."

"What else do you know?"

"That's all, I swear. Straub is a madman. I rue the day we met."

Joe heard the doorbell ring. Wendell looked up with a start. "That's my wife's parents come to visit."

"Don't worry, Wendell, I won't tell them you're a worthless prick." Joe pulled a page from his book and wrote on it. "This is my address in Connellsville. If you hear from Straub, let me know."

Wendell nodded as Joe got up and left the room, passing the arriving guests as he walked out the door.

Chapter 25

Hurrying down the steps to the sidewalk, Joe saw Earl checking his pocket watch. "You get your business attended to, son?"

"Made a good start on it, Earl. Thanks for waiting."

Joe climbed into the carriage and Earl took off. "If we hustle up, I'll be back in time for the two thirty from Philadelphia.

Take me to the Grant Street station. I'm riding the B&O back to Connellsville."

"Connellsville, eh? I got relatives in Fayette County. What do you do for a living?"

For the first time since he was hired, Joe was reluctant to name his employer. "I work for a coke company."

"Your prince of coke is a big shot steel man now."

Joe just nodded. The driver shook the reins and they were off. Joe took a minute to review what he now knew. Wendell met Kurt in early July and agreed to fund a plot to damage Frick in some way. Shortly after, Kurt got a job at Keystone Supply and stole some dynamite. Somewhere along the line, he met Walter Krupp, a man with ties to anarchists. Wendell realized the plan could backfire on him, tried to call it off, but lost control of Kurt. Walter screwed up the job and ended up killing a man. This pissed Kurt off and Krupp ended up dead. Now Kurt most likely had a lot of dynamite and a strong desire to harm Frick.

Earl took a different route back to the B&O station, one that took them through the triangle of land where the Allegheny and Monongahela rivers joined to form the Ohio. It was one of the city's poorest neighborhoods.

"You're in a mite different part of town now, buddy." The driver had to slow down to avoid some children in the street. Joe took a good look at them and the neighborhood. The children were skinny, dirty, and dressed in rags. The street was filled with garbage and worse, the houses sagging little shacks. The air smelled rancid.

"Stop the carriage," Joe said.

Earl pulled back on the reins as Joe waved the children over. They approached slowly, wide-eyed and suspicious. Joe pulled some coins from his pocket and gave a few to each child. They took them silently and ran off.

Earl turned to Joe, smiling. "That's a good thing you did there." Then he snapped the reins and the carriage sped away. In ten minutes they were at the B&O station.

Joe jumped down and reached in his pocket. "How much I owe you, Earl?"

The driver shook his head and extended his hand. "We're square, my friend." Joe and the driver shook hands. With a "Yah!" to his horses, Earl took off.

Joe entered the small station. A southbound train was due in any minute. He bought a ticket and strolled out to the platform. A northbound train sat taking on passengers. Joe walked to the end of the platform to inspect the engine. The fireman walked around the front, oilcan in his hand. Joe smiled and stepped out of his way. "That's a fine piece of equipment you got there." The man nodded and bent to his task.

Joe heard a whistle and saw his train approaching, its headlamp glowing yellow through the smoke and haze. Its chugging slowed until it squealed to a stop at the platform. Joe stood back as the conductor jumped down, placed the step stool on the platform, and helped the arriving passengers off. When the carriage had mostly emptied, Joe hopped up and found a seat. Soon the conductor called, "All aboard," and with a chug and a hiss, the train pulled out of the station.

The train was a local, with three stops between Pittsburgh and Connellsville. The first was Braddock, the site of the earliest settlement in the area. As the train departed, it passed Edgar Thompson Works, one of Carnegie's biggest plants, and his first to use the modern Bessemer process of steelmaking. Joe moved to the other side of the coach to get a closer look.

The plant stretched for miles along the Monongahela River. Dozens of stacks poured thick smoke into the air, while flames shot out of other smaller stacks. Hundreds of railcars sat in a huge yard. Even with the noise of the accelerating train, Joe could hear clanking and banging from the plant. He gave a low whistle.

"Quite the operation Carnegie got there." The conductor stood in the aisle behind Joe. "You should see it at night, looks like hell with the lid off. Ticket, please?"

Joe handed the conductor his ticket as the train moved past the end of the mill complex. He relaxed in his seat and the swaying of the train soon had him dozing.

"Next stop, Connellsville." The conductor tapped Joe's shoulder as he passed through the car. Joe opened his eyes and stretched as the train left Broad Ford, home of Old Overholt, his favorite whiskey. H.C. Frick's first job was in the office there, the distillery owned by his grandfather, Abe Overholt.

It was just past four o'clock when the train pulled into the Connellsville station. Joe barely had enough time to get cleaned up and be at Peggy's by six. *No time for a haircut.* He headed up Water Street, past the hotel. He'd promised Peggy they would eat at The Dinner Bell, so he stopped in to see what the special was and if Johnny's aunt Mary was working.

A bell tinkled as he walked in the side door. The place was empty, lunch long over and dinner service not starting until five. Mary came out of the kitchen, wiping her hands on a big blue apron. She smiled.

"How do, Joe. You're a mite early for dinner. The pork chops are just going in the oven."

"I was passing by, Mary. I'll be coming back around six with a friend. Think you'll have a full house?"

"We do get pretty busy on Saturday night, particularly when stuffed pork chops are the special."

"How about saving me that table back in the corner?"

Mary nodded, and gave Joe a wink. "Bringing a lady friend?"

Joe winked back. "I am, although we're just acquaintances at the moment."

"Well, good luck tonight. See you at six."

"Thanks, Mary, and save some pork chops for us."

Joe hustled home and got cleaned up. Dressed in his Sunday best, he headed down Main to West Penn Terminal. The sidewalks were still crowded with Saturday shoppers, the streets jammed with horses, carriages, and wagons. After turning down Arch, he arrived at the terminal and boarded a waiting car on the South Connellsville line. It soon departed and a few minutes later, he hopped off at the corner of Pittsburgh and Green Street, in the middle of the South Side.

Peggy's apartment building was a three-story structure made of yellow brick. The front corner featured a round turret that ended in a tall pointed slate roof. The ground floor was occupied by Keagy's Apothecary. Joe found the entrance to the apartments and was soon at the door for apartment number four. He took off his cap, smoothed his hair down, and knocked.

"Be right there," he heard Peggy call, and the door opened a moment later. "Good evening, Joe. Let me grab my parasol and we can go." Umbrella in hand, she joined Joe in the hall and closed the door, making sure it was locked.

Joe looked Peggy over. She was dressed in a long golden skirt with a matching high-collared jacket, both trimmed in dark brown. The jacket fit snugly around her tiny waist and closed with a row of small buttons. She wore a light brown hat turned up on one side, adorned with long feathers and a big bow. Her auburn hair was in a bun. "Miss Patterson, I am honored to be your escort for the evening. May I say that you must be the most stylish woman in Connellsville this evening?"

Peggy laughed. "You may say, and you're looking quite dapper yourself. Shall we go?" She held Joe by the elbow as they descended the stairs to the street, Joe enjoying her signature rosewater fragrance. They walked to the corner and waited for the downtown streetcar. Peggy opened her parasol and, holding the handle with both hands, turned to face Joe.

"Thank you for asking me out, Joe. It's been longer than I care to admit since I've gone to dinner and a show."

"It's my pleasure. I don't think The Star will miss me one Saturday night, or you, either." He turned and looked back at her building. "You lived here long?"

"I moved in about three months ago. Daddy has a big house a few blocks from here, but I just decided I wanted my own place, although lately I've been spending many a night back there."

Her sick father. Don't see many young women living on their own. He heard a clang and, looking up Green, saw the streetcar turn from Race Street. "Here's our ride." The trolley stopped at the corner and they climbed aboard for the short ride downtown. After getting off, they strolled up the street, Peggy holding on to Joe's arm again, her parasol resting lightly on her shoulder.

"Been to The Dinner Bell before, Joe?"

"My buddy Johnny Davidson and I were there Tuesday. It's his aunt and uncle's place." When they arrived at the restaurant, Helen closed her parasol and Joe held the door open, then followed her inside.

The dining room was almost full but true to her word, Mary had saved them the table in the corner. She saw them come in, smiled broadly, and hurried over.

"Why, Peggy, don't you look lovely tonight. Joe, you, too. Come on and follow me." She led them over to their table and watched as Joe pulled out a chair for Peggy and scooted it in as she sat down. "And a perfect gentleman, too. How about I get you each a little glass of my homemade elderberry wine?" Before they could answer, she turned and entered the kitchen.

Joe unfolded his napkin and draped in on his lap. "You know Mary?"

"Mary and Mahlon both. We go to the same church, the Methodist Episcopal over on Apple Street. I didn't know she was a Davidson."

Mary returned with two little glasses of wine and a basket of rolls. She put them down on the table. "My stuffed pork chops are the dinner special tonight. How about it?"

"If they're half as good as your pot roast, we're in for a treat. Peggy?"

Peggy nodded. "They sound wonderful."

"You two enjoy the wine. Your dinner will be right out."

Peggy lifted her glass to Joe. "May the face of every good news and the back of every bad news be toward us."

Joe laughed as they clinked glasses and sipped the wine. "You and Lloyd with those Irish toasts. Do you learn them at your Daddy's knee?"

"In my case, it was my mother. She was half Irish."

"I lost my mother when I was thirteen. She was German and Polish. I never saw her touch a drop, and us Poles aren't known for our toasts."

Peggy stared at her glass, swirling the wine as she spoke. "Mother died four years ago. I still think of her every day." She set down the glass and looked at Joe. "How long have you lived in Connellsville?"

"Two years, but I've worked for Frick for six. I've lived all over, from Latrobe to Lemont Furnace."

"Like it here?"

Now it was Joe's turn to play with his wine. He lifted the glass, examined it, then took a sip. "I do. The town's a nice size, and the people I've met here have been friendly."

"How's your eye?"

Joe fingered the bruise. "Mostly healed, I'd say."

"And your investigation?"

"I've made progress, but it's far from being resolved. Funny thing is, the more I dig into it, the more I'm learning about myself."

Peggy gave Joe a long look. "Meaning what, exactly?"

Joe put his elbows on the table and leaned forward, hands clasped. "I'm thirty years old and have lived a blessed life in many ways, though I lost my parents way too soon. Thanks to the love of an uncle, I got a good education. Thanks to that I got a good job as a cop, and thanks to that I have an easy job with Frick. My life has been carefree to this point, no worries and no regrets."

"So how has that changed?"

Joe gave her a grim smile. "I've come to realize that, in a way, my easy life is being paid for by the sweat of every 'dumb Hunkie' that gets off the boat and ends up in one of Frick's mines."

"And that makes you a bad person?"

Joe sighed. "I'm not a bad person. In fact, I'm a good man, or at least I try to be. I've just been wondering if I'm living right."

"Dinner is served, folks." Mary made her way through the other diners with a big tray piled high. "We serve home-style on Saturday." She placed a plate with a stuffed pork chop in front of each, then set down a bowl of mashed potatoes, a plate with three ears of corn, and a bowl filled with tomatoes, onions, and cucumbers in a clear dressing. "Can I get you more wine?"

Joe shook his head. "How about a pitcher of water and two glasses?" Mary headed back toward the kitchen.

Joe and Peggy dug in, mostly silent as they ate. Joe finished the chop and two ears of corn, along with a big mound of potatoes. Peggy smiled as he cleaned his plate. "My, my, I know one thing—the inquiry hasn't hurt your appetite."

Joe wiped his lips with the napkin and pushed back a bit from the table. "Nothing gets between me and a good meal. I always feel better after one."

Mary showed up with a pie on a tray. "I made some of those elderberries into a pie. You folks care to try it?"

Peggy shook her head. "None for me, Mary, although I'm sure it's delicious."

Joe gave a low moan. "I'm 'bout to bust myself and we have a show to get to. We'll just settle up and give you back your table."

Mary put the check on the table. "You young ones have a good time and come see us again."

After Joe put two quarters on top of the check, they left the restaurant and headed south, the sun no longer visible through the haze. Joe said, "We really aren't in a hurry. I just couldn't eat another bite. The show doesn't start until seven thirty. If you have your walking shoes on, we can just take a stroll out Pittsburgh Street."

Peggy once again held Joe by the elbow and gave him a sweet smile. "OK, Joe."

Chapter 26

Joe and Peggy strolled slowly up Water Street toward the bridge, both looking into the distance. A slow coal train was passing by on the B&O, cars rattling and clanking. "If you don't mind, Peggy, can I ask you a personal question?"

"You can ask me anything you like, but I'll not be obligated to answer."

"Fair enough." He paused for a few steps. "Tell me, how is it that an attractive and smart woman like you isn't married?"

When Peggy didn't answer right away, Joe stopped and turned to her. "I'm sorry. I guess being nosy comes natural to me."

She smiled up at him. "No offense taken. I was just trying to figure out the answer." They started walking again.

"I did all of the normal things a young woman does—sat with young men in the parlor, attended the church socials—and met many nice men. I never was in a big hurry, but eventually I did meet a special one and we fell in love."

They climbed the steps to the Main Street Bridge and crossed Arch Street. The stores were closing up and the sidewalks were less crowded, but the noise from the bars was picking up.

"I had just turned twenty-one and we started planning a wedding. A month before we were to be married, he died in an accident at the locomotive works."

Joe saw tears welling in her eyes and felt his own eyes moisten. "I'm sorry for making you remember."

Peggy gave him a little smile. "You're forgiven." They turned south at Brimstone Corner and headed up Pittsburgh Street. "I've met a few good men since then, but couldn't get the spark to flare again. I've been asked, the last time by Henry Brooks. I just can't bring myself to say yes. Deep down I think I've decided that an old maid's life is my fate."

That's enough prying for one night, Joe thought. They walked in silence for a block.

"Now it's my turn. How'd a smart and handsome man like you make it to thirty without settling down?"

She thinks I'm handsome! Joe felt his face flush. "When I was at the courting age, I was already a cop. I got caught up in the nightlife, loved drinking and staying out late. I felt like I was having too much fun to settle down."

"And since you came west?"

"I was still too busy running around for the most part, and the women looking to settle down are all so much younger. I tried the courting and parlor sitting, but in the end I always got cold feet."

They walked in silence again. Joe took his hand and placed it over Peggy's. "Now I have thoughts the same as yours—living the bachelor life is my fate."

Another block passed in silence. A cool wind had picked up from the north, promising a change in the weather. "I'm glad I took a chance on you, Joe. You're not what I expected you to be."

I'm not who I was a few days ago. "And you're all I wanted you to be. If you're willing, we'll do it again."

Peggy laughed. "You are a bold one, and I am willing."

The couple was approaching Green Street again. "What show is playing tonight?" Peggy asked.

"It's called *Shenandoah*. The play ran in New York City for a year. There are two traveling troupes on the road, according to *The Courier*. We're fortunate to have one at our little theatre."

The Colonial Theatre was on the ground floor of a three-story brick building. The upper floors were apartments, and other stores occupied the street level. The building was the business hub of the South Side.

Joe and Peggy walked up to the theatre. Horses and carriages crowded Pittsburgh Street in front. They entered the lobby and waited in line at the ticket counter. From the looks of it, the performance would be a sellout. The line moved quickly and they were soon seated, a few minutes before the curtain came up.

The play was set during the Civil War, and was about two West Point friends, one from New York and the other from Virginia, who came to serve their respective sides. A star-crossed love story was a big part of the plot. *Not my usual cup of tea*, thought Joe, *but I've never enjoyed an evening more.*

After the show ended, they were back on Pittsburgh Street.

"Did you enjoy the play, Peggy?"

"Oh, I did, indeed. And like all good tales, love conquered all in the end."

Joe smiled. "And the world is a better place."

They strolled back to Peggy's building and Joe walked her to the door. "Plans for tomorrow?"

"I have to get up early and visit Father. Then it's off to church. I also teach Sunday school. Then back for Sunday dinner with Daddy. After that I'll have to go catch up on the books down at The Star. And you?"

Joe rubbed his jaw and looked up. "Let's see, church for me, too, then I'm free as a bird. I'm thinking I might try to coax a few trout out of the Yough."

They stood quietly in the hall for a moment, then Peggy took his hands and gave him a kiss on the cheek. "Come see me Monday at The Star." With that, she opened her door and was gone.

Joe stood there for a bit, enjoying the warm feelings the quick kiss had generated. He turned and slowly descended the stairs. Once outside, he looked up at the window of her apartment. *I feel like a schoolboy.* He finally shook his head and walked back toward town, smiling all the way.

Once downtown, he pulled out his watch. It was only ten, and he was too wound up for sleep. He walked past the entrance to his rooms and headed for The Star. *Old habits die hard.*

He entered the saloon and headed for the bar. The joint was packed, with a loud and rowdy crowd well on its way to getting drunk. Joe spotted Lloyd down at the far end and headed his way. He pushed in next to him just as Hiram was bringing a beer.

"You finally showed up. Me and Lloyd was worried about you. The usual?"

"Just a beer for now, Hi, if you please."

Lloyd turned toward him, the crowd pressing them close together. "Look who it is—my old buddy, Joe." Lloyd looked him up and down. "What the hell are you all dressed up for? You been to a wedding or a funeral?"

Joe could tell Lloyd was half in the bag already. His eyes were red rimmed, his hat cocked over one ear. "Neither. I was out to a show at the Colonial."

"I thought you stopped seeing that girl from the bake shop."

Hiram returned with Joe's beer and set it on the bar. Joe picked it up and drank half. "I wasn't with her, Red."

Lloyd leaned close. Joe smelled the whiskey on his breath. "Come on, let the cat out of the bag."

"I was with Peggy."

Lloyd let out a whoop, then slapped Joe hard on the back. "You work fast. You only met her a week ago."

"I surprised myself. She's a fine woman, in my book. We had a great time." Joe wanted to change the subject. "Want to go fishing tomorrow?"

Lloyd put his elbows on the bar. "I got plans already. Going to Soisson Park."

"Who are you going with?"

"I'm meeting some fellas and their wives from work for a picnic. And one woman is bringing her sister."

"Sounds like some matchmaking going on." Joe finished his beer, suddenly tired. "Best of luck, buddy. I'm calling it a night." He threw a nickel on the bar and, after clapping Lloyd on the back, left The Star.

The moon was full and Joe could see some clouds building to the northwest. It looked like that change in the weather was coming. *And change can be good, in the weather and life.*

Chapter 27

J oe stirred on Sunday, and contrary to his habit, lay in bed for some time after. It had rained overnight, although the storm didn't wake him. The morning air was cooler and almost sweet smelling.

He spent some of the time thinking about Peggy, and how much fun he'd had with her. Then his thoughts turned to how good he felt. After some contemplation, he figured out why. Last night was the first Saturday in a long time he hadn't gotten drunk. His thoughts were clear, no headache, no thirst—all in all a welcome change of pace. He felt at peace.

Finally rising, Joe opened the curtains and surveyed the morning. The rain had cleared the air. The sun shined brightly for a change, no haze to be seen. He took a few deep breaths then got cleaned up. Before long, he was out the door and headed across the bridge to St. John's. He arrived right on time for seven o'clock Mass.

The same old ladies were praying the rosary, all together up front. A few people were lighting votive candles. The altar boy came out and lit the candles. Joe took his usual seat in the back, picked up a prayer book, and leafed through it. He had opened it to the three prayers of Faith, Hope, and Charity, and remembered something from the Bible that his mother had taught him as a boy. There are only two commandments—love God, and love your neighbor for the love of God.

After Mass, Joe managed to avoid the Hudaceks, who always sat in front. He stopped by his favorite Sunday breakfast spot, the New Haven House, for pancakes and sausage. After that and two cups of coffee, he was feeling well fortified and ready for a day at the river.

He stopped by his place to change into his fishing pants and vest. He grabbed his rod, tackle box, and creel, and headed for the door. As he prepared to leave, he noticed his revolver sitting on the dresser and, after a moment's thought, put it in the tackle box, too.

A quick stop at the market for some apples and then he boarded the South Connellsville streetcar, sitting in the back with his gear. Just as it pulled out of the depot, a large young man jumped on, wearing dungarees and a red plaid shirt. *He looks familiar.* He looked at Joe briefly before sitting up front. There were only two other riders, a young couple.

The open car headed south and Joe enjoyed the cool breeze. The couple got off at Gibson Avenue. Joe was going to the end of the line at Soisson Park. His favorite fishing hole was about a mile walk from there, just above the dam at the Trotter Water pumping station. The car arrived at the park, and Joe watched the operator flip the power pickup and start his return trip. The park was deserted, not officially open at this hour.

Joe headed for the river. The other rider headed in the opposite direction. Joe turned into the woods, looking up the road before doing so. The man had stopped walking and was watching him from the top of the hill. Joe pulled the revolver from his tackle box and put it in a vest pocket.

The path to the river was steep. The mountains came almost to the riverbank out here. The descent was mostly slipping and sliding, Joe trying not to lose his pole and creel. The path ended at the B&O tracks. Joe jumped over a parked freight train and was soon on the bank of the Yough. A teenage boy was fishing Joe's favorite little pool. He could see several fish tails sticking out of the boy's creel.

Joe approached him quietly. "How's the fishing?"

"Just fair now, mister. They were really biting when I got here, but I'm thinking I caught them all."

Joe smiled and headed upstream. There was another pool around the bend. He heard the freight train clinking rhythmically as the engine pulled the slack from the couplings, and it was soon moving north. Joe arrived at the pool and began casting, enjoying the sounds of the river as it rolled past.

A half hour later, he'd yet to have any luck. He thought he'd see if the boy was still in his spot and headed downstream. Before going very far, he heard a bang and saw the water splash a step behind him. Joe dropped his rod and creel and jumped over the bank, ducking out of sight.

Peeking over the top, he checked the hillside and saw the man from the trolley. Standing next to him was another big blond fellow. *Jake.* Joe watched as the two moved down the hill. They scanned the river up and down, looking for him. Some low trees shielded him, but up ahead the growth cleared out, giving the men a clear field of vision.

No wonder he looked familiar. He's the man who was watching me at Leisenring. Joe stepped into the river and moved downstream. He heard a crack and saw the boy running down the tracks. *Thank God he'll not be mixed up in this.*

"Hey, Zajac. It's me, your old buddy, Jake." Another shot rang out, but Joe didn't even see where it hit. They no longer knew exactly where he was. "I gave Kurt your message. Here's one for you." A third shot hit the water, this time closer to Joe.

Peeking above the bank, Joe saw the men moving down the hillside. They were about fifty yards from the tracks and maybe twenty yards north of Joe's position. Looking downstream, he saw a stone drain running up to and under the tracks. *Time to go.* Joe crept into the culvert and, staying low, was soon under the roadbed. Chancing a glance, he saw the two men standing close to the tracks.

Joe jumped out of the culvert and took his time leveling out the pistol. He squeezed off two rounds and dove back into the ditch, hearing a man scream.

"I'm shot, Jake." Knowing he'd hit at least one, Joe ran for the river. He tucked the gun into his waistband and dove in, hearing several more rifle shots. He took a deep breath, kicked to the bottom of the river, and swam downstream. About a minute later, he surfaced and looked toward the tracks. Jake was a bit behind and saw Joe but didn't shoot. Instead he started running. Joe was about fifty yards from the swinging bridge to the pump house. Jake intended to beat him there and pick him off from the deck.

Taking another deep breath, Joe dove again, this time moving closer to the shore. Thanks to the rain, the river was muddy. If he could clear the bridge, and make it over the low dam just past it, he'd be safe. He held his breath until he thought his lungs would explode.

Once again Joe had to surface, close to the bank and just under the bridge. He could see Jake leaning over the rail in the middle of the span, watching the water. Joe drifted behind a big round rock. Jake still hadn't spotted him.

Diving again, Joe headed for the breast of the dam. A minute later, lungs near bursting, he made it and flopped on top. Another shot rang out but he was gone, sliding down the face of the dam and diving again. When he had to surface, he looked south and saw Jake standing with the other man, tending to his wound. Safe for now, Joe turned onto his back and kicked gently down the river. He caught his breath while letting the current move him along. *Son of a bitch! That was a close call.*

A half hour later, Joe pulled himself out of the river near Connell Run. Dripping wet, he headed down Arch Street, once again attracting the stares of passersby. He paid them no mind and strolled home, happy to have survived the morning. He dried off, got into some dry clothes, and cleaned his pistol. After reloading, he stuck it in his pocket and headed out.

Joe's next stop was City Hall, home of the local jail and police station. He was looking for Johnny. The officer on duty was eating lunch and reading a newspaper at his desk, in an open area outside the jail cells. Joe didn't recognize him.

"Howdy, Officer, name's Joe Zajac. I'm looking for Johnny Davidson. Is he scheduled in today?"

The policeman looked up, sandwich in hand. "State your business."

Joe smiled. "No business. He and I are pals."

The man pointed to a chalkboard on the wall. "There's the duty roster." He took a bite of his sandwich and returned to the paper.

"Thanks. Enjoy your lunch." Joe walked over to the board and saw that Johnny was off that day. He decided to pay him a visit.

Johnny owned a small house off of Fairview Avenue, behind the cemetery. It only took a few minutes for Joe to walk there. He knocked on the door and, getting no answer, walked around back. Johnny was in the yard, picking tomatoes from some healthy-looking vines in a small garden.

"Looks like I'm just in time for lunch."

Johnny looked up, a big red fruit in each hand. "Hey, Joe, you sure are. Let's go inside."

Joe followed him into a small kitchen in the rear of the house. Johnny put the tomatoes on the table, pulled a loaf of bread out of the bread drawer, and a knife from the drawer above it. "Have a seat. Ever eat a tomato sandwich?"

"Can't say as I have, but I'm not one to turn down food."

They both sat down and Johnny cut off four slices of bread. Then he cut the tomatoes into thick slabs, arranging several on two of the slices of bread. After salting the tomatoes, he covered them with the remaining bread, picked one sandwich up, and took a big bite, juice running down his chin.

"Help yourself. There's nothing better than a fresh tomato sandwich."

Joe bit into his sandwich. "Who taught you how to grow tomatoes, H.J. Heinz?" Johnny just smiled. They ate in silence and in a minute the sandwiches were gone.

"What brings you by, Joe?"

"I got a favor to ask. I was out fishing above the Trotter Water pump house this morning and ran into my pal, Jake."

"The fella from Friday night?"

"Him and another fellow who's been tailing me. They were looking for a payback." He filled Johnny in on the events of the morning, including his swim to town and soggy walk up Main Street.

"You sure are squeezing a heap of fun out of life."

Joe nodded. "Now I want to go back out there and pick up my rod and creel. I'd like some company just in case those boys are still around."

"Glad to." Johnny went into the other room and returned wearing a holster and .45 revolver. "Let's go."

They left Johnny's, walked down to West Penn Terminal, and were soon on their way. A half hour later they were at Joe's fishing hole. They found his pole broken, and his wicker creel smashed. Joe picked up the rod, frowning.

"That no-good bastard. It's bad enough he's trying to kill me. I've had this rod for twelve years. Uncle Stan bought it for me." He tossed it in the weeds and kicked the creel. "Now I am pissed off."

Joe turned and looked up the hillside toward where he'd first seen Jake and the other man. "Let's take a little stroll."

They walked to the tracks, then down past the culvert to where Jake's trail came out. Scanning the area, Joe soon found a spent brass cartridge. "Look here, Johnny."

"Looks like a .30 caliber to me." Joe handed him the cartridge, which Johnny put in his pocket after examining it. "I'll check this out later."

Joe looked up the path. "Let's see where they came from." They hiked up the hill, finding two more spent cartridges where Joe had first seen the men. The path went further up, and about a hundred yards on they came to a split. One path headed north, the other kept going up the mountain.

"That way surely takes you back to South Connellsville," said Johnny. They kept climbing for another hundred yards or so, seeing nothing of interest. Rocky outcrops were starting to appear.

"Watch out for rattlesnakes, Joe. These woods out here are lousy with them, especially around the rocks."

"Where do you think this path leads to?"

"Hard to say. The land back here keeps climbing all the way up to Springfield Pike. There's not much up there except a small stone quarry and a few farms. There's an old dirt road past Soisson Park runs up that way."

Joe pulled out his handkerchief and wiped his brow. "Feels like the nice weather is leaving us. The heat is building again." Joe turned down the hill. "I've seen enough."

The two men walked back to the fork and headed south. Sure enough, the path came out close to the park. "You get a chance to mention me to Henry Snyder?"

"I did. He says he'd be happy to see you. Stop by his office anytime tomorrow."

"Thanks, buddy, and thanks for keeping me company. Let's go get us an ice cream, my treat."

Chapter 28

Monday dawned hot and sticky, the cool spell blown away by the south winds. Joe woke early and planned his day. He'd go to Scottdale and report to Mr. Lynch, and he needed to check in at some of the mines he hadn't visited recently, a few up Uniontown way. His usual duties had taken a backseat to the investigation. He wanted to tell Sheriff Miller about Kurt, and should stop by Leisenring, too. He'd go by the *Courier* office in the afternoon, and was looking forward to seeing Peggy that evening.

But first, breakfast. He finished his morning routine, grabbed his gun, and was off. A few minutes later he arrived at City Lunch. Two other early birds had beaten him in but his favorite spot was empty. He headed down to the end of the counter.

Tony came out of the kitchen with two plates for the other customers; then he poured Joe a cup of coffee and brought it to him.

"Hiya, Joey. How's life treating you?" As usual, Tony wore a big smile and a dirty apron.

"Tolerable well, Tony, and you?"

"Enjoyed my day off and let Momma do the cooking for a change. Worked in my garden and took a nap." He stood and stared at Joe, still smiling. Something was up.

"What? Come on, spit it out."

Tony laughed. "I was closing up Saturday, just after six, and guess what I see? Some fella all gussied up with a fancy dressed lady on his arm walking down the street."

In spite of himself, Joe smiled at the memory. "Swear to God, Tony, you should be the detective. Your place was dark when we walked by."

"I don't think you see me. Who's your new lady friend?"

"Her name's Peggy."

Tony kept staring, arms folded.

"Her Pap owns The Star. We just met last week."

"You no wasting your time, then, eh, my friend? I'm happy for you." He took a rag and swiped at the counter. "Now what you want for breakfast?"

"Two scrambled hard with a slice of ham, potatoes, and a short stack."

Tony shook his head. "How you eat so much and don't get fat?" He turned and disappeared into the kitchen.

The bell on the door rang and in walked Dave Norton. He saw Joe and joined him.

"Morning, Norton. What brings you in so early?"

"Got a meeting at the bank before we open, and Martha ran out of eggs. How's the investigation?"

Joe gave him a quick report, ending with the events of the previous day. Norton listened without interrupting, shaking his head.

"You've been darned lucky so far. Maybe you should turn this over to the police or sheriff."

"Did I tell you those bastards broke my favorite rod? No, I have some unfinished business with Kurt and those farm boys."

Tony appeared with Joe's breakfast, on two plates. He slid them onto the counter and turned to Norton. "What can I get you, Davy?"

"Two over easy."

"You got it, boss."

Joe wolfed down his meal like it was his last, listening to Norton talk about his children. His friend was clearly contented. Joe took a last bite, wiped his mouth, and turned toward him. "You were right the other night. I'd consider myself a lucky man to have a home life like you, and it is past time for me to settle down some." He finished his coffee, tossed a quarter on the counter, and got up. "See you later, pal."

He left Norton with his mouth hanging open and headed for West Penn Terminal.

He arrived at the Frick offices just after eight. Polly was at her desk, but otherwise the front office was deserted.

"Morning, Miss Polly. What's new at Frick?"

"We've got another big meeting this afternoon. Looks like a quiet morning, though."

"Is Mr. Lynch in? I'd like to give him a report."

"I'll go see." Polly went upstairs. Joe looked over some papers on her desk. One was an agenda for the afternoon meeting. From what he could tell, it looked like Carnegie had made his deal with the Frick shareholders.

Joe heard the front door open and looked up to see Cliff Sellers walk in. Cliff saw Joe and fixed him with a hard stare.

"What are you doing here, Zajac?"

"Top of the morning to you, Cliff." Joe gave him a big smile. "I just stopped by to give Mr. Lynch a report."

"You can tell me and I'll pass it on."

Joe shook his head. "Mr. Lynch asked me to report to him directly."

Cliff's face reddened, his fists clenched.

"And what are you doing here?" Joe asked. "I figured you'd be out digging dirt."

Cliff took a step toward Joe. "Keep it up. I'm gonna enjoy knocking you down a peg."

"What are you waiting for? There's no fence around me."

Cliff took a deep breath and stepped back, his hands relaxing. "All in good time."

"Looks like the old dog is all bark."

Cliff went around Joe and headed upstairs, passing Polly on the way.

"Mr. Lynch will see you now, Joe."

"Thanks, Polly." Then in a whisper, "You were a big help on Friday. I had an interesting meeting with Wendell on Saturday."

Polly blushed. "Glad to help."

With a tip of his cap, Joe went up to Lynch's office. His secretary nodded and pointed to the chair at his desk. Joe sat and waited as Lynch shuffled through some papers. He made a note, set the papers aside, and looked up.

"Good morning, Mr. Zajac. What have you to report?"

"I had a busy weekend. Can I speak freely?"

Lynch gave his secretary a nod and she left, closing the door behind her. "Go on."

"I'm hot on the fellow Kurt's trail, found out his last name—Straub. He was working out at Keystone Supply in Dunbar up until last Wednesday. And who do you think I ran into out there on Friday? Our man Wendell."

Lynch took off his glasses and sat up straight. "Interesting development. Go on."

"I went down to Pittsburgh on Saturday and stopped by Wendell's place for a visit. I put some heat on him and he sang like a bird. He knows Straub."

"Wendell is behind the murders?"

"He claims not, and I'm inclined to believe him. He *was* looking to stir up trouble, but not anymore."

Lynch smiled. "And with good reason. The deal with Carnegie is done. He's become a wealthy young man. Anything else?"

"I've got Straub's attention. His gang took a shot at me yesterday. And someone is stirring up labor trouble. I'll learn more about that this afternoon."

Lynch stood up and came around the desk. Joe stood to meet him. "This man Straub—he's got the dynamite from Standard?"

"That and more, I believe, sir, and he's determined to use it against Frick."

"What can I do to assist you?"

"Let all of the superintendents know what's going on. Have them report anything suspicious directly to you, especially any labor agitation. Tell them I'm to receive their complete cooperation and assistance if needed, and keep Cliff Sellers out of it."

Lynch nodded. "It will be done immediately. And on top of that, the company is announcing a five thousand dollar reward to anyone that helps us recover the stolen explosives." Lynch returned to his seat and the papers he'd put aside. "If you need anything else, let Polly know."

"Yes, sir." *Five thousand dollars! That's five years' pay.*

An hour later, he arrived at the Lemont mine complex a few miles from Uniontown. He toured the works, checking incoming railcars and inspecting the explosives storage shed. Then he headed to the company store. The superintendent, Ralph Vogel, was in his office there. He rose from his desk as Joe entered. "Morning, Zajac, long time no see."

"How do, Ralph. I've been thrown off my regular rounds, should have been by last week. Anything going on?"

"I'd say. Just got off the telephone with Polly over at Scottdale. Sounds like you got a full plate."

Joe nodded. "Speaking of food, anybody stirring the pot with the workers?"

"Now that you mention it, yes. A man we hired on about a month ago. I hear he's talking up a new union."

"Does it have a name?"

"Not that I've heard."

Joe took out his notebook and pencil. "What's the fellow's name?"

Vogel shuffled some papers around, finding the weekly payroll. "Wilmer Steward, a brattice man."

Joe looked up. "Have the fire boss keep a close eye on him. The man that most likely killed the fire boss at Leisenring was a newly hired brattice man." Joe put away his notebook and got up to leave. "We have over a thousand pounds of missing dynamite in the hands of a violent man looking to harm Frick. Until this is decided, I'm adding to the watch at all of the mines. Tell your bosses to keep their ears open. You hear anything, let Polly know right away. Don't start a panic but be vigilant."

Joe left Lemont and was soon on the streetcar to Uniontown. It was getting on toward the lunch hour and Joe figured he knew where to find Sheriff Miller. It was right before noon when he walked into Greenie's. Miller was at his favorite table, a fat sandwich in his hands and a beer on the table.

"Morning, Sheriff. What you got there?"

Miller chewed for a bit, swallowed, then took a big swig of beer. "Liverwurst, with a big slice of onion. Can't be beat."

Greenie showed up at the table. "You need anything?"

"Just a coffee."

Miller raised an eyebrow. "You sick?"

Joe smiled. "No, just off the sauce until those boys that's trying to kill me get locked up."

Greenie brought his coffee, and Joe spent the next five minutes relating the events since Wednesday as the sheriff worked on his sandwich. They both finished up at the same time.

"So Krupp is really Schmidt and Kurt Straub is the man behind it. Son, sounds like you're on to something big here. What's your angle on it?"

"Straub intends to use that dynamite. He's going to blow up anything he can with Frick's name on it, and he's not working alone. Can you spare your son-in-law some?"

"I'd say. Horace is over at the house painting my porch."

"I'd like him to visit a few of the other mines up this way—not the Frick ones—see if any of the other operators are having labor trouble or missing dynamite. Give them a heads-up to keep their eyes open, but nothing too noticeable. We don't want to tip Kurt's crew off. And spread the word about him."

"I'll see to it, and I'll put a call into Thornton if we turn anything up."

Joe finished his coffee and got up. "Much obliged, Sheriff."

Next stop, Leisenring. Joe made it there in less than an hour, finding Jim Thornton in his office, on the telephone.

"Yes. He just walked in the door. Will do." Jim hung up the phone and rose to greet Joe. "You sure got someone's attention over at Scottdale."

"Let me guess—that was Polly telling you I'm the new king of the hill."

Jim laughed. "Pretty much."

"We have a lot more than a couple of murders to contend with, Jim. You got some time?"

"Like the woman said, you have my complete cooperation."

Joe brought Jim up to date on the investigation, including what he'd just learned at Lemont. "So I figure Straub has men all over."

"What do you want me to do?"

"Let the superintendents at the other Leisenrings know what's going on. See if they know of any troublemakers, especially anyone hired in the last month or so. Tell them we're going to be bringing in more watchmen, twenty-four hours a day."

"You going to deputize men into the Frick police?"

"No, those boys stick out like a sore thumb, and they're hard to control. Besides, most of them are well-known to the workers. I'm going to round up my own special force, every old-timer I can find in the county, men that worked in the mines."

Jim nodded. "That's smart. We'll use them like gophers, have them doing maintenance jobs and the like. There's always plenty needing done. I have a few in mind already."

"Get them hired. Send their names over to Polly. We'll get them all together as soon as I can make a plan."

"OK, Joe. We're not going to let the likes of this Straub blow up our mines."

"I'll be back soon as I can. I need to get the word out to all of the mines in the Connellsville field."

Chapter 29

Joe hurried back to Connellsville, arriving at *The Courier* plant on Apple Street around three. He entered the business office, introduced himself to the woman at the front desk, and asked for Henry Snyder.

"And what would this be about, Mr. Zajac?"

"Tell him I'm Johnny's friend, come about the letter he got on Saturday."

She disappeared down the hall, and in a minute came back following an excited-looking man wearing thick glasses. He had ink stains on his shirt.

"Mr. Zajac, pleased to meet you. Come on back."

Joe followed him down the hall to a big cluttered office. The back wall was a window that looked into the printing plant. Henry cleared off a chair and motioned to it. "Have a seat."

Joe sat down and watched as Henry pulled a rag from a desk drawer and wiped his hands.

"I'm the editor and chief press repairman, it seems, Mr. Zajac."

"Joe's fine, Henry. You publish a good newspaper. I read it every week."

"I plan to publish it more frequently, maybe even a daily. I think the town's grown enough to support it."

"If not now then soon, I'm sure." Joe took out his notebook and pencil. "So Johnny says you got a letter on Saturday?"

"Sure did, and as it turns out, I'm not the only one. Similar letters were sent to every newspaper from Latrobe to Uniontown." He shuffled the stack of papers on his desk, finally finding it. "See for yourself."

Joe opened the clearly printed letter and read:

Capitalist robber barons take heed. The forces of righteousness are upon you. Your reign is coming to an end. The time has come for you and your agents to reap what you have sown. For 30 years you've planted the seeds of human misery, watered them with the sweat and blood of honest working men and grown wealthy while subjecting your labor to senseless risk and an early death. Enjoy your mansions while you can but be warned; The Harvest is coming.

We demand union representation and fair pay for all workers.

—The Reapers

"What do you make of it, Henry?"

Henry pushed his glasses up on his head. "Seems clear enough. Sounds like a threat to me."

"Ever hear tell of these folks before?"

"Never have, neither hereabouts nor any place in America."

Joe took a minute to copy the message into his notebook. He put it away, got up, and walked to the window, watching the men working in the plant.

"I'm poorly informed about such matters. I was a cop before coming out here to work for Frick, and there haven't been any strikes or such since I started. But I've come to know firsthand the hatred that working men harbor for Frick, Carnegie, and the like."

"I've been around long enough to have seen some terrible events, Joe, violent strikes with men and women getting killed on both sides. You've heard of the Homestead Strike, I'm sure."

"Some. I know men died, and someone tried to kill Frick."

"That was a historic moment in the lives of most every man working in the mills and mines of Western Pennsylvania. Frick ended up the most hated businessman in America, and Carnegie not far behind."

Joe stroked his chin, wondering how much he should tell Snyder about what was going on. Before he continued, Henry got up and joined him by the window.

"What do you think happened to that dynamite stolen from Standard?"

Joe sighed, and turned toward him. "I think it's in the hands of a madman that hates Frick with a passion." Joe looked at the note again. "You going to publish this?"

"I am, and I was already prepared to speculate that it is somehow related to your investigation."

"I know it is. I was attacked last Tuesday, and the fella that did it used the same words or damn similar." Joe took out his notebook. "He said, 'As you sow, so shall you reap' as he was trying to stick a knife in me."

"Can I use that in my story?"

Joe thought for a minute. "I don't think it matters. Write what you want. If we haven't stopped this by Saturday, you'll have a bigger story to cover." Joe headed for the door. "Much obliged to you, Henry."

Joe's stomach rumbled. He'd had a big breakfast but skipped lunch. He headed for Tony's for a bite and a chance to do some thinking. He walked into a near empty room, Tony sitting at the counter eating a bowl of soup. Joe sat down next to him.

"Back again, Joey? That breakfast you ate shoulda last you all day."

"I've been running hard, Tony. No hurry, but when you finish, how about you make me a ham sandwich?"

"You got it, boss." Tony slurped up the last of his soup, wiped his mouth on his apron, and headed to the kitchen.

Joe got out his notebook and started a list. Early the next day, starting with Alverton and Standard, he'd visit every big Frick mine in the Connellsville field. He'd meet with the superintendent, look for troublemakers, and see how fast he could get the extra watchmen in place. *I bet Caleb can find me some men.* He would let Lynch know of the plan. *I reckon there's about two dozen mines I need to visit. Take me two days.*

Somehow he needed to flush out Kurt, who could be anywhere. *I bet he's close to town and riding the West Penn all over just like I do.* Time was getting short; Kurt probably wanted to blow up Leisenring yesterday. *I'll wager he plans on striking within a week.*

Tony arrived with Joe's sandwich, and a plate of fresh tomato slices. "You gonna like the tomatoes, picked fresh this morning. You wanna beer?"

Joe shook his head. "No thanks. How about a cup of coffee?"

Tony's eyes widened, but he remained silent. He poured Joe's coffee and went to tend to the other customers.

Joe's thoughts returned to Sunday. Jake's accomplice was obviously following him and knew he was going fishing. It hadn't taken very long for the two of them to show up at the river. *How did Jake get there so fast? I'm going back out there and follow the path up the mountain.*

He put away the notebook and ate his sandwich, finishing it off quickly. After drinking his coffee, he put a dime on the counter and got up. "Got to run, Tony. See you tomorrow."

Tony gave a wave and Joe was out the door. Thirty minutes later he was at the fork in the path. Turning up the hill, he trudged on, past where he and Johnny had gone yesterday. Joe stopped, pulled out his pistol, and slid a round into the empty chamber. He'd carry it from here on.

The going got even tougher as the slope increased and the ground became rockier. Joe took his time, being as quiet as possible. The path was hard to follow over the rocks. He started breaking branches to blaze the trail back. Finally the ground flattened out a bit. Joe saw a clearing ahead, a small cabin sitting in the center. There was a stable in back and two horses in a small corral. One was saddled. A broader path led away from the cabin up the hill.

Winded from the climb, Joe stopped behind a tree and caught his breath. The woods were quiet. He could not go any closer without risking being seen from inside the cabin. His stomach churned a bit. *And I have to take a piss.* Surveillance was not his strong suit.

Now he could hear voices coming from inside and suddenly the door opened. A man walked out, his arm in a sling. Jake's partner in crime. Jake soon followed. "Be careful, Charles. You've been spotted."

"Some big brother you are, got me shot up. Momma was right."

Charles opened the corral gate, led the saddled horse out, mounted awkwardly, and rode off.

They're brothers. No wonder they look alike. Joe retreated down the hill, stopped when he could no longer see the cabin, and relieved himself. Breaking open the revolver, he removed the round from under the hammer and tucked the gun back in his pocket. By the time he got back to Connellsville, it was after five.

Joe stopped by his place, cleaned up, and changed clothes. He was looking forward to seeing Peggy, and felt edgy and happy at the same time. *Best I've felt in a long time.* He got to The Star at six, saw Johnny sitting alone at the table in the corner, and joined him.

"You're just the man I want to see."

"I came in looking for you, Joe. I've been worried about you."

"Don't blame you, buddy. I'm worried myself."

Nell showed up at the table. "Shot and a beer, Joe?"

Joe thought for a moment. "Just the beer, Nell. You got any pickled eggs back there?"

"'Course we do. How many?"

"You want any, Johnny?" Johnny shook his head.

"Two will do."

Nell left to get the beer and eggs. Joe pulled up close to the table. "I did some exploring this afternoon, back up that path by the river, past where we stopped yesterday."

"See anything sheds some light?"

Joe rubbed his hands together, smiling. "Jake and the other fellow are holed up in a cabin about a half mile further up the hill from where we stopped yesterday. And I found out that they're brothers."

Johnny smacked the table with his open hand, making beer slosh out of his glass. "Hot damn. Let's go swear out a warrant with the Connellsville Township constable and pick them up."

Nell returned with Joe's beer and pickled eggs. He took a sip and ate one egg in two bites. "Don't want to do that."

"Why not? The man tried to kill you."

"We're better off him not knowing we're onto him. Might work in our favor. I'm going back out there to watch the place some this week. You got any time to spare?"

"I can make time. What say I go out there early tomorrow and see what I can see?"

"I'd be much obliged, Johnny. Go armed. The path gets hard to follow for a bit over the rocks. Look for my blaze."

Johnny nodded, and finished his beer. "Meet me here tomorrow night." He stood to leave.

Joe rose, and they shook hands. "Be careful, my friend."

Johnny left and Joe sat back down, finishing his second egg. While sipping his beer, he looked over the patrons and watched the door. *Would Kurt show up here?*

A few minutes later Peggy walked in, looking good in a long skirt, blouse, and straw hat. She saw Joe and walked over to his table.

"Hello, Joe. I was hoping to see you here."

Joe stood up and removed his cap. "Good to see you, too, Peggy. Care to join me?"

She smiled and shook her head. "You know I rarely sit with the patrons." Heading toward her office, she said over her shoulder, "You can come on back, though."

Joe left the remains of his beer on the table and followed Peggy to the office. She took her hat off, shook out her hair, and sat down. Joe sat in the chair across the desk.

"It's only been a week since I sat here and met you for the first time. It's hard to believe."

Peggy nodded. "It's been a full week for you."

"Full and special. I can't remember when I enjoyed an evening more."

Peggy smiled, some color rising to her cheeks. "I feel the same."

They sat in silence for a moment, staring and smiling at each other. Joe smelled roses, and was delighted. Finally he spoke. "My investigation has heated up. The next few days are going to be busy. You may not see much of me."

"I understand. Just be careful."

No sense telling her about Sunday. "You can depend on that. We're still on for Saturday right?"

"We're still on."

Joe fidgeted with his hat, wanting to say more. *Time enough for that after.* He stood up to go. "I'll let you to your books, Peggy. I'm going to call it a night."

Peggy nodded, got up, and came around the desk, taking his hands in hers. "Stop by at least for a bit tomorrow. I'd like to know that you're still in one piece." She leaned forward and kissed Joe's cheek. "Now get going."

Joe gave her hands a squeeze, moved a step closer, and whispered, "Thanks for giving this old dog a run."

Chapter 30

After a restless night's sleep, Joe woke just after six. The air hadn't cooled down much overnight, and his sheet and pillow were damp. After cleaning up and dressing, Joe took a few minutes to plan his day. He'd stop by Alverton, then Standard, and then report to Lynch. This afternoon he'd visit more mines, starting near Latrobe and working south.

He pocketed his notebook and revolver and headed out. As he walked down Main, a water wagon went by, washing the recently paved street and flushing the mess into the sewer that ran to the river. *Someday we'll all be riding around in those new automobiles. No more horseshit in the street.*

It was a little past seven when he walked into City Lunch. Tony was standing behind the counter and for once wasn't smiling. Joe was about to ask Tony what was wrong when he noticed someone sitting on his favorite stool, a cup of coffee in front of him. The man had short blond hair and was staring straight at Joe; a slight smile on his thin lips. He was well-dressed and clean shaven. Joe's mind raced. *Is this the gent I've been looking for?*

Joe turned to Tony. "Morning, pal. I see I'm not the only early bird today."

Tony came over to Joe and spoke softly. "I asked him to sit somewhere else. He said it was OK, you wouldn't mind. You know him? I never see him before."

"It's a free country. I think I know the fellow. How about a stack of pancakes and a cup of coffee?"

Joe walked down the counter and sat on the third stool, leaving an empty one between him and the man. He turned the stool to face the stranger. "How do. You're Kurt Straub?"

"My, my, you are quite the detective."

"And you are one daring gent."

Kurt was holding his cup of coffee in both hands. He blew on it, then took a sip. He spoke to Joe without turning. "I told Jake you weren't just another dumb Polack."

Joe laughed and slid back his cap. Tony came out of the kitchen with his pancakes and coffee, still not smiling. He slid the plate in front of Joe, put down the coffee, and retreated to the front of the restaurant, watching the two of them. Joe turned to the counter and began eating.

Kurt set down his coffee and turned to Joe. "You've been making a nuisance of yourself, Mr. Zajac, from the moment we first observed you last week."

The man at Gmitter's was Jake's brother. Joe put his fork down, took a swallow of coffee, then turned to face the other man. They eyed each other evenly. "You're a cold-blooded killer, Kurt, or whatever your real name is. You're crazy, too. You've tried to get me twice, and I'm sitting here wondering why I shouldn't just shoot your ass and be done with it." Joe turned back to his plate.

Kurt gave a high-pitched laugh. "Take your shot, then, but be warned. You might stop me but you won't stop the harvest." He looked down the counter at Tony and waved him over. "The pancakes, if you please. A short stack." Tony nodded, his eyes darting between the two men, and disappeared into the kitchen.

"And when it comes to murder, I'm a piker compared to your beloved Mr. Frick. He's killed more men in the last twenty years than anyone in America, except for maybe his henchman Carnegie. You must be proud to work for such a magnificent fellow."

Joe finished his pancakes and coffee. He fished a dime out of his pocket and slid it under the plate. Turning to Kurt again, he whispered, "I'm determined to put an end to your scheme and see you in jail." He turned and headed for the door.

Kurt laughed again, and yelled after him, "A thousand pounds of dynamite and one stick with your name on it."

Joe strode out the door and headed to the terminal. The man's got nerve, but why show himself? Joe couldn't figure that out. What's to be gained by it? Ten minutes later he boarded the Alverton streetcar. As the trolley turned up Main, he saw Kurt standing outside City Lunch, still smiling. *He's either crazy or sure of himself.*

On the ride to Alverton Joe thought about what Kurt had said. Frick didn't pull the trigger—or in Walter's case, swing the club—but was he responsible for the deaths that occurred in his mines? Kurt thought so. *But he will not be the judge and jury. I'll be damned if I'm going to let him use the dynamite.*

It was a little after eight when he arrived at Alverton. He headed over to the supply shed, and saw Caleb walking up from the ovens. Joe waved him over. "Morning, Caleb. You're just the man I need to see."

"Morning, Mr. Zajac. Another long night at the works. I'm bushed."

"Thanks for your loyalty. I'm putting you in for a raise when I see Ed."

"Much obliged. What brings you here?"

Joe told Caleb all that had happened since Saturday. They walked up to the company store while talking, and sat down on the steps. Caleb fished out his pipe and fired up.

"You sure do live an exciting life. I'll do whatever I can to help. What's your plan?"

"We need to increase the security, but not so as anyone watching might notice. You know any old-timers, men with mine- or coke-yard experience that could use a little work?"

Caleb took a big draw and blew the smoke up in a slim stream. "Sure do. I still got plenty of old buddies hanging around the cracker barrel down the store."

"I'll see that the men are well paid, but they need to have a good head on their shoulders, and be willing to use firearms if necessary. We're going to watch the mines twenty-four hours a day. These boys we're up against might try most anything."

"I'll line some men up. Who are they to report to?"

"I'll be talking to Ed and he'll let you know tonight. Most likely I'll set up a meeting somewhere away from the mines so we can make a plan in private."

Caleb gave him a thumbs-up. "Will do, boss. Now if you're done with me, it's time for my nap."

Joe clapped Caleb on the shoulder and handed him some coins. "Here's some tobacco money, buddy." He headed for the offices.

He found Ed Connelly behind his desk. Ed looked up as Joe entered and stood to greet him. "Morning, Joe. I guess you've solved your problems with Sellers."

Joe laughed. "I guess so. Me and Mr. Lynch are getting along fine without him in the middle. I asked Mr. Lynch to keep Cliff out of my way, and he agreed."

"You'll be Sellers's boss before this is all said and done."

Joe shook his head. "I told you Saturday me and the Frick company would most likely be parting ways when this is over. I still feel that way. Meanwhile we got us a big challenge to meet."

"What do we need to do?"

"First off, you got any troublemakers you know of?"

"No more than usual. There's always a few men talking up a union, trying to organize."

"I'd like you to draw up a list of everyone you've hired since the first of July, and call the names over to Polly at headquarters. We know for a fact that the man behind all of this has planted his confederates in some of the mines. I suspect there's one here."

Suddenly, loud steps could be heard on the steps. A moment later Caleb burst into the office, a piece of paper in his hand.

"Mr. Zajac, Ed, looky here what I found over at the washhouse." He handed Joe the paper. It featured a shadow drawing of the Grim Reaper at the top, followed by the same message delivered to *The Courier*.

Joe handed it to Ed, who read it and threw it down on his desk. "What kind of horseshit is this? You see who left it, Caleb?"

"No, sir, but I seen what looks like others posted around. Want me to go check?"

Ed nodded and Caleb left.

"Well, Ed, I'd say this proves 'The Reapers' got a man here. Work up that list and start keeping an eye on them. And we're adding to the watch, too, going twenty-four hours and two men at all times."

"You bringing in Frick men?"

"No, I'm bringing in old-timers, men that know their way around and won't draw attention like a Frick bull with a gun on his hip."

Ed sat back down, rubbing both hands over his face. "OK, Joe, like Lynch said, you're calling the shots. I'll get the list together first thing."

"Caleb will be bringing some of his buddies by. Put them on the payroll and tell them we'll meet on Wednesday. I'll let you know where later on today." Joe headed for the door. "And one more thing—give Caleb a raise. He's proven his value."

Joe headed for the streetcar stop. When he got there, he saw another of the pamphlets posted on a telephone pole. No sense tearing it down. *They're likely all over.* The trolley soon arrived and he was at Standard by nine thirty.

Superintendent Caspar Brown had also gotten his orders from Scottdale. He and Joe took a walk around the works. The pamphlets had been posted here, too. "Harvest indeed," said Caspar. "These boys sound like union organizers, pure and simple."

"I wish that was the case, but I have my doubts. These fellows are as much interested in bringing Frick down. Now here's what we're going to do." Joe laid out the plan and asked for his list of new hires.

Casper shook his head. "That will be a long list here. We got men coming and going all the time."

"We need to check them all out. If you have reason to trust them, all well and good. If not, we need to keep an eye on them until this is decided. I'll be sending extra watchmen over Wednesday. Put them to work doing maintenance and keep them moving around the property."

"You're the boss on this. You really think they'd try something here?"

"Standard is one of the jewels of Frick's operation. I'd wager that the odds are high she'll be a target. Call that list over to Scottdale as soon as you can."

After shaking hands, Joe headed back to the streetcar stop. He arrived in Scottdale around eleven. Polly greeted him warmly as he walked in.

"Hello, Joe. I got the word out to every mine superintendent. You here to see Mr. Lynch again?"

"Yes, Polly, is he in?"

"He canceled a trip to Pittsburgh to meet with Carnegie so he could be here. Come on up."

Joe followed her up the steps and they headed to the conference room. "Mr. Lynch asked me to have you wait here. He'll be right with you." She closed the door and left him alone.

Joe sat down and tried to relax. His meeting with Kurt had affected him more than he realized. Leaning back in the chair, he closed his eyes for a moment.

The opening door made him jump. He was standing when Lynch walked in, carrying a familiar pamphlet. He closed the door behind him.

"Good morning, Mr. Zajac. You have some news?"

"Yes, Mr. Lynch. I see The Reapers have been to Scottdale."

"And every other Frick mine, I suspect. We've been getting reports all morning."

"The same message was mailed to every newspaper in the area. I saw one yesterday at *The Courier*."

Lynch sat down at the table and Joe joined him. "I finally found Kurt Straub, or he found me, I should say. He's getting bold."

"Did you have him arrested?"

"What for? I can't prove he's done a thing at this point. He wasn't carrying a bloody club, or a stick of dynamite. I threatened to kill him and he just laughed, said that wouldn't stop 'the harvest.'"

Lynch nodded, took off his glasses, and rubbed his eyes. "You're right, of course."

"Besides, I got an angle he doesn't know of. I found the hideout of his man Jake, the fellow that shot at me on Sunday."

"You're keeping it under surveillance?"

"Some, yes. But we need to be careful not to tip our hand. I suspect Kurt will be showing up there in due course."

"What's your plan, Mr. Zajac?"

"We're increasing the watch at all of our biggest mines and we're doing it quietly. I'm hiring a band of old-timers to do it, and need to pay them well."

"Bring on as many as you see fit and spend what you need. Just keep Polly informed."

"We need to check out every new hire since the first of July. That's when Kurt started his plan, I reckon. I figure he's got at least one man in each of the big mines, maybe more. The superintendents will be calling in names to Polly."

Lynch nodded again. "Anything else?"

"I need a place to meet with my new men, someplace away from the mines. Any ideas?"

Lynch thought for a minute, and nodded once more. "There's a grange hall not far from Pennsville—Pleasant Valley. It's close to the streetcar line. I can make it available for you tomorrow evening, say seven."

"Our scheme has to be kept quiet if it's to succeed. Don't let anyone know what we're doing, and keep up business as usual. In the meantime, we'll see if we can't get Kurt to tip his hand." Joe stood up and headed for the door. "I have a dozen mines to visit today and more tomorrow. I'll check back on Wednesday."

He paused at the door. "One more thing. If I were you, I'd advise Frick to watch himself and his family."

Chapter 31

And so it went for the rest of the afternoon. Starting near Latrobe, Joe stopped at every large Frick mine in Westmoreland County. His plan was simple and well received. All of the superintendents had old-timers to help. The men would come to the Pleasant Valley grange on Wednesday evening at seven.

Tired and grimy, Joe rolled into town near seven. He jumped off the streetcar at Brimstone Corner and headed straight to The Star. Johnny was at their usual table. Joe got a beer and joined him, quickly glancing over to see that Peggy was in her office.

Joe took a drink of his beer, smacking his lips. "Ah, that's tasty. Evening, Johnny."

"Hello, buddy. Make any progress today?"

"I'd say. Guess who I had breakfast with?"

"Don't tell me that Jake made another move?"

Joe shook his head. "Better than that. I walk in the joint and none other than Mr. Kurt Straub is sitting in my spot."

Johnny's eyes widened. He slapped the table, sloshing the beers. "Damn, Joe, what did you do?"

"Nothing. We had a little talk. I'll give him this—he's a bold one." Joe took another sip of beer. "Did you make it out south this morning?"

"Sure enough. I was there at the crack of dawn. Not much happened. I saw Jake and his brother. A couple of other men were there, too. They mostly stayed inside except for going in and out of the stable some. I could only keep watch a couple of hours, then I had to go to work."

"Can you go out again tomorrow?"

"Sure, Joe. I'll hit it early again." Johnny took a pull at his beer, then tugged a paper out of his pocket. "I took this off a pole down by City Hall." It was the Grim Reaper pamphlet. "There's more put up all over town."

Joe pulled his own copy out. "Saw this on a pole out Alverton. I was at a dozen Frick mines today and this had been posted at every one. It's the same message that was sent to *The Courier*."

"What do you make of it?"

"It's a threat, maybe a warning, and without a doubt the work of Kurt and his boys."

They sat in silence for a bit. Joe slouched back, beer in his hands. "I'm going back out there tonight."

"Be careful. That's a tricky climb even in the day. Full moon was Friday so you should have some light, long as the clouds don't roll in."

Joe nodded, finished his beer, and leaned forward. "Let's think this through from Kurt's angle. He's got twenty cases of dynamite. That's a good wagonload. He's got it stashed somewhere. Think it's up at that cabin?"

Johnny rubbed his jawline, thinking. "Might be. The stable's big enough to hold it. But what exactly is he going to do with it?"

"If I'm right, he has confederates planted all over. He was going to blow Leisenring by detonating a charge down a ventilation shaft. But Kurt most likely knows I'm on to that scheme. We've been keeping a close eye on the shafts and nothing suspicious is going on."

"Maybe he'll be planting charges inside? The best target would be the main shaft in the deep mines."

"That might be, but he'd need men with explosives experience to at least rig up the charges beforehand."

"Do you really think he's planning on blowing up mines all over the Connellsville field? That's a good long haul from Latrobe to Uniontown."

"I do, and if so, he'd need to start getting the dynamite into place in advance." Joe shook his head. "All I know is he'll make his move before too long. In a way, time is working for us."

Johnny finished his beer and pushed back from the table. "I promised Pap I'd stop by for a bit tonight. Watch yourself. I'll pick up the case again tomorrow close to dawn as I can make it."

"Much obliged. See you tomorrow."

Joe looked up to see Peggy smiling at him from her office, and it made him smile, too. *She's beautiful.* Her hair was piled on top of her head, a few strands falling over her face. Feeling energized, he headed back to her office. He entered and closed the door behind him. "No need for those barflies to be watching the show."

Peggy smiled. "Hello, Joe. Busy day?"

"Yes, indeed. I was feeling worn out but I'm better now. How about you?"

"I spent most of the day with my father. He doesn't seem to be getting much better." She closed the book of accounts in front of her. "The Star's doing well, though. The men of Connellsville sure do drink their share."

Joe laughed. "I admit I've done my part. Say, I'm hungry. You got time to join me for a bite?"

She frowned and bit her lip. "I'd love to, but I need to finish up the books and get an order ready."

"That's all right. I still got some business to attend to."

Peggy was still frowning. "I talked to Johnny when I came in. He told me about Sunday. Why didn't you let me know?"

"Didn't want you to worry about me, and don't you fret. I got this mess on the run."

Peggy finally smiled weakly. "I lost one man that was special to me. I don't want that to happen with you." She got up and came around the desk.

Joe rose to face her. They held hands for a moment, then kissed. "You're a fine woman, Peggy."

Joe could feel his face redden, surprised by his own boldness. He felt flush. Smiling, he shook his head. "I think I'm coming down with something."

They moved apart, Peggy tucking her hair behind her ear. "I'm afraid it's contagious. Get going now, but come see me again tomorrow so I know you're still alive."

Joe nodded and left the office. He stopped Nell as she walked by. "How about a roast beef sandwich and wrap it up?"

He went up to the bar and stood at the end, watching the crowd. Hiram saw him and came over. "What's your pleasure?"

"Nothing else tonight; I'm still working. Just waiting for a sandwich."

Hiram smiled as he wiped off the bar. "You know what they say about 'all work and no play,' don't you, Joe?"

Joe smiled. "That's good advice I intend to follow before too long."

Nell brought Joe his sandwich, wrapped in brown paper. He paid her, waved to Hiram, and left.

Joe stopped at his place, ate the sandwich, and changed into a dark shirt. He checked his little pistol and, after some consideration, pulled out the .45 and holster. *I need something with more punch than that little peashooter.* He left his shirt out, somewhat concealing the weapon. Pulling on his cap, he headed out for the terminal.

It was almost nine as Joe walked down Main. The street was nearly empty, the sun no longer visible in the hazy evening light. The air was still, with a few clouds drifting across the red sky, and the moon rising in the east.

Arriving at the terminal, he hopped on a South Connellsville car and twenty minutes later was walking into the woods at the end of the line. The moon cast a pale light, enough for Joe to make it up the now-familiar path. He was soon at the edge of the clearing and saw the cabin lit inside. He could hear men talking. Several horses were tied at a rail and a delivery wagon stood on the side. *Something's going on.*

A cloud drifted across the moon. Joe decided to use the darkness to crawl a bit closer, and was able to hide behind a woodpile near the side of the cabin. He sat on the ground, pulled out the .45, and slid a bullet into the empty chamber under the hammer. He sat unmoving as a half hour passed.

Voices rose and fell inside, but Joe was still unable to make out the conversation. Without warning, the front door opened and four men stepped out. *There's Kurt.* They spoke in a low voice, and then the three other men mounted up. Kurt waved as they turned their horses to leave, calling out, "Until Saturday."

Kurt went back inside and closed the door. After a few minutes, the voices quieted and the lights dimmed. Joe removed the round under the hammer, holstered the .45, and crawled back out of the clearing. Thirty minutes later he was back at Soisson Park, but just missed the last car back to town. Tired but still excited, he started walking, knowing that the events were heading to a resolution one way or another.

Chapter 32

Connellsville was a dream town, too, and here the dreams were coming true, visible in the successful businesses downtown, obvious in the elegant new houses being built on Pittsburgh Street, palpable in the spirit and energy of the people who lived there. But realization of the dreams was coming with a price, sensed in the choking air that covered the town, evident in the unclean water that filled the streams, and noticeable in the faces of the worn-out men who paid the bill.

Joe Zajac was also a dreamer. Today he was dreaming about a woman. He and Peggy were having a picnic in the park. A gingham cloth lay on the ground, a wicker basket open upon it. A plate of fried chicken sat before them as they smiled and held hands. Suddenly, behind Peggy a blond man appeared. He had something in his hand—dynamite! He lit the fuse and tossed the charge. "The harvest is upon you."

Joe woke with a start, heart racing, and in a cold sweat. Looking around, he realized it was only a dream, but one grounded in fact. Kurt Straub stood between him and whatever the future might hold for him and Peggy.

Getting up, Joe looked at his watch. It had been after midnight by the time he got to bed, but despite this he was wide awake. The watch said six thirty.

He rubbed his face and the dream faded. One thing was certain—he'd not let Kurt stand between him and his vision of a better life. He got up, completed his morning ritual, and was at City Lunch just after seven, openly wearing the .45 on his hip.

Tony was standing behind the counter, arms folded across his chest. Not smiling, but not frowning, either, he eyed Joe, eyes widening when he noticed the pistol. Looking down the counter, Joe was not surprised to see Kurt again, sitting on the third stool.

"Morning, Tony. Looks like you got a new regular." Joe walked down the counter and took his usual spot. Kurt caught his eye, and regarded the pistol on Joe's hip.

"I feel like I'm in the Wild West."

"You are. Wild Western Pennsylvania."

Kurt was already working on a plate of scrambled eggs. Joe waved Tony over. On his way down, he got Joe a cup of coffee. "I got a busy day ahead of me, Tony. How about two over easy, sausage, biscuits and potatoes?"

"You got it, boss."

Kurt spoke as he shoveled eggs. "This is a good spot, Zajac, and Tony's a fine fellow. I can see why you start your day here."

"There's none better than Tony." Joe took a sip of his coffee and turned to Kurt. "What brings you here?"

Kurt paused, fork in the air, and looked at Joe. "Even a madman has to eat."

Joe smiled. "I got a deal for you. How about you just drop that dynamite back over to Standard, no questions asked."

"And I have a deal for you. How about you help me blow the H. C. Frick Coke Company out of business? You surely understand by now that he's an evil man."

"And you're a violent murderer. Why'd you kill Walter?"

Kurt finished his eggs, and took a drink of coffee. "Walter was stupid. There was no need to kill Goretsky. He had no real proof. But Walter panicked, was going to turn himself in, and me too, most likely."

"So you just took the matter into your own hands?"

Kurt sat up straight. "I did. True justice is rare. I saved the county the trouble."

"And the next case on the docket?"

Kurt smiled, rubbing his hands together. "The workers of America versus Henry Clay Frick."

Tony showed up with Joe's breakfast. He retreated to the front of the counter without comment.

"You sound like a college man. What's behind your hatred of Frick?"

"I'm not a 'college man,' as you say, but I know enough to distinguish which side I stand on." Kurt rose and departed, handing Tony a dollar as he headed out. Turning at the door, he smiled. "See you tomorrow."

Tony looked at the bill and joined Joe. "He's a crazy man. Give me a dollar for a ten-cent plate of eggs and a cup of coffee."

"Crazy like a fox."

"I never see you wearing a gun before, Joey. Now I worry about you even more."

Joe smiled at his friend. "I worry about me, too." He finished his breakfast and headed out. "See you tomorrow."

Joe boarded a southbound streetcar, took out his notebook, and planned his day. He made a list of the ten biggest mines in the Uniontown area. He'd visit them all, then go to Scottdale. He needed the list of new hires and would talk to Mr. Lynch. He had to catch up with Johnny and meet with the old-timers at seven. Even though his day was full, somewhere in there he wanted to see Peggy. *I want to meet her father.* Writing her name in the book gave him pleasure. He underlined it twice and smiled.

The West Penn ran by every mine on Joe's list, part of the grand design for working the Connellsville Coal Field. Trains for the coal and coke, streetcars for the workers, company towns and stores all helped build the boom times of the last few years.

Joe's calls were accomplished by midafternoon. All the superintendents were on board, new hires identified and old-timers recruited. Joe decided to stop by Leisenring No. 1 on his way to Scottdale. He found Jim in his office, and tapped on the doorframe as he entered.

"Got a minute?"

Jim looked up, eyeing Joe's pistol. "Ready for action, looks like."

Joe nodded. "Prepared to defend myself." He sat down across from Jim. "You call in the new-hire list yet?"

"No, I was just getting to it." He riffled through a stack of papers and handed two pages to Joe. "Here it is, for all three Leisenrings."

Joe counted thirty-seven names, too many to watch. "We got to cull this down. If the man is known to someone, he's not likely in with Kurt. We can only watch a few men at each mine."

"OK. I got my old-timers coming by in a bit. Want to talk to them?"

"We're meeting tonight over at the Pleasant Valley grange hall, seven o'clock. They all need to show up."

Jim nodded. "Anything else?"

Joe thought for a moment before replying. "I'm trying to figure out Kurt's plan. He has the dynamite to do plenty of damage, but I doubt he has the experienced men to hit all the mines. I figure he'll go after a few of the bigger targets. Since Leisenring was his first choice, I figure it's one of them, and maybe Standard and Alverton, too."

"When do you figure he'll make his move?"

"I don't think he wants to hurt the workers. Putting out that pamphlet was both a threat and a warning, as I see it. I wager he strikes on Sunday, when the mines are empty."

"We'll be ready for him. I'll pass the word on to Number Two and Three."

Joe got up to leave. "I'll plan on being right here from Saturday afternoon on."

They shook hands and Joe left him working on the list. An hour later Joe arrived at Frick headquarters. Polly jumped up as he entered, holding some papers.

"Here's your list of new hires, Joe, and here's another of some of the men you can expect at your meeting."

"Thanks, Polly. I'm going to need you to keep in close contact with the superintendents. We'll be better prepared after tonight." He looked up the steps. "Lynch in?"

"He is, and H.C. himself, too. They're in Lynch's office. Go on up to the conference room and I'll let them know you're here."

"What's Frick here for?"

Polly just shrugged and headed up the stairs. Joe followed, went to the conference room, and stood by the window, cap in hand. A moment later Lynch walked in, followed by a shorter man with a full beard. Looking at the picture on the wall, Joe realized who it was. *Frick himself.*

The two men sat at the conference table. Lynch motioned at a chair. "Please join us, Mr. Zajac." Joe sat down with his papers in front of him, hands folded and resting on the table.

"Mr. Frick has asked to be included in our discussion."

Frick nodded. Joe nodded back and started up. "I've been busy since we last spoke, visited most every Frick operation from Latrobe to past Uniontown. I spoke with the superintendents and we're all on track."

"For the benefit of Mr. Frick, go over your plan."

Joe cleared his throat. "I'm sure that Kurt Straub is behind The Reapers. He's responsible for at least one murder and stole the dynamite, which he intends to use against the company. I think the attacks will come on Sunday."

Turning to Frick, Lynch broke in. "Straub has shown himself to Mr. Zajac but we have nothing on him." He turned back to Joe. "Go on."

"I've met him twice now. He joined me for breakfast again this morning. I suggested that if he returned the dynamite to Standard, we'd let the matter end there."

"And what was his response?"

"He tried to enlist me in his plan." Joe looked from Lynch to Frick. "I refused."

"What is your impression of the man?"

"He's trying to present this as something being done for the workers, but I don't buy that." Joe paused for a moment then fixed Frick with a cold stare. "I'd say he's motivated as much by a personal hatred of Mr. Frick here."

Frick held his stare and nodded. Joe continued, holding up his papers. "I have my list of recent hires and my old-timers brigade. We'll meet tonight. The men will be in place tomorrow. I'm guaranteeing them a month's work, even if we resolve this before."

"It's your call. Do what you need to do," Lynch said.

"I'm encouraging them to bring weapons if they're willing." Joe addressed Frick. "These boys tried to shoot and stab me. The men need to be ready to defend themselves." Then to Lynch, "They won't be carrying them around like I've taken to doing, but they need to have them handy."

Lynch nodded. "You've done a fine job with this. I'd expect you have a bright future in the business, Mr. Zajac."

Joe bit his tongue. Time enough later to decide on his future.

Lynch turned to Frick. "Henry, do you have any questions?"

Frick's hands were folded, and he was tapping two fingers together. "This fellow Straub—what does he look like?"

"He's about my age, around thirty, somewhat shorter with blond hair and blue eyes, German blood maybe. He's educated, clean, well-dressed."

"And you think I'm in personal danger?"

"Yes indeed. You're a murderer in Kurt's eyes, and he's planning your judgment day."

Frick started stroking his beard. "He's got plenty of company in that regard. Rest assured I've taken some measures. My wife and children are no longer in Pittsburgh."

Joe straightened his papers, ready to move on. "Anything else?"

Frick set his hands on the table. "As of tomorrow, the H.C. Frick Coke Company will be owned in its entirety by Carnegie Steel. And Mr. Lynch has been running the place for years. But understand, I still love the firm dearly. It's been my life for quite some time. I don't want to see it damaged. I'll be in your debt if you can stop it."

He rose, as did Lynch. They exited the room, leaving Joe alone with his thoughts.

Chapter 33

Joe left Frick headquarters and decided to grab lunch at a stand down the street. He ate two hot dogs and washed them down with a root beer. Well-fortified for the evening, he headed to Pleasant Valley, arriving after six thirty.

The hall was about a quarter mile down a dirt road from the West Penn line. The front door was open. Joe entered to find a young man pushing a broom. He stopped sweeping as Joe approached.

"Help you, mister?"

"I'm Joe. Mr. Lynch made arrangements for me to use the hall this evening."

"I'm Raymond. Thought I'd clean up a bit while I was waiting for you. What time you think you'll be finished?"

"By eight, I'd say, maybe a bit later."

"I'll be back at eight thirty to lock up." Raymond returned to his sweeping. Five minutes later he put away the broom and left.

The hall was one big room, with folding chairs set up for the meeting. A wooden table with two chairs sat up front. Joe took a seat there and arranged his papers in front of him.

Men started trickling in before seven. Seeing Caleb arrive, Joe motioned him forward. "How about you sit up here with me, Caleb? I could use some help with my papers."

"Sure enough, Mr. Zajac. Looks like we're filling up."

Joe saw Caspar from Standard and a few other familiar faces from the regular night watch, but most of the men were unfamiliar. They were definitely older for the most part, but looked to be in good shape. At 7:10 Joe rose to start the meeting. He counted almost sixty men in attendance.

"Evening, men, my name is Joe Zajac, and I work for Frick. We got us a problem and need your help. Anybody been told exactly why you're here?"

One man stood up. "Just that there's work to be had, but no particulars." The other men nodded.

"Here's the particulars. You all heard about the dynamite gone missing from Standard."

Caspar piped up, "Sure did."

"There's a man looking to use it against Frick, to settle some personal grudge, likely. I intend to see that he's stopped and need your help."

A man stood in the rear, arms crossed and looking wary. "What's the pay?"

"Generous, but before we get to that, how many of you men worked in a mine or coke yard before?" Almost every man raised his hand. Joe nodded. "Good. Now how many know how to use a firearm?"

Once again nearly every hand went up. Joe walked to the front of the table. "I need able-bodied men, familiar with mines and coke yards, to help me stop this man. He's got others working for him, and they've demonstrated a willingness to use violence. If any of you men have concerns for your safety, the work might not be for you."

The man in the rear stood again. "What's the pay?" Laughter echoed through the hall.

Joe smiled and approached the first row of seats. "The pay is two dollars a day, first week paid in advance, with twenty-four days of work guaranteed."

The man in the rear said, "And all I got to do is get shot at maybe? Sign me up, boss." The men laughed again, and mumbled their agreement. No one left the hall.

Joe walked back and forth across the room, looking various men in the eye as he spoke. "I've got twenty mines need watching, and some suspicious characters at each mine to keep track of. If you're in, I'll assign you a mine as close to your home as possible. If you need to ride West Penn, I'll pay your fare. You'll report to the mine superintendent at eight tomorrow morning, but some of you will be working nights. Be prepared to work this Sunday. Take a weapon if you have one. You'll draw your first week's pay and be assigned a cover job, most likely painting or maintenance. As we know more, we'll point out some men to you, men we suspect of being in on the scheme. You'll keep an eye out for them at all times. If you see them anyplace they shouldn't be, you'll let someone know. Other than that, you'll be walking the works, watching for anything that doesn't belong—person, package, or equipment. I'll be by each location at least once Thursday or Friday. Be prepared to give me a report." Joe walked back behind the table. "Any questions?"

The men were talking among themselves, their voices loud and excited. They pay was very good for men too old to work the hard jobs anymore. Finally, an old man in the middle stood up. "This is all well and good, but why should I risk my neck for Frick? What's he ever done for the working man except put his boot on their neck?" Several of the men shouted their agreement.

"That's a fair question, and one you'll each have to ask yourself. But remember this—if the plan succeeds and mines are shut down, Frick will still be eating. He'll still have a roof over his head. The men put out of work won't be so lucky."

The men considered this. Another fellow stood up. "How do we know this guarantee part is good? Ain't nothing in writing."

Caleb stood up. "This man's word is good, I'll speak to that."

The crowd seemed to be satisfied that one of their own backed Joe up. He gave them a minute then started up again. "I'll call your name from this list. If you're here, stand up and I'll give you your assignment. If I don't call your name, stick around and come up after. And one more thing—the true purpose of your job is to remain a secret. Anybody asks, you're hired temporary to do maintenance."

Joe split the list with Caleb, and for the next thirty minutes, they called roll and made assignments. The men drifted away after and soon it was only Joe and Caleb. "Looks like we got us an old-timer brigade for sure, Mr. Zajac. I think these fellas will do right by us."

"Time will tell. At least we've got a plan."

Joe and Caleb walked together back to the streetcar line. The sun was setting, the western sky glowing red and orange. Even out there one could smell the ovens.

The men walked silently for a while, past farms and little cottages. Caleb finally broke the quiet. "This was all fine property when I was a boy, all German farmers for the most part. The air was sweet; all the little streams ran clear. Now you'd not catch me taking a drink from any of them. And a man can't walk a mile without getting sooty. The land's been spoiled, all in the name of progress." He kicked a stone down the road. "Don't seem like progress to me."

Joe walked a step ahead, kicked the same stone a bit further. "Poland was clean but we had nothing—no work, no money, only the food we grew on our little piece of land. Winters were hard. I'd not go back."

"You're a lucky one and I guess you know it." They arrived at the stop, Joe heading one way and Caleb the other. Caleb's car came first. He gave Joe a wave as the car departed and Joe was left alone.

Joe collapsed on a bench, the nervous energy he'd been running on all day gone. In the gathering darkness, he had doubts about his strategy, but the plan was launched. He'd work out the details as best he could.

A familiar clang rang through the night. Joe saw a lone headlight glowing up the line. He rose so the operator was sure to see him.

It was just after nine when he got to The Star. Glad to see Johnny still sitting at a table, Joe grabbed a beer at the bar and joined him.

"I 'bout gave up on you, Joe. You're running late and I'm bushed."

"Thanks for waiting, buddy." Joe took a swallow of beer and set it down. "Did you make it out south today?"

"I did, at the crack of dawn again. That's why I'm worn out."

"See anything of interest?"

"The place got busy early. I saw two other men there besides Jake and his brother. I don't think either one was Kurt Straub from the way you described him. These were older men. Both had long mustaches and slicked-down hair."

"What were they up to?"

"They spent most of the time I was there in the stable. The horses were in the corral so they weren't tending to them. I was only able to stay two hours, had to get to work."

"I'd like to get in that stable."

Johnny finished his beer. "That's hard to do with them around. It's too close to the cabin." He stood to go. "I got things to do tomorrow morning before work. Dad wants me to stop by. You going out there tonight?"

Joe shook his head. "I'm dog-tired like you. I'll not be hiking up that hill tonight. Tomorrow morning will be soon enough." Joe stood and offered his hand. "I'm much obliged for your help. You got plans for Sunday?"

"Nothing yet."

"How'd you like a day of work for Frick? I need some experienced backup. You can name your price."

Johnny gave Joe a weary smile. "I'm in. And I'll let you know after what it'll cost you."

Joe watched Johnny trudge out the door, feeling as exhausted as his friend looked. Finishing his beer, he looked to the office. The door was closed, no light showing. Joe headed to the bar and waved Hiram over. "Where's Miss Patterson tonight?"

"Gone, left about eight thirty, said if you came in to tell you she was sorry but she had something to do."

"Thanks, Hi. I'll be back by tomorrow earlier, you can tell her."

Joe left The Star and walked slowly up Pittsburgh Street, feeling down because he missed Peggy. *But tomorrow is another day, and this mess won't last forever.*

Chapter 34

Mighty men do as they must, hostage to what's in their hearts.

Good or evil, their paths are fixed. Life sets the scene, each plays his part.

Joe woke with renewed vigor, anxious to get going. Last night he'd planned on being at the cabin early, but this morning changed his mind. He felt compelled to see Kurt again, found him intriguing, in fact. Joe dressed quickly, strapped on his .45, and headed to City Lunch.

He entered to find Kurt already there, sitting on the third stool, watching the door. Joe heard Tony in the kitchen. Sauntering down the counter, feeling calm and relaxed, he took his seat and turned to face his foe.

"I met your friend Frick yesterday."

"I'd love to have the chance."

"This 'Reaper' bull—I don't buy it. This is all about you and Frick."

"I admit to my personal hatred, and I have my reasons, but it's more than that."

Tony appeared with a plate for Kurt, ham and eggs today. He set it down and turned to Joe. "You guys are making me nervous. You gonna shoot each other?"

Kurt laughed. "No, Tony, I'll not bring violence to your establishment, and I'm sure your friend Joe feels the same."

Tony wiped his face with his apron. "Joey, you hungry?"

"I'm kinda keyed up today. Coffee, two donuts, and an egg sandwich wrapped up."

Tony got Joe a cup of coffee and the donuts, then returned to the kitchen.

Joe and Kurt both ate for a few minutes, then Kurt put down his fork. "Here's the heart of it, Zajac. America has plenty of rich men now, and plenty of poor ones, but few in the middle. The distance between the two is great, and therein is the essential injustice."

"Tell me, then—how is blowing up Frick's property going to help? You'll just be putting men out of work. Who's going to feed their families?"

Kurt was finishing up his meal, wiping up egg yolk with a piece of biscuit. "There will be work in the reconstruction business, and there's a larger battle to be waged. Men like Frick and Carnegie have to know they live in a world where consequences exist, even at their lofty height."

Joe shook his head. "Noble words can't justify immoral deeds. Consequences run both ways."

Kurt rose, putting a dollar on the counter. "Our courses are set, then, aren't they?" He turned to leave. "I regret that I won't be able to join you again for breakfast for a few days. Give my regards to Tony."

Kurt walked out the door as Tony brought Joe his sandwich. "Who is that guy, Joey?"

"That's the fellow behind all of the trouble. He sends his regards."

Tony's eyes widened. "He's a killer?"

Joe nodded. "But that's the last you'll see of him, I reckon."

Joe took his sandwich, paid for his meal, and walked to West Penn Terminal. Twenty minutes later he was back in the woods at the end of the line. He hiked the path to the edge of the clearing, loaded the empty chamber in his .45, sat down, and ate his egg sandwich.

Five minutes later he heard men talking. Peeking over the rise, he saw Jake and Charles with the two men Johnny had described heading for the stable. Soon they all came out, the older men carrying a canvas bag that they placed carefully in the bed of the wagon. They hitched up two horses and, after some whispered words with Jake, departed.

Damn, the dynamite is in the stable and it's on the move already.

Jake went back in the stable and came out with small pack on his back. He saddled up the two remaining horses, mounted one, and took off. *There goes some more.* Finally Jake's brother came out, arm still in a sling. He mounted the last horse and rode slowly up the track.

Joe sat still for fifteen minutes. Hearing nothing, he decided to take a chance on the cabin being empty. He had to see what was left in the stable.

He moved around the edge of the clearing until he was behind the building. There was a window in the back wall. He crawled to it and slowly rose until he could peer inside. Though the light was dim, he saw some crates. He could make out the writing on the one closest to him: VULCAN POWDER COMPANY. *I was right; it is here.*

Joe counted the crates—ten. Two were open, the rest stacked. He sat with his back to the wall, trying to decide on a course of action. Before he could think of anything, he heard a horse snort. He began backing away from the stable on his hands and knees, gun in hand. He made it to the edge of the clearing just as Jake's brother rode back in.

Joe lay low until Charles dismounted and went inside the cabin. Then he retreated to the path, and headed down the hill. Within half an hour he was back at the end of the line, a streetcar waiting there. He headed to Uniontown for some mine visits, first stop being Lemont. He found Ralph Vogel in his office at the company store.

Joe entered and had a seat. "Morning, Ralph, did my man show up?" He pulled out his papers. "Moses Whitehead?"

"He did, and I put him to work painting the supply shed. I brought on my Uncle Kutch, too." Ralph pointed to an old rifle leaning in the corner. "He showed up with that."

Joe smiled. The rifle looked to be Civil War era. "That's an old seven-shot Spencer. Looks serviceable. Let's move it into the supply shed and make sure the men have a key." Joe consulted his list of new hires. "Find anything out about Wilmer?"

"I did. He's a mite too curious for me. The fire boss says he's found him poking around places he had no business being."

Joe made a note on the list. "Make sure Moses and Kutch know what he looks like." Joe folded up the papers and stuck them back in his vest. "Here's our plan. It will be up to you to execute it. First off, I'm expecting the action to start late Saturday, any time after the men come out of the mine. It's possible nothing will happen until Sunday, but plan on being here the whole time. Enlist some of your bosses to back you up. Second, these fellows are likely armed and willing to use their weapons." Joe slapped his holster. "Arm yourself."

Ralph nodded, pulling a similar .45 out of his desk drawer.

"Another thing—I found out just this morning that explosives are already on the move. Go check Wilmer's cubbyhole and don't let him work alone the rest of the week. He might have already planted something so do some inspecting. I'd say the prime targets would be the main shaft and cage, the tipple, and the power house."

Ralph was making some notes. "OK, anything else?"

"Call Polly with any news or questions. She'll go direct to Lynch with it." Joe stood to leave. "Keep our plan as quiet as you can. We want these fellows to make their move so we can end this."

"Got it." Ralph came around and offered his hand. "Good luck to us all."

Joe nodded and left. Before leaving Lemont, he stopped by the supply shed, saw Moses painting the rear wall at a leisurely pace. "Good to see you made it. Did you draw your pay?"

Moses smiled. "Sure did, boss. Much obliged."

"You and Kutch make sure to check in with Ralph later. He'll go over the plan."

"Will do." The men shook hands and Joe was on his way.

The next five hours were much the same. Joe visited Leith, Redstone, Oliphant, Wynn, Kyle, and Youngstown. All his men were in place, all superintendents given the same orders. A few potential agitators had been identified at each mine. By three Joe was on his way back to Scottdale.

He entered Frick headquarters hungry but satisfied. His plan was far from foolproof, but the execution would be well coordinated. Polly was at her desk, frowning as he entered.

"Howdy, Polly. Why the long face?"

She leaned forward, speaking softly. "Mr. Sellers is here. He's been in with Mr. Lynch. You'll be meeting with them both in the conference room."

Joe smiled. "Old Cliff doesn't worry me anymore. Bring them on."

Feeling almost eager, Joe headed for the conference room. He smiled in at Cliff as he passed his office. Joe welcomed the showdown. He'd be done with Cliff soon enough.

Mr. Lynch soon arrived, Cliff on his tail. They both sat opposite Joe, Cliff looking smug and pleased. Joe sat quietly, waiting for someone to begin.

Lynch spoke. "Before we get started, Cliff has expressed some misgivings regarding your plan. I'd like you to hear them and express an opinion."

Joe nodded. "Sure, Mr. Lynch." He turned to Cliff. "Speak you piece."

Drawing himself up, Cliff began. "I was out at some of our properties today, talking with the superintendents, and got wind of your plan. I got to hand it to you, Zajac; it's a doozy. Where'd you dig up these codgers, the old folks' home?"

Joe smiled. "These old-timers know a damn sight more about our properties than you do. What's your point?"

"Only an idiot would turn the safety of our works over to a bunch of coots. What we need to stop this trouble is a show of force. I can have a hundred new Frick police deputies in place by Saturday morning, all packing .45s. Your boy and his henchmen will think twice about trying anything."

Joe sat silently for a bit before responding. "Anything else, Cliff?"

"We should come down hard on any men we're suspicious of. Let me talk to a few of them, and we'll soon find out where this dynamite's at."

Joe nodded at Cliff before turning to Mr. Lynch. "Cliff here is an exceptional fellow. It's rare to find a man as stupid as he looks."

Lynch smiled in spite of himself. Cliff blew up. "You need to fire this wiseass and let me handle things the right way."

Lynch held his hands up, palms out. "All right, gentlemen, that's quite enough. We're all colleagues here, simply trying to arrive at a sound decision about our course of action. Mr. Zajac, what's wrong with Cliff's plan?"

Joe took a calming breath; he'd not let Cliff plant the needle. "What's wrong is that we want these plotters to make their move. We'll get them out in the open and recover the explosives. All he'll do is delay the day of reckoning. We can't keep our mines ringed with armed men forever. And as for Cliff strong-arming information out of these men we suspect, well, they're just that at this point—suspects. We got nothing on them yet."

Lynch nodded. Cliff muttered, "Horseshit."

Joe felt bulletproof. "And as for finding the dynamite, I've already located quite a bit of it. We'll stop it from ever being used."

Lynch turned to Cliff. "I'm inclined to agree with Mr. Zajac. His plan isn't perfect, but I trust him. Thank you for your advice, Cliff."

Cliff knew he was being dismissed. Red-faced, he glared at Joe before stomping out of the room, slamming the door behind him.

Lynch shook his head. "Cliff is past his prime, I fear. Now where do we stand?"

Joe spent the next ten minutes reporting on the events of the last day, including the marching orders he'd given the superintendents. Lynch listened without comment, nodding occasionally. When Joe was done, he offered one observation: "I'd watch the pumps, too. It wouldn't take long for some of these mines to fill up without them."

They ended their meeting with Joe promising to come by the next day for one last report before the weekend.

Joe hurried out the door with a wave to Polly. Once again he stopped at the lunch counter before boarding the streetcar. He had to talk to Johnny and definitely didn't want to miss Peggy again. He wanted to move their dinner to the next evening, because it looked like Saturday night he'd be at Number One.

It was six thirty when he hopped off the streetcar. Entering The Star, he was glad to see Johnny at his table and Peggy in her office. He grabbed a beer and sat down with Johnny.

"I got good news and bad news, Johnny."

"About the cabin?"

"Yeah. I went up early and everyone left. I was able to get a look-see inside the stable. I counted ten cases of dynamite inside."

"Just like we figured it was. What's the bad news?"

"Two crates have been opened. Those older fellows must be his bomb makers. They left in the wagon with a big canvas bag, and Jake hightailed out of there with a pack on his back."

"So they're moving it closer to the mines, or maybe even planting some of the bombs."

"What should we do about it, you think?"

Johnny stroked his chin. "We can't let it all get out of there."

"But I don't want to jump the gun before they've made their move. I know they're planning a meet Saturday. Maybe we wait until then to go after them. I'm going out there again tomorrow morning and see what I can see."

"OK. There's some risk but I see what you're getting at." He looked at his watch. "Time to scoot. I'm meeting a friend for supper. It's pot roast night at The Dinner Bell." He gave Joe a wink, drained his beer, and took off. Joe finished his and headed for Peggy's office.

She looked up smiling as he entered and closed the door. Her smile disappeared when she saw the .45 on his hip. "What's that all about, Joe?"

"Just being careful, is all." He sat down at her desk. "Sorry I missed you last night. I had a late meeting."

Peggy put down her pen and closed her ledger book. "When will this all be finished? I'm worried to death over it."

"I'm betting it's all resolved by Sunday, and don't you worry too much. I got a good plan and good men helping out."

She shook her head but remained silent.

"One thing, though, we have to change our plans for Saturday. I'll likely be at Leisenring all night and Sunday to boot. You have plans for tomorrow?"

"No." She brightened. "Can I make you dinner?"

"You sure can. What time should I come over?"

"Not at my place, at Dad's, say seven. I'd like you to meet him."

Joe beamed at her. "I've been thinking I'd like to make his acquaintance. What's the address?"

"Two twelve Patterson Avenue on the South Side, a block up from the streetcar line."

"Dinner with the Pattersons of Patterson Avenue. Sounds like I'm moving into high society."

Peggy came around the desk and took Joe's hands as he rose. "I don't know about that, and my cooking is only fair, but I'm looking forward to it." They kissed. "Now get going. And please don't get hurt."

Joe strolled home, walking on air.

Chapter 35

Duty a stern master is, calling men to pay the price.

Those that sense it have no choice but to respond, and toss the dice.

The whistle of a passing train roused Joe early from a deep and dreamless sleep. Awake but not wanting to get up, he lay unmoving, eyes closed. His mind floated, detached from his body. Scenes drifted in and out of his vision, moments from his life, both good and bad. At first pleasant, the visions became too intense. Joe shook himself and rose.

Sitting on the edge of the bed, head in his hands, Joe's mind worked to grasp the here and now. The fog receded and he got up. He'd been a fortunate fellow so far, like Caleb said. *Let's see if my luck can hold through Sunday.*

Joe got ready to face the day, still feeling adrift. With little awareness of the walk, he found himself at the door to City Lunch. Once again the first customer, he entered an empty room and made his way to his stool. Tony heard the bell and came out of the kitchen. His smile back in place, he poured Joe a coffee.

"Hello, Joey. Everything back to usual today, your killer no show up."

"That's good, Tony," Joe replied in a monotone. "I've had enough of him."

Tony studied Joe's face. "What's the matter, you no sleep good?"

"Slept fine, but the last two weeks are catching up with me."

"I got just the thing to pep you up, a special treat. I'm making waffles today. I got one coming right up for you." He returned to the kitchen as Joe nursed his coffee.

A few other patrons came in, regulars Joe recognized but didn't really know. The door opened again and in walked Henry Snyder carrying a paper. He saw Joe and came down to join him.

"Good morning, Mr. Zajac. Johnny told me I'd likely find you here. I wanted to show you today's edition, hot off the presses."

Joe took the offered paper and opened it to the front page. The headline story was not a surprise: "New Group Threatens Violence." Beneath that: "Frick Mines Targeted." The message from The Reapers was reproduced, and Joe was quoted as saying, "Missing dynamite is in the hands of a madman."

Joe put down the paper as Tony brought his waffle, golden brown and buttered, with two fat sausages. Tony placed a little pitcher of warm maple syrup beside it.

Henry eyed the plate. "I'll have the same, Tony."

Joe poured syrup over his waffle, then turned to the editor. "I got to hand it to you, Henry. You're one hell of a newspaperman. You'll be selling out today's edition, I suspect."

"We printed twice as many as we usually do. What with the pamphlets showing up all over, it's the biggest story we've had in quite some time."

Joe ate his waffle while reading the rest of the story, finishing both at the same time. *God bless Tony*. Between the waffle and the newspaper, Joe had finally shaken off his stupor. In its place were peace and a clear focus on what he needed to accomplish. Draining his coffee, he stood to leave. "Much obliged for you showing me the paper, Henry. Come Monday we'll know how it ends."

"I'll want to hear the story."

"You'll be the first to hear it." With a wave to Tony, Joe left for the terminal. He boarded a South Connellsville streetcar, traveled to the end of the line, and headed for the woods.

Looking up the hill, he saw a wagon coming down a rutted lane. It was being carefully driven by the men Joe thought of as the bomb makers—the old men with slick hair. Joe watched as they came to the end of the lane and turned up past the park toward town. He saw a big canvas sack on the bed as they headed away.

More explosives on the move. Joe hated to think where they might show up. *Maybe I should have shut it down. How much is still up there?* He hiked down the path and climbed rapidly to the clearing, where voices could be heard coming from the cabin. Joe sat down just over the rise.

After ten minutes Joe grew impatient. The voices had quieted down but the men were still in the cabin. *If they'll stay in there, I can take a look.* He began moving around the edge of the clearing toward the stable. When he was the closest he could get, he moved at a low crouch to the stable window. Peeking in, he was relieved to see seven crates still there.

A screen door banged, and Joe heard men walking toward him. "How long you gonna be, Jake?"

"I aim to be back by midafternoon. The men won't start showing up much before seven."

"Bring some bread."

"I will, Charles. You already asked."

Joe sat, back pressed against the wall, his pistol drawn. *He's leaving Charles alone.*

"You forgot yesterday. I'm tired of staying up here."

And Charles doesn't sound so tough.

Joe heard a horse whinny, then a "giddyup." Jake had departed.

Joe glanced around the corner just in time to see Charles, his arm no longer in a sling, reenter the cabin. Joe backed out of the clearing, returned to the path, and hiked back to Soisson Park. He had a few minutes until the car arrived. Sitting on a bench at the stop, he got out his notebook and started a fresh page, titled "Schedule."

1. Find Johnny
2. Scottdale
3. Mine visits
4. Dinner with Peggy and Pap
5. Observe cabin, count heads
6. Saturday dawn—raid camp

He had a full day. *We'll give the boys a big surprise.*

Entering the police station, Joe found Johnny talking to the chief. Lawrence Kelly was a big fella with red hair and freckles, about forty years old, Joe figured, but looked much younger. He and Joe had only met on a few occasions.

"Morning, fellas."

The men turned to him. "Say, Joe, we were just talking about you. Been back to the cabin?"

"I have. How about we talk in your office, Chief?"

"Come on."

Joe followed the men down the hall to a spacious office on the corner. The river and tracks were visible through windows on the rear wall. The three of them sat around a small table in the corner.

Chief Kelly started off. "Johnny's been keeping me up on your investigation. From the sounds of it, events are coming to a head."

"They are, and I need your help." Joe related the events of the morning. "So here's my line. I'm going back up there tonight to see how many men we're dealing with. Once we know that, we'll need to pull together a crew. We can't let the rest of that dynamite, or those fellas, out of town tomorrow. Too much of it has already been moved out, and we can round up a bunch of the gang in one fell swoop."

The chief nodded. "We can help, but the cabin is in Connellsville Township. We'll need to get the constable involved and let Sheriff Miller know, too."

"Sheriff Miller knows me and will help. Someone with authority needs to take the reins, else I'll have to get a gang of Frick police deputies involved. I'd rather avoid the bloodshed."

The chief went over to his desk, where he had his own telephone. "I'll call the sheriff. You got a battle plan?"

"I doubt we'll be dealing with more than a dozen men, but they'll likely be armed. Let's aim for twenty men on our side. We need to be in place by dawn so we meet here at five. Six of us will come up below the cabin and the rest spread at the head of the lane. Soon as the men start to leave, we'll move in."

Chief Kelly made a few notes. Picking up the phone, he gave Joe a thumbs-up.

Joe turned to Johnny. "What time do you get off today?"

"Six."

"I'll meet you here at five thirty." Joe pulled out his pocket watch. "I need to get moving. Lynch needs to know what I'm up to."

Joe walked into Frick headquarters at noon. Polly gave him a big smile and handed him a several sheets of papers. "These are all for you, reports from the mines."

Joe tucked them in his vest. "Thanks for all you're doing, Polly. Is Mr. Lynch in?"

"Sure is, and he's been looking for you." She crooked her finger at Joe and headed upstairs. Joe followed and headed to the conference room, where Lynch soon joined him, carrying his own notebook.

"Good morning, Mr. Zajac. Where do we stand?"

Joe liked working with Lynch, appreciated his no-bull style and concentration. "I was back to the cabin this morning. Seven full cases of dynamite are still there. You can depend on it never being used."

"What's your plan?"

"Connellsville's Police Chief Kelly is organizing a force. Kurt's men are assembling there tonight, but by seven tomorrow morning they should all be in custody, and that store of dynamite recovered."

Lynch made some notes. "You'll be with them?"

"Those boys tried to get me twice. I wouldn't miss it."

"What are your plans for the rest of today?"

"I'll be going to more mines up this way, make sure every super-intendent understands our scheme. Tomorrow after the raid, I'm going to Leisenring."

"We still have no idea where the rest of the dynamite is?"

Joe shook his head. "It's wherever Kurt is holed up."

Lynch looked through his papers. "Here's something for you. We've already stopped one man, Mr. Steward of Lemont. He was found to have a charge in his possession, and is now residing in the Uniontown jail."

Joe rubbed his hands together. "I knew he was hooked up in this."

"It was your old-timer that got him. Mr. Whitehead."

"So far so good, then." Joe checked his pocket watch. "Time for me to get moving. Anything else?"

"I'd like a report and final meeting after the raid tomorrow. We can meet in Connellsville."

"Meet me at City Lunch at ten, corner of Main and Arch across from City Hall."

Lynch and Joe stood. Lynch put his hand on Joe's shoulder. "You've got a good head on you, Mr. Zajac. Best of luck."

Joe left the Frick offices, spending the rest of the afternoon visiting mines in Westmoreland County: Hostetter, Whitney, Standard, Alverton, and a few of the smaller operations. All the superintendents were well prepared, with new hires and critical areas of the properties under surveillance. All would have their men in place from six in the evening on Saturday through Sunday night. With nothing left to do at the mines, Joe headed back to Connellsville, arriving at City Hall just before five thirty. Johnny was sitting on the steps, and stood when he saw Joe approach.

"Hello, Johnny. What's news?"

"The chief was able to round everybody up. Looks like we'll have about two dozen men, counting us. Sheriff Miller will be heading up the force."

"He probably figures it'll help his reelection campaign."

Johnny laughed. "He'll be Sheriff of Fayette County until he kicks the bucket."

"Everything's ready on the Frick end. Lynch is coming to town tomorrow after the raid." Joe pulled out his pocket watch. "Can you go out to the cabin with me tonight?"

"Sure. What time?"

"Say around ten. How about I meet you at the terminal?"

"OK. See you then." They shook hands and went their separate ways.

Chapter 36

Who's to say why two attract: a smile, sweet words, shared hope and sorrow. Of human nature love's a fact.

Two people bond and face tomorrow.

Joe was now in a big hurry. He still had to get cleaned up and be at Peggy's in about half an hour. He ran up Main to his place, washed, changed clothes, and was back at the terminal just before six. Fifteen minutes later, cap in hand, he was knocking at the door at 212 Patterson Avenue, a two-story yellow brick home with a wide front porch.

A smiling Peggy opened the door, wearing a lace apron. "Welcome to the Pattersons', Joe." She stood aside and waved him in, touching his arm as he passed. "Daddy's in the parlor."

Joe followed her down the hall and into the parlor. A frail-looking man sat in a red easy chair, his feet on an ottoman. A cane rested against the chair. He was reading *The Courier*.

"Daddy, I'd like to introduce you to Joe Zajac. Joe, meet Andrew Patterson, my wonderful father." Mr. Patterson put down the paper and rose, his hand extended. "Welcome, Joe, but just call me Andy."

"How do, Andy. Thank you for having me to dinner."

Peggy pushed a strand of hair off her face with the back of her hand. "If you two will excuse me, I need to finish dinner." She left them in the parlor.

Andy gave Joe a once-over. "Have a seat, young feller."

Joe sat on the sofa. *Maybe I'm not too old to play the parlor game.* The room was familiar looking. The sofa matched the easy chair, doilies adorned the end tables and furniture tops. A gas fireplace was in the center of the far wall, a maroon carpet on the floor.

Joe was nervous, turning his cap around in his hands. Then, feeling self-conscious, he put it down on the end table. He finally fixed Andy with a firm stare. "You have a wonderful daughter."

Andy smiled. "Don't I know it? She's been the best child a father could hope for. Her well-being is my main worry."

Joe relaxed a bit. "We only met two weeks ago, but I already recognize that she's a special woman."

"She's got herself a strong personality, Joe. Can be stubborn as a mule, too. She's doing a man's work, running The Star since I took sick."

Peggy returned to the parlor, apron off and looking great in a long blue dress. "And who's to say what a man's work is? I'll not be living my life ruled by such thinking. Come on, then, dinner is ready."

Joe and Andy shared a smile, rose, and followed her into the dining room. A pot roast and all the fixings sat on the table. The three chatted through dinner, Joe enjoying stories from Andy's youth.

After apple pie for dessert, Andy excused himself. "That was quite the meal, honey. If you two don't mind, I'll be heading up for a little rest."

Peggy accompanied Andy to his room. When she returned, Joe had already started clearing the table. Together it took only a few minutes to finish the job. "It's good to see a man not afraid to pitch in around the kitchen."

Joe leaned against the sink, drying his hands on the dish towel. "After my mother died, I learned how to cook, clean, and even sew up holes in my socks."

Joe followed Peggy back to the parlor, where they sat together on the sofa, quiet for a moment. Then he took her hands in his, and they gazed into each other's eyes. First she smiled; then he laughed, which made her start giggling.

"You make me feel like a schoolboy, Peggy."

"You make me feel like an ingénue, and I like it."

Joe moved closer, putting one arm around Peggy, the other still holding her hand. She leaned over, her head resting on his shoulder. They sat for a bit, passion building. Joe put his hand under her chin, tilted her head up, and kissed her, not the quick pressing of lips they'd shared before, but a deep tender joining that left both breathless. They broke it off and regarded each other almost warily before embracing again.

After finally breaking apart, Peggy gave Joe another smile. "You'll think me forward, but I'm too old to play the schoolgirl."

"And I'm way past playing parlor games."

For the next hour they sat on the sofa, talking about life and sharing tender moments. Then he saw by the clock on the mantel it was nine. *Time to go get ready to meet Johnny.*

Joe moved away from their embrace, sitting forward on the edge of the sofa. "I need to leave, Peggy."

"Where are you going?"

"There are some ruthless men that need to be watched. Johnny and I are going scouting."

"When will I see you again?"

Joe shook his head wearily. "Maybe not until Monday. If we're lucky I'll be by Sunday evening, if that's fitting."

Peggy handed him his cap. "It is more than fitting. I'll be anxious until this trouble is over." They stood, walked to the door, and, with one final embrace, parted.

Joe hurried down Patterson Avenue, deciding to walk back downtown. The night air would help clear his head. *Damn, I got it bad.* Twenty minutes later he was back outside City Hall waiting for Johnny, wearing his .45. Soon Johnny came riding down Main Street astride a big black horse, with another tied and following. Joe walked to the corner to meet him.

"No streetcars tonight?"

"I borrowed these from Pop. We'll make better time."

Joe mounted the other horse and they trotted through Arch Street. Fifteen minutes later they were tying up the horses in the woods and heading up the hillside. Climbing quietly, they soon reached the edge of the clearing.

Looking over the rise, Joe saw a small fire burning in front of the cabin. A group of men sat around it, talking in low tones. Two more men arrived on horseback, tied up their horses, and walked to the fire. One of the men was Kurt Straub.

Leaning toward Johnny, Joe pointed and whispered. "The short one's Kurt." Kurt walked into the cabin and came out with Jake, Charles, and several others. As they all gathered around the fire, Joe counted fifteen men. Kurt stood on the cabin steps and addressed the crowd.

"Men, we stand on the brink of an important moment, brothers joined together against injustice." A few of the men cheered; most sat quietly.

Kurt walked down the steps, joining the men around the fire. All stood together. Kurt looked around at them, and began again. "Soon we strike a blow against those that would enslave the powerless, robbers growing rich while labor pays the price. Soon Frick and Carnegie will pay the price, blood for blood. It's time for the harvest." This time the men cheered, fists shaking.

Joe got goose bumps. Kurt was a powerful speaker.

"I'm honored to know each and every one of you. Now, let's prepare for the reaping."

Kurt returned to the cabin. Over the next half hour, the men went in two at a time, coming out after about five minutes, each carrying a piece of paper. They began laying out bedrolls, preparing to spend the night.

Joe nudged Johnny and pointed down the hill. They retreated silently and were soon on their horses heading back to town.

"I tell you, Joe, that fellow Straub would make a fine preacher."

"He's got the passion of a true believer, and his hatred gives resolve."

They rode quietly to Johnny's, where they dismounted and tied the horses to the porch rail.

"I hope he's there tomorrow, Johnny."

Chapter 37

The conflict starts. Surprise is ours, men taken at first light.

Foul deeds upset, good wins the morn, and we push on with the fight.

As it turned out, Kurt was not there Saturday, but at five in the morning Joe was still hopeful. Two dozen men were assembled in the police station, Sheriff Miller standing in front of them, a wad of tobacco in his cheek. All were armed, most with a rifle and pistol. Joe had his holstered .45 and the smaller pistol tucked in his belt. He recognized Miller's son-in-law, Horace Etling, but the rest were strangers.

"All right men, listen up," Sheriff Miller said. "There are more than likely about fifteen men up at the cabin. Here's the idea. Joe will take four men and approach from downhill. They'll cut off any retreat in that direction. The rest of us will assemble at the cabin road, block it with a wagon, and move in a line down the hill. If we're lucky we'll catch them groggy. If not, we bring heavy force of arms to bear. Don't take any chances with these boys, and try not to shoot up the stable, else we'll all be knocking on the pearly gates. Any questions?"

The men stood silently, grim-faced. Miller nodded, and launched a stream of spit into the spittoon. "Let's go shut 'em down."

The team left, some boarding wagons, the rest on horseback. It took them fifteen minutes to get to the end of the streetcar line, where they split up. Joe and Miller conferred.

"How long for you to get in position Joe?"

"Give us twenty minutes. We'll be watching for your move."

They shook hands and Joe headed into the woods with his squad. Soon they were back at the edge of the clearing, Joe peeking over the rise. He saw that most of the men were still down, only one up drinking coffee. He heard a whinny and saw Jake in the corral, saddling up a horse. He ducked down and whispered to Johnny, "I'm going over by the stable."

Johnny nodded and Joe started moving in that direction, crouched low. Before he could get there, he heard a shout, "Intruders!"

The one awake saw the men advancing and pulled out a pistol, but it was too late. The men moved in loudly, shouting, "Sheriff! All surrender!"

Joe watched Jake enter the stable and come out with a rifle. Jake knelt down and fired, hitting one of the sheriff's men. Gunfire erupted, and the first man with the pistol went down, struck in the leg and shoulder. The sleeping men stayed down, arms up.

Sheriff Miller led the charge. "Watch out for the stable." Some of the bullets sent Jake's way were hitting the building. Joe ran faster, getting a line on Jake. At a point where he could safely fire, he knelt and squeezed off two shots, both missing their mark. Jake wheeled and returned fire, forcing Joe to roll down the hill. He got up and moved around the clearing, getting behind the stable.

Gunfire burst from the cabin, and the sheriff's men dove for cover. Then Johnny and his men joined in, striking the cabin with a volley of fire. Windows exploded and a man howled. The gunfire from the cabin stopped.

Miller called from the edge of the clearing, "You men inside come out hands up. You are surrounded."

After a minute, the front door opened. Four men walked out as directed.

Joe heard a horse snort. Above him, Jake was riding all out and right toward him, rifle raised. Jake squeezed off two shots as Joe dove behind a fallen tree. With a "hiyah!" he slapped the horse and rode through the woods, heading farther up the mountain and away from the cabin. Joe took a few futile shots at him, then headed for the cabin.

Sheriff Miller was strutting around the yard, watching his men tie up the prisoners. Joe counted thirteen men, including Charles, who'd been hit while inside the cabin. The bullet struck him in the same shoulder Joe had got him in, and the wound was bleeding badly.

"Go bring the wagon down, Horace. We'll see if we can't get this one to the hospital before he bleeds to death."

Joe clapped Miller on the shoulder. "Good work, Sheriff. Too bad the big bird already flew the coop."

The wounds of the first man with the pistol were minor, as was that of the sheriff's man Jake hit. The plan had succeeded better than expected.

Eventually Miller had his prisoners tied up and strung together on a long line. He prodded the first with his rifle. "Get going." They trudged up the hill, heads down, Miller's men riding beside them.

"We'll clean up here, Zajac. You got things to do, so go ahead and do them."

"Leave a few men here with the dynamite until we can get it moved out."

Miller nodded, and headed back up the hill. Joe decided to inspect the stable.

Inside he found a long table, a dozen assembled charges sitting on it. Two of the dynamite cases were empty; the third had a few sticks still in it. The other seven were unopened. *He had more dynamite than he knew what to do with.*

When Joe left the stable, two men were already standing outside the door. He entered the cabin, which had one big room with a sink and wood stove. He poked around the mess until he found Jake's duffel. He dumped it out and picked through the contents, finding a Frick ID card issued to Jacob Krouse. *So that's his last name.* He'd worked at Standard at some point.

What I need is to find out where the rest of the dynamite is stashed. He looked through some papers. One was a map of the Frick mines in Fayette and Westmoreland County. Looking closely, Joe noticed that some were marked, either circled or underlined. He counted six of each. Standard, Alverton, Whitney, Hostetter, United, and Calumet were underlined in Westmoreland County. Lemont, the three Leisenrings, Oliphant, and Redstone were circled in Fayette County. Joe stuffed the map inside his vest and quickly looked through the rest of Jake's belongings. After finding nothing of importance, he left the cabin and found Johnny waiting.

"Ready to get out of here, Joe?"

"Let's go. I want to catch up with Charles."

The two returned to their horses and rode out of the woods at the end of the line. They were just in time to see the twelve men come out of the road, shuffling along. Sheriff Miller was already waiting at the streetcar stop, talking to the operator, as they passed by. "West Penn's going to give these boys a ride to the clink, Joe."

"Where's the wounded man?"

"They took him to South Side Hospital."

Joe and Johnny rode to the hospital and found Charles being treated, one of Miller's men at his side. The doctor had stopped the bleeding but Charles was near delirious. "Come back in an hour or so. He should be somewhat recovered," the doctor said.

The men went to Johnny's house, left the horses, and walked down to the terminal. The streetcar with the prisoners had just arrived. Sheriff Miller had them all lined up again and marching up Arch Street to City Hall, with the sheriff in the lead and Horace Etling following. A crowd of boys tagged along, hooting and hollering. Joe and Johnny fell in behind the procession.

Chief Kelly stood waiting for them, with Henry Snyder standing at his side. A small crowd had gathered. Sheriff Miller ascended the steps and spoke in a loud voice. "Chief Kelly, would you be kind enough to lock up these prisoners until such time as they can be moved to the Uniontown jail?"

"Sure, Sheriff. They'll think twice about causing trouble in Fayette County again."

The crowd cheered, Miller tipped his hat, and the prisoners were led inside. Joe watched as Henry Snyder interviewed Miller, who gave a reasonably accurate account of the successful raid. When they finished, the newspaperman scanned the crowd, saw Joe, and headed his way.

"Hello, Joe. Looks like you nipped your troubles in the bud. Congratulations."

"There's no congratulating to be done yet. We've only accounted for half the dynamite, and the man that hatched the plot is still free."

Joe turned and left the festive crowd, crossed Main, and entered City Lunch. Tony stood smiling behind the counter.

"You catch the bad guys, eh, Joey? Good work."

Joe just nodded, walked down to his seat, and flopped down. Tony followed with a cup of coffee. "You hungry?"

"I'm getting there, my friend. How about a short stack?"

"You got it, boss man."

Joe pulled the map out and spread it on the counter. *These have to be the targets. But why the different markings?*

Joe heard the doorbell tinkle, and saw Mr. Lynch enter, searching the room. Joe stood, caught his eye, and waved him back.

Lynch was casually dressed, for the moment not looking like the president of the largest coke manufacturer in the world. He came over to Joe.

"Good morning, Mr. Zajac."

"Morning, Mr. Lynch." They shook hands and sat down.

"How goes your plan?"

"So far so good, but Kurt Straub wasn't there. We recovered seven full cases of dynamite and some already rigged to explode. We need to get a Frick crew up to the cabin."

"All right. Any of the men injured?"

"One on our side, not serious. Two on the other, with one in the hospital."

Tony arrived with Joe's pancakes. He put them on the counter and turned to Lynch. "You need a coffee, my friend?"

"Yes, indeed, and your pancakes, if you please."

Tony served Lynch his coffee and returned to the kitchen.

Lynch added cream and sugar to his coffee and took a sip. "No deaths in the action is welcome news. Have you interrogated the men you captured?"

"Not yet. Kurt's lieutenant escaped. The guy's brother is the fellow in the hospital. I'm going to question him as soon as he's able to talk."

Joe finished his pancakes, and, pulling the map out of his vest, turned to Lynch. "I found this in the cabin." He spread the map out on the counter.

Lynch pulled out his glasses and bent to examine it. "Looks like we know what mines he's targeted."

"Most likely we do, but why the different markings?"

Lynch pondered that for a moment, drinking his coffee. "The dynamite was divided, and the ringleader of this wasn't at the cabin. He's most likely with the remaining dynamite. I suspect that these targets have been divided by county, half for him and half for his lieutenant."

Joe smiled. "You'd make a good detective, Mr. Lynch." "Now if we only knew where the men you stopped were heading." Tony arrived with Lynch's pancakes, and he dug in with gusto. "Mrs. Lynch rarely makes these."

Joe folded the map and returned it to his vest. "When you're finished, we'll head back to the hospital and see what we can get out of Charles Krouse."

Thirty minutes later they arrived at South Side Hospital. They found Charles in a private room, awake but in obvious pain. His guard spoke up as Joe and Lynch entered. "This here's one mean pup. Hasn't stopped running his mouth since he woke up."

"Take a break, buddy." Joe said. "We want to have a little talk with your prisoner."

"I'll go grab a bite."

The guard left as Joe and Lynch stood at the bed, one on each side. Charles eyed them warily.

"You can both go to hell. I'm not talking."

Joe shook his head. "I'm sorry about your brother. He should have given himself up."

"What are you talking about? He got away."

Joe shook his head again. "I clipped him. We found his horse, saddle all bloody. We're looking for his body now."

Charles wilted, his eyes glistening. "I told him running with Straub would lead to no good."

"You'll be moved to Uniontown tomorrow and charged with attempted murder."

Charles sat up a bit, wincing. "I didn't try to kill anybody."

"You and Jake tried to kill me on Sunday."

"That was all Jake's doing."

"That's not the way I saw it."

Charles slumped back down, eyes closed.

"Where's Straub holed up?"

"Only Jake knew that. I never was to his hideout."

"You were going to hit the Westmoreland mines with Jake?"

Charles opened his eyes and nodded.

"You cooperate with the investigation and I'll forget about Sunday."

Joe and Lynch stayed with Charles until the guard returned, then walked back downtown.

Lynch checked his watch—just past twelve thirty. "That was a good piece of work back there. I'd not have thought to play it like that."

"I've always been good thinking on my feet. We can't let our guard down entirely, though. Jake's still out there, probably with dynamite, too."

"What's our next move?"

"Back to City Hall. Let's see what we can find out from our prisoners."

Chapter 38

No one sees the future. You live life day to day.

But lucky is the person that finds the righteous way.

Downtown Connellsville had a festive air about it on the afternoon of Saturday, August 18. Main Street was abuzz with news of the raid. A small crowd of men was still gathered at City Hall, smoking and talking. Joe and Lynch strode through them, entered the building, and headed for the chief's office. They found him sitting at his desk. Joe rapped on the doorframe and Kelly waved them in.

"Chief, I'd like you to meet Tom Lynch, president of H.C. Frick."

Kelly stood and extended his hand. "How do, Mr. Lynch." Turning to Joe, he said, "I got some news for you. We've questioned each of the prisoners. Quite a few are ready to tell the tale." He picked up a stack of small cards from his desk. "And looky here, most all of them were carrying these."

Joe took the cards and shuffled through them. Frick IDs, each man working at a mine in Westmoreland. "This ties in with what we learned from Charles Krouse, the wounded prisoner. These fellows were heading to Westmoreland County." Joe handed the stack to Mr. Lynch. "Let's make a list and see if any match up with the men we've been watching."

Joe turned back to Chief Kelly. "You'll need to keep a guard on Krouse overnight. We should be able to lock him up tomorrow."

"Will do. Anything else?"

"Where's Johnny?"

"He's having lunch somewhere, said he'll meet you here at three."

Joe and Lynch sat at the chief's table, made their notes, returned the ID cards to Chief Kelly, and left City Hall. Pausing on the steps, Joe made their final plan. "Take those names back to Scottdale and check them against our list. Get word to the mines involved. They still need to keep alert, but I suspect most of the mines are safe. We've only Jake and Kurt to worry about."

Lynch nodded. "Where do you think Jake will strike?"

"The jewel of the Frick crown—Standard."

"You've been right so far. How about we move some of the old-timers from the other mines there?"

"Makes sense. Send Cliff over, too."

Lynch smiled. "That should keep him busy." They shook hands and Lynch turned to leave, adding, "The company is in your debt for the first-rate work you've done."

Joe watched Lynch cross Arch and head for West Penn Terminal. It was two o'clock. *Time to pack my bag and head to Leisenring.*

A half hour later, bag in hand, Joe was back at City Lunch. A few late diners sat at the tables with the checkered cloths. The two ceiling fans turned slowly. Tony stood smiling behind the counter, red stains on his white apron. Joe walked down the counter to his spot and Tony followed.

"I think you must be hungry again, eh, Joey?"

"Sure am. You know me well. What's the special today?"

He pointed to his apron. "What do you think? Spaghetti and meatballs."

Joe laughed, relaxing a bit for the first time that day. "Ah, the rhythms of life. I'll have it, and a glass of milk."

"You got it, boss man."

Joe thought about the many meals he'd had with Tony. *He's become a good friend.* He thought about Johnny Davidson, Dave Norton, and Lloyd McCormick, good friends all. *Connellsville has become my hometown.* Finally he thought of Peggy, a woman he hadn't even known two weeks ago. *If it wasn't for the murder, we'd likely never have met.* Now she was one of the most important people in his life. He felt like his existence had been condensed, months of living jammed into two weeks. *And more to come.*

Tony arrived with his lunch: a mound of noodles covered in a thick red sauce with two fat meatballs perched on top, a plate with two thick slices of crusty bread, and a glass of milk. Joe licked his lips and looked up at Tony expectantly. Before he could say anything, Tony said, "I go get you some cheese."

Joe buttered his bread and took a bite, chewing slowly. Despite the action still to come, he felt at peace. Tony returned with a bowl of grated cheese and joined Joe at the counter. Joe sprinkled some on his spaghetti and dug in.

"I like to watch you eat, Joey. You got some great appetite."

Joe finished chewing a mouthful and took a drink. "You know, Tony, I like Connellsville. I'm going to settle down here for good, so you're going to watch me eat plenty."

Tony smiled, rose, and patted Joe on the back. "That's good news, my friend." He left to attend to other customers.

Joe finished his meal as the clock on the wall chimed three. He dropped a quarter on the counter, picked up his grip, and headed for the door, waving at Tony as he left. He crossed Main Street just as Johnny came walking up the rear sidewalk of City Hall carrying a small pack.

"Ready for a long night, Johnny?"

"All set to put an end to this."

"Let's head to Leisenring."

The two caught the next streetcar going there, and were at Jim Thornton's office by three thirty. As they entered, Joe saw a rifle standing in the corner. Jim was shuffling through a stack of papers and smoking a pipe. He set the items aside.

"Hello, Joe. Who's your sidekick?"

"Jim, meet my buddy Johnny Davidson, one of Connellsville's finest coppers."

Jim got up and came around the desk, hand out. "How do, Johnny. Many thanks for your help."

"I aim to make sure my pal doesn't get shot up or something. He's been attracting the wrong kind of attention lately."

"Why don't you boys drop your baggage here and we'll take a little stroll."

Joe and Johnny put their bags in the corner and followed Jim outside. From the hillside where the company store stood, they could see most of the mine and coke works across the road. The tipple and shaft entrance were directly in front of them, rows of coke ovens stretched out in two directions. The power house sat next to the tipple. Railroad tracks ran behind the ovens, and the streetcar track ran along the other side of the road.

Jim pointed toward the end of the row of ovens to the left. "I got one of your old-timers pretending to be rebuilding an oven down there. From where he's set, he can see down the road and the tracks. I got another fellow over at the other end."

Joe shielded his eyes and looked in both directions. "This spot is as good as any for observation."

"My front porch is even better. Plan on camping out there tonight."

Joe got out his notebook and turned to a fresh page. "What time does the shift end today?"

"The men get off at five. They're mostly out of the bathhouse and gone by five thirty."

"Who else you got involved?"

"Tonight it's just us, your two men, and my nephew I got watching the ventilation shafts. Tomorrow at dawn you'll have half a dozen bosses volunteered for duty."

"How about Number Two and Three?"

"I met with both superintendents this morning. We're all as ready as we can be." Jim looked back at the store. "I need to finish up my production report. Come up to the house around six. The missus made a batch of fried chicken."

Jim went back to his office, and Joe turned to Johnny. "Let's walk the property. I want to talk to the men."

They walked down the smoky road to the end of the ovens. The coke yard was near empty, ovens unloaded long ago. Only a few oven tenders were visible. Joe saw his old-timer, sitting inside a half-built oven. He jumped up as they approached.

"Howdy, Joe. Didn't know you were coming by here."

"We'll be here with you all night. What's your name?"

"I'm Abe Fautlinger. Spent fifteen years working here until they put me out to pasture."

"Abe, pleased to meet you. This is my buddy Johnny. You see anything funny since you came on?"

Abe tipped his cap. "How do, Johnny. I seen some men down the tracks a ways. Don't know what they's up to."

"We'll take a look-see. Meanwhile, I'd like you to circulate around some. The men will be getting off soon. Keep an eye on the tipple and power house."

"Sure enough."

"You armed?"

Abe lifted his shirt. A small pistol was tucked in his belt.

"Be ready to use it. We're dealing with violent men."

Joe and Johnny walked down the tracks about a hundred yards, just past where they left Frick property. No one was around, and nothing looked suspicious. They looped around the rear and walked up Possum Run to the other row of ovens. Joe's second man was nowhere to be seen. They climbed the bank and began walking back toward the tipple on the lorry tracks.

"You fellas hold it right there."

Joe and Johnny froze.

"Now hands up, and turn around nice and slow-like."

Turning, they saw an old man holding a rifle at the ready.

"Oh, it's you, Joe. Wasn't expecting you. Sorry about that." The man lowered his weapon.

Joe and Johnny exhaled sharply. *We're two fine cops*, Joe thought, *letting an old-timer get the jump on us.*

"Nice work, buddy. What's your name?"

"Ben Rogers. I got me a little hidey hole in them trees over there. Got the whole line of ovens in my sights."

"Good work, Ben. Scout down the creek every so often, too."

"Will do, Cap'n."

Joe and Johnny continued up the lorry tracks, walking through the oven smoke. Arriving at the tipple, Johnny started to cough. "Damn, that's some rough stuff."

Joe was hacking now, too. "Don't know how the men bear it."

The sky, never really bright around most of Fayette County, was darkening even more. A rumble of faraway thunder rolled in. Dark clouds had built up in the western sky. "Let's head back to Jim's," Joe said.

Joe spotted Abe with a scythe, mowing down weeds around the bathhouse. He heard the lift start, and in a few minutes the cage emerged from the mine shaft, filled with workers. It jerked to a halt and the men trudged out, most as black as the coal they mined. They moved in silence toward the bathhouse as the cage descended, their work week finished.

Joe and Johnny followed them across the road. They saw Joe's first suspect, Tomas Smida, eyeing them coldly as he entered the building. Smida's anger and resentment was palpable. *I'm a changed man, Tomas*, Joe thought.

Lightning flashed and thunder pealed again, closer now. The first drops of rain dimpled the dusty ground. Joe and Johnny ran to the company store, arriving just as the storm broke. They stood in the front entrance and watched the rain. "We need the rain," Joe said, "but it'll make the night miserable for my men."

Johnny filled his lungs with the sweet damp air. "I love rain, love the way it cleans everything up, especially the air. At the rate it's coming down, I doubt it will last long though."

Joe nodded. "Let's go find Jim."

Jim was on the telephone as they walked into his office. He nodded to them as he spoke. "OK, Chief, they just walked in. I'll let them know." After hanging up, he rubbed his hands together.

"That was Chief Kelly. They've been working on a few of the prisoners, finally got one young fella to spill the beans. The plan was for the men to work in teams of two for the most part. They were to stay out of the mine today and lie low. The action was to commence tomorrow morning at dawn. Each man had a target at their mine. This fellow was to blow a railroad bridge at Whitney. His partner was to go after the power house."

Joe clapped and rubbed his hands together like Jim. "If we can believe him, then we can stand down for the evening. What do you think, Jim?"

"I'd say it makes sense."

"I'll go tell Abe and Ben to get some rest and be back here at five. That'll give us two more men tomorrow. I'd bet my bottom dollar that Number One is the target of Mr. Straub."

Chapter 39

The final episode unfolds, Leisenring the goal.

A clever foe proves hard to stop; three dead men pay the toll.

Joe and Johnny spent the night on Jim's porch anyway. Joe's instincts were solid, too. Kurt had singled out Number One for some special attention. But at 4:00 a.m. on Sunday, Joe didn't know that for sure.

The rain lasted longer than Johnny thought, continuing until almost midnight. Afterward, cool dry air blew in, another little break from the dog days of summer. Joe drifted awake at four, the night sky glowing orange from the flames of the ovens. He pulled on his shoes and used the outhouse, then sat on the porch steps planning the day.

Dawn would break around five. The men would be in place soon after. *Kurt will make his move by noon.*

The screen door opened and Jim appeared, a cup of coffee in his hands. "Morning, Joe. The missus is making breakfast, and coffee is on the stove."

Johnny rolled over, sighing. "That time already?"

"That time, buddy. Today will end this, one way or another."

Johnny got up and dressed. The three men devoured a platter of scrambled eggs, then got their gear together. They were at Jim's office by four forty-five. Ben, Abe, and the bosses were already there waiting. Joe recognized only Bob Finnerty among the latter.

Jim made a round of introductions then said, "This is your battle, Joe. What's the plan?"

Joe took out a map of the mine complex he'd gotten from Jim and laid it flat on the desk, pointing as he spoke. "Abe, you go back down to that oven you were working on. You'll have some cover there. Watch the road and tracks. Ben, use that hidey-hole you jumped us from yesterday. You can see along the creek from there and to the west. Either of you see anything suspicious, fire one warning shot.

"Jim, how about you taking a ride first thing, check out the ventilation shafts. Bob, you and one other hole up in the cage. Johnny, you and a second make your way up to the top of the slate dump. You'll command the high ground there." Joe pointed to two of the other bosses. "You two work in among the railroad cars." Pointing to the last man, he said, "We'll be in the bathhouse."

The men moved out right after five, the sun cresting in the eastern sky. The next hour passed slowly and Joe was getting antsy. He left the bathhouse and circled around the building, stopping near the trolley tracks. The first streetcar of the day rolled toward the end of the line, only the operator on board. Joe recognized him and waved as he passed, watching until the car disappeared around the bend.

As Joe turned away, a thunder-like boom rolled through the little valley from the west. Joe looked up to a cloudless sky, then to the west. A plume of smoke and dust could be seen rising in the air. Joe's pulse quickened, and a sick feeling roiled his guts. *The action has begun.* He ran toward the slate dump, calling to Johnny, "See anything?"

Johnny shook his head. "Only smoke."

Joe saw Jim returning from his rounds and waved him over. "Sounds like the action has started up, Jim." A second explosion echoed down the valley, this one more distant. "Call over to Number Two and Three. See what you can find out."

Jim wheeled his horse around and rode off. As he departed, a third explosion thundered, this one closer.

Joe returned to the bathhouse and called out his man. "Head on down the tracks a ways and watch the road." Then he ran up to Jim's office, arriving as Jim got off the phone. "Number Two and Three have both been attacked. They hit the power house at Number Three. The charge blew too fast, took their man out with most of one wall. The men at Number Two saw them coming and headed them off. They were able to blow a railroad bridge and some ovens before retreating."

"Grab your rifle and let's go."

The two hurried back to the road, one watching each way. A shot rang out to the west, followed by several more in a volley. Joe ran down the tracks as the streetcar came round the bend, traveling slowly. As Joe watched it approach, a man leaned out of the car, pistol in hand, and fired. Joe dove for the ditch and pulled his pistol.

The car stopped thirty yards from Joe. He could see Kurt at the controls, a West Penn cap perched on his head. Four other men were inside, all leaning out, guns drawn. They started firing as Kurt advanced the car, stopping across from the tipple. One of the men jumped out and ran to the tipple, carrying a charge. He laid it at the base of the structure and lit the fuse. As he turned to run, Bob Finnerty emerged from the cage and fired, dropping the man in the middle of the road. The streetcar accelerated again toward Joe, its occupants firing in all directions.

Joe retreated toward the bathhouse. As he did, a huge explosion filled the air, knocking him to the ground. He rolled behind a tree and looked up in time to see the tipple fall, tons of coal and the debris covering the road and tracks. Rifle fire started up from the slate dump, and another of Kurt's men slumped over.

The streetcar stopped again, halfway down the row of ovens. Another man jumped out, charge in hand, and ran toward them. Mounting the lorry tracks, he lit the fuse. Joe saw Abe pop up from his oven, rifle at the ready. The old-timer fired, dropping the man, charge still in hand. The explosion came seconds later, the man disappearing in a cloud of dirt.

The streetcar took off again, stopping at the end of the ovens. Kurt jumped off and ran toward the railroad tracks, his last accomplice laying down heavy fire toward Abe's oven. Joe ran to the store, jumped on Jim's horse, and took off in pursuit. The men in the railcars were running toward the streetcar, firing as they did. Kurt's last man stopped firing, jumped to the controls, and took off.

Joe turned at the end of the ovens just in time to see Kurt mount a horse that had been tied in the woods, a hundred yards down the tracks. Kurt turned, saw Joe, and slapped his mount's rump, taking off down the tracks. Joe took a moment to reload his .45 and followed him.

Kurt was the superior horseman, and Joe was unable to close the gap. At one point Kurt disappeared around a bend. Joe slowed as he came to it, dismounted, and proceeded slowly. As he rounded the bend, a shot rang out. Joe heard it whistle past and dove for cover. He waited a minute before peeking out. Seeing Kurt on the move again, he remounted and continued the chase.

They rode on for miles, with Joe not gaining much ground. Ahead, he could see the B&O bridge over the Yough. Kurt dismounted at the end of the span, and pulled a charge from his jacket. Running with it, he began to cross the bridge.

Joe reached the bridge and dismounted, following Kurt with his pistol in hand. Halfway across, Kurt stopped and turned toward Joe, who kept walking until only twenty yards separated them.

"That's far enough, Mr. Zajac. Our little contest is done for the day."

"Not until I take you into custody."

Kurt smiled and shook his head. "That's not going to happen. I'm prepared to die first." He held the dynamite up, his pistol barrel pressed to it.

"Haven't enough men died for your cause today?"

"I'm willing to add two more to the tally."

Keeping his eye on Kurt, Joe took a step forward. His foot slipped between the open railroad ties and he fell, managing to hold on to his gun. A sharp pain shot up his leg. Looking up, he saw a train approaching the bridge from the other side.

Kurt laughed. "Looks like fate has had its say." He climbed over the bridge railing and looked to the water below.

Joe shouted, "Why do you hate Frick?"

Kurt's smile vanished. "I'm his bastard son."

Kurt tossed the charge in Joe's direction, shot at it, and missed. Joe fired back as Kurt leaped from the bridge, and saw the man flinch before dropping.

The bridge rumbled as the train began to cross. Joe struggled to free his ankle. He could see the engineer, heard him hit the brakes. Joe's foot finally popped loose and he rolled to the edge of the bridge, holding on tightly as the train screeched by.

It was a short one, a yard engine pulling a dozen empty gondola cars. After the last car passed, Joe jumped up but fell to his knees, his injured ankle unable to support him. He looked over the side of the bridge and saw nothing.

The train had stopped on the other side, the engineer out running toward Joe, who holstered his gun and took a deep breath. The engineer hollered as he approached, "What's going on here?"

Joe smiled and struggled to get up, holding on to the railing. "Just the end of the line for one crazy bastard."

Chapter 40

Joe told a bit of the story as the engineer helped him off the bridge. Joe tried but was unable to mount his horse.

"Climb on up and I'll run you back to Number One," said the engineer, as he tied the horse to a tree. "We'll send someone back for your mount."

Joe struggled up into the cab of the steam engine and leaned out the window. The engineer climbed aboard, released the brakes, and eased the throttle forward. With a chug, the little engine moved.

Halfway back, Joe saw Jim heading down the tracks on horseback. "Slow down, Chief. I need a word with this fellow."

The engine slowed to a crawl, then stopped. Jim rode up, his horse shying away from the engine. "Good to see you're in one piece, Joe. Where's Straub?"

"Jumped in the river. I messed up my ankle, and my horse is tied down by the bridge. This fella here's running me back to Number One."

"I'll go get him and see you back there."

The engine started back up and soon arrived at Leisenring. Joe saw men gathered near the tipple. Old women and young children were busy loading canvas sacks with the dumped coal. *The coal bins of Leisenring will all be full by tonight,* Joe thought. With the help of the engineer, he limped out. Johnny ran over to greet him.

"Thank God you're alive. Jim just took off looking for you."

"We saw him. He's gone to get my horse."

"What happened to Straub?"

"Help me across the road first. I need to find a place to sit down."

Joe surveyed the damage as Johnny helped him. The tipple was totally demolished. It would have to be rebuilt, and Number One would be out of production until it was. There'd be no streetcar traffic past Leisenring for some time. The two men made it to a bench by the ball field and sat down. Joe told his story, leaving out the part about Kurt being Frick's son.

Johnny whistled when Joe finished. "The Yough is pretty shallow under that trestle. You think he made it?"

"I don't know. The river was running high, thanks to the rain. I'd feel better if we're able to find his body." Joe surveyed the mine again. Two men were digging down where the fellow got blown up. "What's the final tally here?"

"All three of Straub's men are dead; the one's in pieces. On our side, only the fellow up the tracks got it and he'll survive."

"His warning saved us some misery." Joe stood again, still unable to put any weight on his injured foot. "Soon as Jim comes back ,we'll head to town. I need to get this ankle looked at."

Johnny helped him walk toward Jim's house. "Wonder how the rest of the mines made out?"

"It'll be tomorrow until we find out the whole story."

The two sat on Jim's porch until he returned. They borrowed his wagon, loaded up, and headed back to town. By ten they were finished at the hospital. Joe's ankle was badly sprained, not broken, and he left on crutches.

Johnny helped him onto the wagon. "Where to?"

Wonder where Peggy is? "Take me home."

In fifteen minutes, Joe was back at his place and lying on the bed. He occasionally dozed throughout the rest of the day. When awake, he thought about his future. Of one thing he was certain—there had to be a better way to make a living than working for Frick.

By five he was hungry, and with some difficulty made his way to The Star. He hobbled in, pleased to see Peggy there, standing with Hiram. She turned as he entered, ran over, and wrapped her arms around him. Unable to return the favor, Joe stood unsteadily as she hugged him. After a minute she let go and backed away.

"Is it over, Joe?"

Joe nodded. "It is. Let's sit down. I need one of your famous roast beef sandwiches."

Peggy helped him to the corner table and left to make his sandwich. Hiram brought him a beer. "Need a shot, Joe?"

Joe shook his head. "I'm having a hard enough time walking as it is."

Peggy returned with his sandwich and put it in front of him. They sat quietly as he made short work of it.

She smiled as she watched him eat. "It's good to see your appetite hasn't been harmed."

He took a few sips of beer, wiped his lips with the back of his hand, and smiled back. "Seeing you is strong medicine. My ankle feels better already."

For the next half hour, Joe told Peggy his story, including the part about Kurt being Frick's son. "I'm not going to be telling that part to anyone else, excepting Mr. Frick if I see him again."

"I'll not tell, either. That's quite a story."

"If someone told me that over a beer, I'd figure he was pitching the bull."

"What's next?"

"A good night's sleep, then off to Scottdale tomorrow to wrap this up."

Peggy walked back with him, helped him to his room, and, after a kiss, left. Joe was suddenly exhausted, and was soon asleep.

A few miles away, a dark form emerged from the B&O stockyards.

***

Monday morning found Joe in fine spirits. He'd still need the crutches for a few days but he could deal with that. He was up and out by seven, and on his favorite stool at City Lunch a few minutes later, Tony at his side.

"So you done getting shot at and beat up, Joey?"

"I'd say. I'm likely to be out of the investigating business for good."

"You did some good work on this one. You save the day, I hear."

Joe smiled. "All I know is I'm a lucky guy."

Joe was eating when Henry Snyder stopped in. "Morning, Joe, mind if I join you?"

"Have a seat, Henry. What can I do for you?"

"I'm working on a story for Friday's paper about the events of the weekend. 'Frick Cop Saves the Day' or something like that. I'd like to hear your version of the battle at Leisenring. I've already talked to Johnny."

"I'll do it, but give me a day to get caught up. And there'll be none of that 'Joe Saves the Day' headline, either. Credit goes to all of the men that stopped Straub and his gang."

"OK, fair enough."

"What do you hear about the other mines?"

"Straub's men did some damage at Redstone and Kyle but they got away. Some got nabbed moving in at Leith and Wynn. There was some action at Standard. All in all, Frick got away lucky, even with what happened at Number One."

"Any word of a body showing up in the Yough?"

"None so far."

Joe finished his breakfast, clumsily rose, and headed toward the door on his crutches. "I'll stop by tomorrow afternoon if that's good for you."

"That's fine, Joe. Much obliged."

Joe made his way to the terminal and was soon in Scottdale. Polly jumped up as he entered the office. "Welcome, Joe. Are you hurt seriously?"

"My ankle got sprained pretty badly, but it's already much better."

"Mr. Lynch said to send you right up to his office. Do you need some help?"

"I'd appreciate it if you'd carry my crutches."

Joe hopped up the steps with Polly right behind. At the top she gave him his crutches, and he made his way to Lynch's office. Lynch looked up from his desk as Joe walked in, then got up and came around to greet him.

"Joe, I heard from Jim you were somewhat the worse for wear." He pointed to a small table with two chairs. "Let's have a seat."

They sat down, Lynch taking the crutches. "The H.C. Frick Company owes you a debt of gratitude. Had it not been for your fine work, we'd have suffered much greater damage."

"Thank you, Mr. Lynch. Let's not forget about the old-timers. Without them, we'd not have fared as well." Joe took out his notebook. "Abe Fautlinger and Ben Rogers both provided exceptional support at Leisenring."

Lynch took out his notebook and wrote their names. "They, and the rest, will be receiving double pay for their service."

"They deserve it. Now fill me in on Sunday. You've heard from all of the mines?"

"Yes, we have, and as I said, it could have been much worse. Leisenring incurred the worst damage."

"What about our men? Anyone hurt badly? What happened at Standard?"

"The worst injury was to Cliff Sellers. He went up against your man Jake, had to kill him. In the process he was shot twice, in the leg and stomach. He's lucky to have survived but is facing a long convalescence. The damage at Standard is not inconsequential. Jake and three others carried the attack. They were able to roll a coal wagon loaded with dynamite into the slope entrance, which collapsed in the explosion. We'll have to excavate a new entrance a bit down the ridge."

"We're still missing some dynamite, too."

Lynch smiled. "The fellow injured at Number Two revealed the location of Straub's hideout. We recovered almost eight more cases."

"And the rest of the Fayette County mines?"

"All minor damage, most of Straub's gang captured. The fellow that left Leisenring in the streetcar seems to have made a clean getaway."

"Number One is out of service for some time, though."

"It is, but we've already got plans on the table to replace the tipple. We're going to erect a more modern design, one made mostly of steel."

"But we've not found Kurt's body."

"I suspect it's only a matter of time. At any rate, I doubt he'll be causing us anymore trouble."

Lynch rose and walked over to his desk, returning with an envelope with Joe's name on it. "This is for you, Mr. Zajac."

Joe opened the envelope. Inside was a check for twenty-five hundred dollars. "What's this about?"

"It's your reward for the partial recovery of the dynamite on Saturday. Think of it as a bonus for a job very well done. You saved the company potentially ten times that."

Joe couldn't contain a big grin. "Much obliged, Mr. Lynch."

"And I have another offer for you. As Mr. Sellers will not be able to return, we've retired him with a small pension. His job is yours if you want it, and personally I hope you do."

Joe's grin faded, his head spinning a bit at the news. "What I'd like most right now is a week off. The offer is gratifying, as is your confidence in me."

"Take the week; you've earned it. Come back on Friday and we'll talk again." Lynch rose and returned to his desk. "If you like, I'll have a man take you back to Connellsville in my carriage."

Joe rose and headed for the door. "No thanks, Mr. Lynch. The streetcar suits me fine."

Chapter 41

Saturday the twenty-fifth of August found Joe off his crutches, a slight limp the only sign of his injury. Late afternoon found him at the Pattersons', sitting in the backyard with Andy, shucking corn. Peggy decided that a celebration was in order, and had invited Johnny, Lloyd, and their girls over for a picnic dinner.

Andy sat on a covered swing while Joe shucked. "Son, I think my daughter is mighty fond of you. She's not been this happy in a long time."

Joe smiled at the old man, enjoying his company. "And I'm mighty fond of her. Being with her makes me feel peaceful."

Andy nodded. "A good woman brings out the best in a man, and vice versa." His eyes glistened. "My bad heart's not going to get better. When my time comes I'll go easy, knowing that my girl has found a mate."

Peggy picked that moment to come outside. "We're all ready for our guests." She looked at her father. "Are you all right, Daddy?"

Andy pulled out a handkerchief, mopped his brow, and wiped his eyes. "Never been better, honey."

She sat next to Joe and started shucking. "Take your time, Joe. Get all of those little hairs off." She finished one ear and showed it off. "Like this."

Joe smiled and nodded. Peggy picked up another ear.

"How did Mr. Lynch take the news yesterday?"

"He was surprised and honestly disappointed, I'd say. I felt complimented by that. But he wished me well and said to come see him if I ever changed my mind."

"You like him, don't you?"

"He's a good fellow. H.C. might be hateful, but Mr. Lynch is a fair man."

"You didn't tell him what Straub said?"

"I'll not be passing on the ravings of a madman."

"So are you going to become a man of leisure, then, with your windfall?"

Joe shook his head. "I need to stay busy. You know what they say about an idle mind."

"Looking for work? I can always use a good man down at The Star. I'll even show you how to keep the books."

"I'd love to help when I can, but I got other plans." Joe finished his ear, holding it up for inspection before putting it in the pot. "I always enjoyed school; reading and learning comes easy to me. I've come to the understanding that there's plenty going on in the world I'm ignorant of. My intentions are to remedy that. Monday I'm going down to Allegheny City to visit the University of Western Pennsylvania. If they'll have me, I intend to start studies there in September."

Peggy dropped the ear of corn she'd been shucking, reached over, and took Joe's hands. "You are a man of many surprises. That's a wonderful idea."

Joe gave her hands a squeeze. "A man is never too old to live a better life."

About the Author

Jim Oglethorpe is a native of Connellsville, Pennsylvania and a descendent of miners and cokers. A true son of the "Keystone State", he is a 1972 graduate of Penn State University.

Jim and his wife Jean moved to Fort Myers, Florida in 2007. Jim began writing in 2009, initially blogging about politics. This is his first book.

www.ingramcontent.com/pod-product-compliance
Lightning Source LLC
Chambersburg PA
CBHW071150170626

46809CB00002B/849